I0764505

THE PATH OF DUTY

AND OTHER STORIES

MORE WILDSIDE CLASSICS

Dacobra, or The White Priests of Ahriman, by Harris Burland
The Nabob, by Alphonse Daudet
Out of the Wreck, by Captain A. E. Dingle
The Elm-Tree on the Mall, by Anatole France
The Lance of Kanana, by Harry W. French
Amazon Nights, by Arthur O. Friel
Caught in the Net, by Emile Gaboriau
The Gentle Grafter, by O. Henry
Raffles, by E. W. Hornung
Gates of Empire, by Robert E. Howard
Tom Brown's School Days, by Thomas Hughes
The Opium Ship, by H. Bedford Jones
The Miracles of Antichrist, by Selma Lagerlof
Arsène Lupin, by Maurice LeBlanc
A Phantom Lover, by Vernon Lee
The Iron Heel, by Jack London
The Witness for the Defence, by A.E.W. Mason
The Spider Strain and Other Tales, by Johnston McCulley
Tales of Thubway Tham, by Johnston McCulley
The Prince of Graustark, by George McCutcheon
Bull-Dog Drummond, by Cyril McNeile
The Moon Pool, by A. Merritt
The Red House Mystery, by A. A. Milne
Blix, by Frank Norris
Wings over Tomorrow, by Philip Francis Nowlan
The Devil's Paw, by E. Phillips Oppenheim
Satan's Daughter and Other Tales, by E. Hoffmann Price
The Insidious Dr. Fu Manchu, by Sax Rohmer
Mauprat, by George Sand
The Slayer and Other Tales, by H. de Vere Stacpoole
Penrod (Gordon Grant Illustrated Edition), by Booth Tarkington
The Gilded Age, by Mark Twain
The Blockade Runners, by Jules Verne
The Gadfly, by E.L. Voynich

Please see www.wildsidepress.com for a complete list!

THE PATH OF DUTY
AND OTHER STORIES

H. S. CASWELL

WILDSIDE PRESS

THE PATH OF DUTY AND OTHER STORIES

This edition published in 2006 by Wildside Press, LLC.
www.wildsidepress.com

CONTENTS

CLARA ROSCOM; OR, THE PATH OF DUTY

CHAPTER I.

A Sudden Bereavement.

"Awake, my dear child, awake!" These were the words I heard: I started up, gazing in a bewildered manner into the face of my mother, who had, with some difficulty, succeeded in arousing me from the sweet, healthful sleep of childhood. My mother drew nigh to me and whispered, "My dear Clara, your papa is dying." With a frightened cry, I threw my arms around her neck, and begged her to tell me what had happened. I was unable to comprehend the meaning of her words. Since my earliest recollection, my father had never experienced a day's illness, and so the reader may be able to form some idea of the shock occasioned by her words — uttered, as they were, at the hour of midnight. When my mother had succeeded in soothing me, in some degree, to calmness, she informed me, in a voice choked with sobs, which, for my sake, she tried to suppress, that my father had, two hours since, been stricken with apoplexy, in so severe a form that his life was despaired of. She further informed me that his attending physician thought he would not live to see the light of another morning. Well do I remember the nervous terror with which I clung to my mother as we entered my father's apartment, and the icy chill which diffused itself over my body, as I gazed upon the fearfully changed features of my father. I had never before seen death in any form. I believe the first view of death is more or less terrible to every child; it certainly was terrible for me to first view death imprinted upon the countenance of a fond father. I have ever since thought that my father recognized me when my mother led me to his bed-side; but power of utterance was gone. It was a fearful trial to me, who had seen but ten years of life. After the first shock, a strange calm took possession of me. Though many years have passed since that period, I remember, as though it were but yesterday, how I sat during those long hours, scarcely for an instant removing my eyes from my father's face, but shed not a tear; for, after the first burst of grief, tears refused to come to my relief. Just as the day began to dawn I heard the physician say, in a whisper, to a kind neighbor who stood by, I think he is going. At that moment my father opened his eyes, and, looking upward with a pleasant smile, expired without a struggle. I could never clearly remember how I passed the intervening days between my father's death and burial. I have an indistinct recollection of the hushed voices and soft footsteps of friends and neighbors, who kindly came to aid in performing the last offices of love and friendship to the remains of my departed father. I also remember being led by my almost heart-broken mother into the darkened room, where lay the lifeless body of my father, now prepared for the grave; but I have a more vivid recollection of standing with my mother beside an open grave, and hearing our pastor, in a solemn voice, utter the words, "Earth to earth — ashes to ashes — dust to dust." Oh! the falling of that first earth upon my father's coffin, shall I ever forget the sound? Child as I was, it seemed to me that my heart would break; but tears, the first I had shed since my father's death, came to my relief. Those blessed tears. I may well call them blessed, since the physician afterwards told my mother that they saved either my reason or my life. Kind friends besought my mother and me to allow ourselves to be conveyed home and not await the filling up of the grave. But no. We could not leave the spot till the last earth was thrown upon the grave, and a mound covered with grassy sods was to be seen, where a little before was only a mournful cavity. Then indeed we felt that he was gone, and that we must return to our desolate home — the home which ever before his presence had filled with joy and gladness.

I must pass over, with a few words only, the first year of our bereavement, as even now I shudder to recall the feeling of loneliness and desolation which took possession of us, when we found ourselves left alone in the home where everything reminded us so strongly of the departed one. There was a small apartment adjoining our usual sitting-room which my father was wont to call his study, and, being fond of books, he used there to pass much of his leisure time. It was quite a long time after his death before my mother could enter that apartment. She said to me one day, "Will you go with me, Clara, to your father's study?" I replied, "Can you go *there*, Mamma?" "Yes, dear," said my mother, and led the way to the door. No one had entered that room since my father left it on the last night of his life, the door having been locked on the day succeeding his death. As my mother softly turned the key and opened the door, it seemed almost that we stood in my father's presence, so vividly did the surroundings of that room recall him to our minds. There stood his table and chair, and his writing desk stood upon the table, and several books and papers were scattered carelessly upon the table. The last book he had been reading lay open as he had left it; it was a volume of Whitfield's sermons; it was a book which my father valued highly, and is now a cherished keep-sake of my own. My mother seemed quite overcome with grief. I know she had striven daily to conceal her grief when in my presence, for she knew how I grieved for my father; and she was aware that her tears would only add to my sorrow, so for my sake it was that she forced herself to appear calm — almost cheerful; but upon this occasion her grief was not to be checked. She bowed her head upon the table, while convulsive sobs shook her frame. I tried, in my childish way, to comfort her. I had never seen her so much moved since my father's death. When she became more composed, she rose, and I assisted her in dusting and arranging the furniture of the room; and after this first visit to the room, wc no longer avoided entering it. Since quite a young man my father had been employed as book-keeper in a large mercantile house in the city of Philadelphia, where we resided. As he had ever proved trustworthy and faithful to the interests of his employers, they had seen fit, upon his marriage, to give him an increase of salary, which enabled him to purchase a small, but neat and convenient dwelling in a respectable street in Philadelphia, where we had lived in the enjoyment of all the comforts, and with many of the luxuries of life, to the time of the sad event which left me fatherless and my mother a widow. I had never, as yet, attended any school. My mother had been my only teacher, and as her own education had been thorough, she was amply qualified for the task.

CHAPTER II.
Success At School.

About a year after my father's death, my mother decided upon sending me to school, as she thought I was becoming too sedate and serious for a child only eleven years of age. I had never been very familiar with the neighbouring children of my own age, and after the death of my father I cared still less for their companionship. My chief enjoyment was in the society of my mother; and as we kept no servant, I found many ways of making myself useful to her; and every afternoon she devoted two or three hours to my lessons and needlework. Thus passed away the first year after our great sorrow, when, as I have already said, my mother decided upon sending me to school. It seemed to me, at the time, quite a formidable undertaking — this going to school. I had never been separated from my mother, and the five hours to be spent daily in the school-room seemed to my childish mind a very long time. I had ever been shy and diffident in the presence of strangers, and the idea of entering a large school a stranger to both teacher and pupils, was very unpleasant to me. But when I found it to be my mother's wish that I should go, I endeavoured to overcome my reluctance, and assisted my mother in her preparations for entering me as a pupil at the beginning of the ensuing term.

It was with a feeling of timidity that I accompanied my mother through several streets to the school taught by Miss Edmonds. My mother accompanied me to relieve me from any awkwardness I might feel in presenting myself for admission. It was a select school for girls. As my education had thus far been entirely conducted by my mother, I had of course, never been subjected to the rules of a school-room; and I must confess that I had formed an idea of school teachers in general that was not at all flattering. I fancied them all to be old, sour and cross — a mere walking bundle of rules and regulations, and I was quite unprepared to see the sweet-looking young lady who answered to my mother's summons at the door. Surely, thought I, this young lady cannot be Miss Edmonds; and when my mother enquired if such were her name and she replied in the affirmative, I thought going to school might not be so bad after all. After giving Miss Edmonds my name and age, my mother held some conversation with her regarding my studies, and left me with an encouraging smile. I felt all my timidity return when I thought of entering the school-room with Miss Edmonds, but her kind and friendly manner reassured me. The school consisted of about thirty girls, many of them older than myself. I had feared that my attainments would be inferior to those of the youngest of the pupils, and I was equally pleased and surprised when Miss Edmonds, after a long and careful examination in regard to my acquirements, placed me in one of the higher classes. There was to me an irresistible attraction in the countenance and manner of my teacher; and, from the first moment I saw her I loved her. Although her home is now far distant from mine, and we have not met for many years, I love her as dearly now as when she took me by the hand when a child of eleven years. She conducted her school in a very systematic and orderly manner, and was very particular to require perfect recitations from her pupils; but as I possessed a retentive memory, I found my tasks much lighter than did many of my classmates.

When I had been about a year at school, Miss Edmonds offered a prize, in the class to which I belonged, to the young lady who should write the most able composition upon a given subject. The prize was to be a small gold pencil-case, and was to be awarded at the close of the summer term. The closing day at length came; there was much suppressed excitement when we were called to order that morning. As we expected no visitors till the afternoon, we spent the morning mostly in reviewing our various studies. By two o'clock our school-room was crowded. We first passed a very searching examination in the different studies we had pursued during the past year. I believe we passed our examination in a manner creditable both to our teacher and to ourselves.

The reading of our compositions was reserved, as the closing exercise. The compositions, with the name of the writer, were read by Miss Edmonds. Each person present was at liberty to write down each name as it was read by our teacher, annexing to it the numbers one, two or three, according to their opinion of the merits of the composition, each desk being furnished with paper, pens and ink for the purpose. When the compositions had all been read, the slips of paper were collected and handed to our pastor, who was to read aloud the fortunate name with the greatest number of ones annexed. What then was my amazement and that of all present when our pastor, after carefully examining the papers, rose and said, — "Miss Clara Roscom will please come forward, and receive from the hands of Miss Edmonds the reward of so much merit." I remember I felt a nervous dread of crossing the large school-room alone, when I knew every eye would be directed to me. Composing myself by a strong effort, I rose and walked up to the raised platform, where at her desk sat Miss Edmonds, with our pastor and several other friends. As I bowed low in acknowledgement of the gift, Miss Edmonds, with a few kind words, dismissed me to my seat. I heard many flattering remarks among our assembled friends; but the proudest moment of all, to me, was when I gained my mother's side and she said to me in a low voice, "My dear Clara, this seems to me a token that you will prove a blessing to your poor widowed mother."

Miss Edmonds often remarked that I made wonderful progress in my studies, and these commendations, coming from my teacher, incited me to still greater diligence. I take no credit to myself for superior talent, but I certainly did my best, for, be it remembered, I was studying to please my dear mother, who often said to me, "You must, my dear Clara, make the best of your opportunities for improvement, as the time may come when your education may be your only means of support." My mother often regretted that we did not own a piano, for she was very anxious that I should study music; but our means did not justify the purchase of an instrument, and she thought that lessons without the necessary practice would be useless. The parents of Miss Edmonds resided in the city. They had once been wealthy, but owing to those reverses to which all are liable they had become reduced in circumstances, so much so that Miss Edmonds gladly turned to account the superior education she had received in their prosperous days, and she had for some time been a teacher when I became a member of her school. My mother happened to mention to Miss Edmonds one day her regret that I was unable to take music-lessons, for want of opportunity for the needful practice, when she informed my mother that she still retained her piano out of the wreck of their former affluence, and that, if she wished me to take lessons, I was at liberty to practice daily upon it. My mother accepted for me the kind offer, and I at once began taking lessons. I remained four years under the instruction of Miss Edmonds, with much profit to myself. At the end of this time, Mr. Edmonds removed with his family to the city of New York, having through the influence of friends, obtained the situation of cashier in one of the banks in that city. It was a severe trial for Miss Edmonds to resign the school where she was so much beloved by her pupils; but she thought it her duty to accompany her parents to their new home.

CHAPTER III.
Clara at Mrs. Wentworth's Boarding School.

As it was my mother's intention to give me a thoroughly good education, she began, after the departure of Miss Edmonds, to consider the propriety of sending me to a noted seminary for young ladies, about two hundred miles from Philadelphia, as she learned from various sources of the excellence of the institution. There was but one difficulty in the way, and that was the money needful for defraying my expenses. At my father's death, he left us the owners of the house we occupied, and a sum of money, though not a large one, in the Savings' Bank. Up to the time of which I speak, we had only drawn the annual interest of our money, while the principal remained untouched, my mother having obtained needle-work to eke out our small income; but, in order that I should finish my education according to the wishes of my mother, as well as my own, a portion of the principal must be withdrawn. After some reflection upon the subject, my mother decided that a good education might prove of more value to me than money, so a portion of the money was drawn, and we began the preparations for my departure from home. It was the high reputation which the school sustained that influenced my mother in her decision to send me so far from home. There was a lady residing in the near vicinity of the school who had been a loved school-mate of my mother in their youthful days. My mother wrote to her upon the subject and received a very friendly reply, informing her that, owing to their own early friendship, she would be most happy to fill a mother's place to me, so long as I should wish to remain at school. I should have been much elated at the proposed journey had it not been for the thought of leaving my mother, who had ever been my confidant and adviser. My mother also felt keenly the coming departure, although she strove to conceal her feelings as much as possible. I strongly objected to leaving her alone, but we had as yet been unable to devise any plan to avoid so doing. My mother would have rented a portion of our dwelling, but it was not adapted for the convenience of two families, neither could she endure the disquiet of keeping boarders.

"Clara," said my mother one day, as we sat at work, "I think I will send for Aunt Patience to come and stay with me during your absence."

She laughed outright at the look of dismay with which I regarded her, occasioned by the recollection which I retained of a visit she paid us when I was eight years of age. She was a maiden lady somewhat advanced in years, possessed of a very kind heart and many excellent qualities; but the name of Patience seemed to me a misapplication in her case, for she certainly possessed but a small quantity of that valuable article. Early in life she had passed through many trials, which might have tended to sour her disposition. I remember that during the visit referred to, my mother had occasion to spend a day from home, leaving me in care of Aunt Patience. It seemed a very long day to me. Like all children, I was restless and troublesome, and to one unaccustomed to the care of children it was doubtless very annoying. During the day I received a severe box on the ear from Aunt Patience, for saying to her in an outburst of childish anger, when provoked by her continued fault-finding,

"I don't know what makes them call you Aunt Patience, for you scold all the time."

She informed my mother of it upon her return, and she gave me a reproof for allowing myself to speak disrespectfully to my relative; although, while listening to the relation of the difficulty by Aunt Patience, she found it extremely difficult to repress a smile. However, my mother both loved and respected her, and thought she could live very comfortably with her during my absence; indeed my mother thought her quite a desirable companion, for, setting aside her irritability at petty annoyances, she was a woman of good sense, and was well informed upon most subjects, so I gladly joined in the invitation which my mother sent her, to come and make our house her home for an indefinite period. As she lived only a day's journey by railway from Philadelphia, she arrived a week before I left home. She did not like the idea of my mother spending so much money in sending me to school. To all of her remarks upon the subject my mother replied pleasantly, for she was her own aunt, and she would not treat her with disrespect. During the few days I remained at home after her arrival, I formed a much more favorable opinion of Aunt Patience than I had done during her visit in the days of my childhood; and when I observed how kind she was to my mother I found it easy to love her.

I felt very sad the morning I bade adieu to my mother and Aunt Patience, to go into the world alone. My mother had before given me many kind counsels regarding my future conduct, now she only said, as she embraced me at parting, "My dear daughter, I trust you will improve your time and talents, and conduct yourself in a manner that will not disappoint your mother." As Aunt Patience bade me good-bye, she said, with a countenance of much solemnity, "You must remember, Clara, all the advice I have given you." Sad as I felt, I could not repress a smile, for during the past week her advices regarding my future conduct had been so numerous, that it would have required a memory more retentive than mine to have remembered them all; but I knew they were intended for my good, and I readily promised to try and observe them. I wish not to weary the reader by giving a detailed account of my journey. I arrived safely at my destination, and met with a very cordial welcome at the house of Mrs. Armitage, my mother's friend; two days later I became a member of the celebrated school for young ladies, taught at that time by Mrs. Wentworth, aided by competent assistance.

Mrs. Wentworth was a widow lady, of superior education and noble mind. I spent four happy years in this institution, having visited my mother but once during the time. It was very pleasant for me to find myself once more at home, with the opportunity for rest and relaxation, after four years, application to books. During my absence, my mother and Aunt Patience had lived very quietly, they saw but little company, and were much occupied with their needles as a means of support. During the first three years of my absence my mother enjoyed good health, but, during my last year at school, she was visited by a long and painful illness, through which she was attended, with the utmost kindness and attention, by her aunt; my mother being unwilling to recall me from school, if it were possible to avoid it; and she had been obliged, on account of her illness, to withdraw most of the sum remaining in the Savings' Bank. On my return home I found her enjoying a tolerable degree of health, but I feared that such close application to her needle had been too much for one whose constitution was naturally delicate. She seemed like one weary both in mind and body. After my arrival, however, she seemed to regain her usual cheerfulness, and in a short time seemed quite herself again. It was now I felt it my duty to turn the education which my mother had been at so much pains to give me to account by teaching, in order to assist her, and also to obtain a support for myself. We had decided to offer Aunt Patience a home for the remainder of her life, indeed I felt that I owed her a debt of gratitude for her past kindness to my mother. We therefore told her that so long as we possessed a home, we would gladly share it with her, provided she felt contented to remain with us. She at first demurred a little, as she was aware that our means were limited; but when my mother told her that she would not know what to do without her, it seemed to set her mind at rest, and she gladly assented to our proposal, and it was settled that for the future her home was to be with us.

I had as yet settled upon no definite plan in regard to teaching. My mother wished me to apply for the situation of governess in a family, as she thought that position would command a higher salary, and would prove less laborious than a situation in a school. About this time we noticed in a daily paper an advertisement for a governess, wanted in the family of a Mr. Leighton, residing in the suburbs of the city; the salary offered was liberal, and I thought, with my mother, that I had best apply for the situation.

CHAPTER IV.
Governess in Mr. Leighton's Family.

It was with a feeling of trepidation, such as I never before experienced, that I ascended the steps of the splendid residence of Mr. Leighton. When I found myself at the door, my courage well nigh failed me, but without giving myself much time for reflection, I rang the door bell. After some little delay the door was opened by a domestic, of whom I enquired if I could see Mrs. Leighton. The servant replied that she did not know, but that she would see if her mistress was disengaged. "What name?" enquired the servant, "Miss Roscom," I replied. The servant ushered me into the parlor, and left the room. Being left alone, I amused myself by taking a survey of the apartment. It was evident that I had entered the abode of luxury and wealth. The sofas and chairs were covered with rich velvet, while satin curtains draped the windows. An elegant and costly piano occupied one corner of the room; the walls were adorned by costly pictures, and on the marble centre-table were many books in elegant bindings; and rare and exquisite ornaments were scattered with lavish profusion. Upon the entrance of a tall, and, as I thought at the time, rather haughty-looking lady, I rose, bowed and continued standing, as she said, —

"My servant informs me your name is Miss Roscom."

I replied in the affirmative, and added, "I have the pleasure, I presume, of addressing Mrs. Leighton?"

The lady acknowledged her claim to that name, and I continued, — "Seeing your advertisement for a governess, I have made bold to apply for the situation."

The lady bent upon me a searching look, as she replied, —

"Pray be seated Miss, and we will converse upon the matter."

I gladly obeyed her request that I should be seated, for I felt nervous and agitated. After a moment's silence she addressed me, saying, —

"You look rather young, for the responsible duties of a governess."

I replied that I was not yet nineteen years of age, that I had not as yet been engaged in teaching, having only myself left school three months since, — but that I found it necessary that I should do something for my own support and that of my widowed mother, — and that I would gladly do my utmost to give satisfaction, could I obtain a situation.

Mrs. Leighton, after a moment's thought, said, — "Although you are young for the position, your countenance pleases me, and I feel inclined to give you a trial."

She then informed me that my pupils would consist of two girls, the eldest twelve, the other ten years of age, also a little boy of seven. She added, "I had almost forgotten to enquire if you have brought any references?"

Whereupon I handed her the certificate of qualifications given me by Mrs. Wentworth when I left school. She looked pleased as she replied,

"Your being for four years a member of Mrs. Wentworth's school is in itself a recommendation."

I also handed her the names of several ladies well known in the city, telling her she was at liberty to make any enquiries of them she might think proper. She replied that she felt almost certain she would engage me, but that she would send me a decided answer in the course of two or three days. I thanked her, and, bidding her good morning, set out on my return home, much elated with the success of this my first application.

The salary offered by Mrs. Leighton was a weighty consideration to me, and although aware that my duties would often prove unpleasant and irksome, I felt that I could endure much with the consciousness that I was assisting my dear mother.

My mother advised me not to be too sanguine as I might not obtain the situation; but, on the third day after my application, my suspense was relieved by receiving a note from Mrs. Leighton, saying that she would gladly engage me, if I still wished for the situation; and she named an early day when she wished me to enter upon my duties. I replied that I gladly accepted the situation, and would be ready to begin duties at the day appointed.

Now that I had accepted the position, I began to experience many doubts as to my success in the undertaking. I had no knowledge as yet of the dispositions of the children that were to be committed to my care, not having even seen them; but my mother told me I was wrong to allow such thoughts to trouble me, and that the blessing of God would surely rest upon my labors so long as I continued in the path of duty. I therefore cast away all my desponding fears, and hastened the preparations for my departure to the home of the Leightons.

I was kindly received by Mrs. Leighton upon my arrival; and, when we were seated in the parlor, she summoned the children for the purpose of introducing them to me.

"My dears," said she, addressing the children, "this is Miss Roscom, your governess."

Then, turning to me, she introduced them each by name. I must confess that I was not prepossessed in favor of the eldest of the girls. She was very tall for her age; she had a dark complexion, with very black eyes and hair, and had, as it seemed to me, rather a forbidding expression of countenance. She also gave me, as I thought, rather pert replies to the few remarks I addressed to her. There was not the slightest resemblance between her and her younger sister; her name was Georgania. There was something peculiarly attractive in the countenance and manner of Bertha, or Birdie, as she was called by all the family. She was indeed a child formed to attract the admiration and love of all who saw her. Her complexion would have appeared almost too pale but for the rose-tint on either cheek; she had beautiful eyes of a dark blue, and her soft brown hair fell in luxuriant curls upon her shoulders. She came forward as her mother called her name and placed her hand in mine. I thought at the time that I had never before seen so lovely and engaging a child. The little boy, Lewis, was a manly looking little fellow for his age, although I feared, from his countenance that he might possess a temper and a will not easy to be controlled. He somewhat resembled his sister Georgania, as his complexion and eyes were dark; but he had a more pleasing expression of countenance. When Mrs. Leighton had dismissed the children from the room, she turned to me, remarking that probably I would like to retire for a time to my own room, she called one of the servants and requested her to show me to my apartment. As I was leaving the parlor she informed me that tea would be ready at half-past six o'clock. The room appropriated to my use was very pleasant, and was also tastefully furnished. At the tea-table I was introduced to Mr. Leighton, whom I had not before seen. I was very much pleased by his manner, which had none of that patronizing condescension with which the rich so often address the poor. I found him a gentleman, in the truest sense of the word.

After tea, Mr. Leighton requested me to favor them with some music. Accordingly I seated myself at the piano and played several pieces, with which he seemed much pleased. He remarked that they were quite at a loss for music since their eldest daughter, Laura, left home for school, as their two youngest daughters had but recently commenced taking lessons. As I rose from the piano, Mrs. Leighton enquired if I sang. I replied that I sometimes sang to oblige my friends. She asked if I would favor them with a song. Resuming my seat, I began the first song which occurred to my mind. It chanced to be that much-admired song, by Foster, called "Willie, we have missed you." When I concluded I was surprised to find Mrs. Leighton in tears. She informed me, by way of apology, that their eldest son's name was Willie, and that he had been absent for some months in England, on account of the death of a wealthy uncle, who had made him his heir. She remarked, further, that he was the life of their dwelling, and they had indeed missed him very much. I said that I was sorry to have given her pain. She replied that the song had afforded her a pleasure, although, said she, "I could not refrain from tears while thinking of my absent Willie."

In order to change the subject, Mr. Leighton remarked that they were fortunate in securing a governess who could both sing and play, as he was very fond of music.

When I left Mrs. Wentworth's school I was called an excellent performer on the piano, for I was very fond of music, and had devoted much time to practice. We also enjoyed some very pleasant conversation during the evening, and the more I saw of Mr. and Mrs. Leighton I felt disposed to like them. When I retired to my own room I kneeled and thanked my Heavenly Father for directing me to a home where I had a prospect of being useful and happy.

It is not my intention to give a detailed account of the events of the next two years; and a few words must suffice for that period of time.

If I had trials of temper to endure from my pupils, — and who ever yet was a governess and had not, — I also enjoyed much pleasure in their society. The eldest of my pupils gave me more trouble than did both the others. Her memory was not retentive; she had also a certain listlessness of manner during lessons which was at times very annoying. But it was a very pleasant task to instruct Birdie; she drank in knowledge eagerly, and possessed an excellent memory. In music she made astonishing progress, for a child of her years; and she was of a most affectionate disposition, which made the duty of imparting knowledge to her doubly pleasant. The progress of little Lewis was equal to that of most boys of his age. I found less trouble with him than I had at first anticipated. I found him to be a child that would never be controlled by harshness, but he was easily restrained by kindness.

As often as I could do so conveniently I visited my mother and Aunt Patience. Aunt Patience seemed happier than I had ever before seen her. I think the quiet of her home tended to soften her somewhat irritable temper.

CHAPTER V.

Willie Leighton's Return from England.

Soon after I became a resident in the dwelling of Mr. Leighton, they received a letter from Willie, informing them that the estate of his deceased relative could not be finally arranged in less time than a year, perhaps longer; and he thought that instead of returning to Philadelphia he would enter a College in England, and devote the intervening time to study. His parents could not object, knowing it to be for his interest, as he had not, when a boy taken very kindly to study. A year passed away, and Willie did not return, but they received frequent letters from him. Near the close of the second year he wrote, informing them that he intended leaving England on the tenth of the month following, as the matters pertaining to the property left him were now satisfactorily arranged.

About this time Laura returned home from school, having finished her term of study. Mrs. Leighton intended sending Georgania to the same institution where Laura studied, but she was not to go till the coming autumn. She wished, however, that I should remain with them till Birdie and Lewis should be old enough to send from home. I had been very, *very* kindly treated in the home of Mrs. Leighton, and had become strongly attached to my pupils, especially the two younger of them; and I was glad of the opportunity of remaining near to my mother.

As the time drew near when they looked for the return of Willie, all the family were busy with their preparations for giving him a joyous welcome.

When I observed the eagerness with which they looked forward to his return, I could not at times help feeling a pang of regret that I had neither brother nor sister of my own. Had it not been for my surviving parent, I should have felt entirely alone in the world. Not that I envied the Leightons — far from it — but I could not help sometimes contrasting my position in life with theirs. They being blessed with the love of fond parents, brothers and sisters, along with the possession of abundant wealth, and every comfort which tends to form a happy home; while I was a poor, fatherless girl, obliged to labor for my own support and that of my mother. I could not help thinking how different all might have been had the life of my father been spared. I do not think that I was usually of an unhappy disposition; on the contrary, I was inclined to be hopeful and cheerful; but I believe with the best of us, the happiness of others more favoured than ourselves will give rise to a feeling of sadness.

The time soon arrived when, according to the letter they had received from Willie, they might daily expect his arrival. None of the family were able to settle their minds upon any employment, and it was with the greatest difficulty that I could obtain the attention of my pupils during the time appointed for their daily lessons, and, being aware of the cause, I could hardly blame them. Their suspense was at length ended by the arrival of Willie. Never shall I forget the joy which was depicted upon the countenance of little Lewis when suddenly he burst into my room, exclaiming,

"Oh! Miss Roscom, our dear, *dear* brother Willie has come at last! Don't you wish you had a brother Willie too?"

Had he known the pang which his childish remark occasioned me he certainly would never have made it. With much difficulty I kept back my tears and tried to appear as much pleased as the child evidently wished me to be. I had been accustomed, since my residence in the family, to spend my evening mostly with them in the parlor; but on that evening I remained in my own room, feeling that I should be an intruder upon that family reunion. I took up a book and endeavored to interest myself in its pages. I could distinctly hear the joyous murmur of voices from below, varied by bursts of laughter, not loud, but strikingly mirthful. I soon heard light footsteps ascending the stairs; the next moment Birdie rushed in, exclaiming,

"Mamma says she has been so much occupied that she had almost forgotten you; but she says you must come down at once;

you mustn't sit here alone when we are all so happy."

I begged to be excused from going down, saying that they would probably prefer being left to themselves on this evening of Willie's return.

"Oh!" said she, "Papa and mamma both expect you to go down."

Fearful of giving offence, and after making some slight alterations in my dress, I accompanied Birdie down stairs and entered the parlor.

I believe most persons feel a kind of embarrassment when meeting for the first time one of whom they have long heard much. I was sensible of this feeling when I entered the parlor that evening.

Willie rose as I entered the room, and Mrs. Leighton, coming forward, said, —

"Miss Roscom, allow me to introduce to you my son Willie."

I felt much relieved by this unceremonious introduction. For a time we engaged in general conversation. The manner of Willie was so genial and pleasant that I at once felt at ease in his society. I had often thought that Birdie resembled no other member of the family, but that was before I saw Willie. He had the same complexion, the same cast of countenance, with the same smile, only in a more mature and masculine form.

After an hour spent in social conversation, he said some music would be very welcome to him, it was so long since he had enjoyed that pleasure in their own home. Laura immediately went to the piano, and sang two or three songs which she knew to be favourites of his. Willie invited me to play, but I begged him to excuse me for the time being, as he had three sisters present, who all played more or less.

After his sisters had each in their turn favored him with some music, he rose, and taking the vacant seat at the piano, asked if we would not like to hear an English song. His sisters laughed heartily, thinking him to be only in jest; but their amusement changed to wonder and admiration when, after running his fingers lightly over the keys, he began playing a soft and melodious prelude. It seemed that when a boy of fifteen, he had as a sort of amusement learned the rudiments of music, but he had not begun with any settled purpose of making progress in the study, and had soon become tired of it. What then was their surprise to hear him sing with much taste and skill, to a beautiful accompaniment, a song he had learned in England.

He explained, that while in England, a class-mate of his, who was an excellent musician, had given him lessons; and that after a time he had become very fond of it, and had practised much during his leisure hours.

It was easy to see that Willie was almost idolized by all the family. During the evening Mrs. Leighton could scarcely take her eyes from the face of her son, and they all eagerly listened to his every word: and any one who saw the noble-looking young man, could not wonder at their affection for him. When he rose from the piano, Birdie and Lewis begged for one more song, but Mrs. Leighton reminded them that it was late, and that their brother must be fatigued. And soon after prayers, the happy family separated for the night.

CHAPTER VI.
An Evening Party.

Previous to the return home of Laura and Willie, the Leightons had seen but little company for a family of their wealth and social position; but now, instead of the heretofore quiet evenings, their superb parlors were thronged with acquaintances and friends, for both Willie and Laura had been favourites with both young and old.

Laura had intended giving a large party, but had deferred it till Willie should return home; and soon after his arrival the invitations were sent, and preparations were commenced for the contemplated party. I did not expect, neither did I wish, to be included among the guests. I had never attended a fashionable party in my life; and I thought, even were I favoured with an invitation, that I should feel strangely out of place amid so much display of wealth and fashion as I should be sure to meet with at a party given by one of the most wealthy and influential families in the city.

I was much surprised when I received from Laura a very cordial invitation to attend her party. I at first declined the invitation, saying that I was unaccustomed to any thing of the kind, and that as most of the guests would be strangers to me, I should prefer not attending; but when Mr. and Mrs. Leighton expressed their wish that I should attend the party, I overcame my reluctance and consented.

The evening at length came, and although I anticipated but little pleasure from the party, I felt a degree of restlessness and expectation when the appointed evening arrived. My wardrobe was not furnished with any superfluities in the way of dress, and my command of money was not sufficient to allow of any extravagance in apparel. Laura kindly offered to present me with a beautiful silk dress for the occasion, but I delicately, though firmly, declined the gift, for I wished not to appear otherwise than in my true position. I therefore selected the most appropriate dress I possessed for the occasion; it was quite plain, though of rich material. The only ornament I wore was a pearl necklace, which had been a bridal gift to my mother.

Laura assisted me in making my toilette, and insisted that I should allow her to place a few natural flowers in my hair, and to please her I consented to wear them. Laura looked very lovely in the costly dress purchased for the occasion; she also wore a set of diamond ornaments, which her father had presented to her on her return from school.

As soon as we had finished our toilettes, we descended to the drawing-room, where Mr. and Mrs. Leighton had already taken their places, as it was near the hour when they might expect their guests to begin to assemble.

I went down thus early to avoid the unpleasantness of entering the brilliantly lighted drawing-room after it should be filled with guests. I had requested of the Leightons that I might receive as few introductions as possible under the circumstances. Truly it was a brilliant assembly which soon filled those spacious apartments. Among the guests who first arrived were a Mr. and Mrs. Lawton, with their daughter, to whom Laura gave me an introduction.

Their kind attentions and lively conversation soon dispelled the feeling of embarrassment with which I first found myself in the company of so many wealthy and distinguished people.

Dancing was soon introduced. Dancing was an accomplishment which I had never learned, as my mother disapproved of the amusement. Willie seemed disappointed when he invited me to become his partner for the quadrille then forming, and I replied that I did not dance. When he learned that I did not dance he introduced to me a young gentleman by the name of Shirley, who was seated near us, and who, for some reason or other, did not join the dancers. Mr. Shirley's conversational powers were extremely good, and we engaged in conversation for some time, in the course of which I enquired why he refrained from dancing? A shade of sadness passed over his countenance as he replied, —

"When a mere youth I was very fond of the amusement, and devoted much time to the practice of it. I believe it is the only thing which I ever knowingly did against the wishes of my parents; but my fondness for dancing amounted almost to a passion, and I often frequented the giddy ball-room when I knew that I was grieving my fond parents by so doing. My father and mother considered dancing a sinful amusement; but as my inclination to follow it was so strong, they finally forbore to admonish me further.

"When I was about twenty years of age my mother died. I was then residing at a distance from home. When mother's illness became alarming, I was summoned home. I was tenderly attached to my mother, and my grief was overwhelming when I saw that she must die. A short time before her death, she said to me one day, when we chanced to be left alone, 'My dear son, there is one subject upon which I wish to speak with you, ere I leave you for ever. You know I have ever considered dancing to be a sinful amusement. There may be no sin in the simple act of dancing, but it is an amusement which certainly has a tendency to evil. I know that you very much enjoy it, but you are now capable of serious reflection, and allow me to ask you if you feel in a suitable frame of mind for prayer and meditation when you retire to your room after having spent the evening in the frivolous amusement of dancing?' This was an argument which I could neither gainsay nor resist, and coming as it did from the lips of my dying mother, I was much affected by it. Before leaving my mother's room, I solemnly promised her that I would never again participate in the amusement of dancing, and that promise I have most sacredly kept. I now often wonder that I could ever have been so fond of an amusement which at the best affords so little real enjoyment to its votaries. I trust you will pardon the liberty which I have taken in talking so long of myself to you, an entire stranger; but when you enquired my reason for not joining in the dance, something in your countenance impelled me to be thus candid in my answer."

We remained for some time longer in conversation, and I really began to enjoy the party. There were several ladies and gentlemen seated near us, engaged also in conversation, and I could not avoid hearing much that passed among them. Presently I heard a lady enquire of a Mrs. Kingsley, a lady to whom I had been introduced in the early part of the evening, —

"Who is that young lady with whom Mr. Shirley has been so long conversing?"

"Oh!" she replied, "she is *only* the governess in Mrs. Leighton's family. A *person*, as I am informed, of good education, but very poor, and obliged to teach as a means of support for herself and mother, who is a widow."

Why should I have felt so indignant at those words, which, if maliciously intended, were certainly true? I suppose the attentions I was receiving at this my first party were causing me to forget my true position. The lady who had first spoken remarked further to Mrs. Kingsley, —

"Don't you think her very pretty — almost beautiful? I think I never before saw so intelligent a countenance."

Mrs. Kingsley replied, —

"I see nothing so very intelligent in her countenance, and if you consider her pretty, I must say that I am astonished at your taste; indeed I think her quite common-looking. I almost wonder that the Leightons should have made her a guest at a party with their friends; but then Miss Laura is kind-hearted, and I presume invited her out of pity — those *poor people* have so few pleasures."

"Hush! She may hear you."

And they changed the subject. I had, however, heard quite enough to spoil my enjoyment for the rest of the evening. I was young and inexperienced then, and this was my first, though by no means my last, lesson in those distinctions which the world draws between the rich and the poor. Had I possessed a little more knowledge of the world I should better have understood the matter, knowing as I did, that Mrs. Kingsley had an unmarried daughter present, of uncertain age, with a fair prospect of remaining for some time longer in her state of single blessedness. I forbear describing Miss Kingsley, and will only say that if Mrs. Kingsley thought me common-looking, I, on the contrary, thought her daughter, Miss Kingsley, to be very uncommon-looking.

After the remarks to which I had been an unwilling listener, I derived very little pleasure from the party. I mentally said, if my poverty is to be made a subject of conversation in parties like this, I wish never to attend another; and I was heartily glad when the gay assembly departed, at two o'clock in the morning.

Thus ended my first party, which would have afforded me much enjoyment had I not chanced to hear those annoying remarks from Mrs. Kingsley.

The party given by the Leightons was soon succeeded by others among their numerous acquaintances. To several of those parties I was favored with invitations, which I invariably declined, for I had decided to attend no more fashionable parties. At length, when urged by the Leightons to give my reasons for steadily refusing all invitations, I informed them of the remarks I had overheard from Mrs. Kingsley on the night of Laura's party. Never shall I forget the look of scorn and contempt with which Willie Leighton listened as I related the circumstance; but he made no remark, as he knew Mrs. Kingsley to be one of his mother's most intimate friends. Mrs. Leighton remarked that Mrs. Kingsley possessed many good qualities, although she was sometimes inclined to make malicious remarks.

CHAPTER VII.
Failing Health of Clara's Mother.

I soon had a far more serious cause for disquiet than the remarks of Mrs. Kingsley or any one else could have occasioned. I had many times during the past year feared that my mother's health was failing. She looked thin and pale, and seemed to lack her usual activity in performing her household duties. I frequently enquired if she were ill, and she had ever replied that she was quite well; only it might be a little fatigued. But the truth could no longer be concealed. My mother was ill, and that seriously. She still attended to her daily occupations, but she was greatly changed; she seemed during the past few weeks to have grown thin almost to attenuation. She was very pale, except at times there was a feverish glow upon her cheeks. I was then too young to detect, as I should now do, the insidious approach of that foe to human life, consumption. Going one day to visit my mother, I was so struck by the change so visible in her countenance, I privately asked Aunt Patience if she did not feel alarmed for my mother? She burst into tears, and was for some time unable to reply. I had never before seen Aunt Patience so much affected. I begged of her to tell me if there was any real cause for alarm, for I had hoped she would be able to dispel all my fears in regard to my mother. Regaining her composure, she told me that consumption was hereditary in my mother's family. I had never before chanced to hear it mentioned, but Aunt Patience now informed me that several of the family had fallen victims to that disease, and that she feared it had already fastened upon my mother.

"I am glad," she said, "that you have spoken to me upon the subject. I have long wished to make known my feelings to you, but I shrank from giving you pain. I have been unable to persuade your mother to call a physician. She imagines herself better; but I can see but too plainly that such is not the case."

I forebore mentioning the subject to my mother at that time; indeed I could not have done so. I was now thoroughly alarmed — almost terrified, and it was with a heavy heart that I returned to the dwelling of Mrs. Leighton.

I had frequently spoken to Mrs. Leighton of my mother's failing health, and I now felt it my duty to resign my position as governess, for a time at least, and return to my mother, that she might be relieved from all care. When I returned to Mrs. Leighton's on the evening in question, I again spoke to her upon the subject, saying that I feared I should be obliged to resign my situation in her family and return to my mother, who evidently needed my attention. Mrs. Leighton expressed much sympathy for me in my trouble, saying that I ought by all means to hasten to my mother; but added that she did not wish me to resign my position, as she was willing to wait for me for any length of time I might find it necessary to remain at home. She said, further, that Laura would be quite willing to give some attention to the children during my absence; and she tried to cheer me up, saying that she trusted my mother would soon be better. I too tried to be hopeful, but the impression that my mother was to die had taken deep hold of my mind.

I visited my mother the next evening, and, to avoid surprising her by suddenly returning home, I informed her that I intended spending a few weeks at home, as I needed rest from teaching, and that Laura would attend to the children during the time I should remain at home. My mother seemed so cheerful that evening that I began to hope that I might have been too much alarmed; but, when I had opportunity for speaking privately with Aunt Patience, her words confirmed my worst fears. She informed me that at her earnest solicitation my mother had that day summoned a physician; that he had prescribed some medicine for her, and given her some advice in regard to diet, walking or riding in the open air, &c. She further informed me that she had herself spoken privately to the physician, requesting him to tell her candidly what he thought of my mother's case. He replied, —

"As you have asked me a plain question, I think it my duty to give you a candid answer. I know not," continued the physician, "how it might have been had I been called six months ago, but now I fear the case of Mrs. Roscom is beyond the reach of medicine. I will gladly do my utmost for her, but I fear that a few months, it may be a few weeks, will terminate her life."

This was *fearful* tidings to me, as I had strongly hoped that the opinion of the physician would have been more favorable. When I became outwardly composed, I rejoined my mother, in company with Aunt Patience. My mother was not aware that Aunt Patience had held any conversation with the physician regarding her illness. She seemed much pleased at the prospect of my return home. I informed her, before leaving, that she might expect my return in the course of two or three days.

She failed rapidly from this time; and, shortly after I returned to my home, was obliged to give up all employment, however light. We often reminded her of the physician's wish, that she should walk in the open air; but it was seldom she felt equal to the task of walking even a short distance.

Mrs. Leighton and Laura often called, and brought many little delicacies to tempt the appetite of my invalid mother. Mrs. Leighton told my mother that she would be happy to send her carriage as often as she felt strong to ride out. My mother replied that on fine days she would gladly avail herself of her kind offer; and, so as long as my mother was able, the carriage was sent every fine day to give her the benefit of a short ride in the open air.

I presume that, on ordinary occasions, I should have felt some embarrassment in receiving a visit from Mrs. Leighton and Laura in my home, which appeared so humble, compared to their own elegant residence; but now it never cost me a thought, for, in the presence of a great sorrow, all trifling considerations vanish away.

It was in the month of May that I returned home, and by the last of June my mother was entirely confined to her room, and much of the time to her bed. She suffered much from nervous restlessness, and at times her cough was very distressing. She would allow no one, as yet, to sit with her during the night, but I gained her consent that I might sleep on a lounge which stood in her room.

There was no end to the kindness we received from the Leightons; no day passed without some one of the family calling to enquire for my mother.

Soon after this time my mother appeared much better. She was able to sit up more than formerly, and her cough was far less troublesome. I remember one day saying to Aunt Patience, when we chanced to be alone, that I began to think my mother would yet recover, she seemed so much better.

"My dear Clara," she replied, "I hope your mother may recover; but you must not build hopes which I fear will never be realised. This seeming change for the better is only one of these deceitful turns of her disease by which so many are deceived. I do not wish to alarm you needlessly, but I dare not cherish any hopes of her recovery."

The idea that my mother would die had been impressed upon my mind from the first; yet, when I observed her improved appearance, I thought that the physician, as well as ourselves, might have been deceived.

CHAPTER VIII.
A Bright Dream and Peaceful End.

The seeming favorable turn of my mother's disease proved, as Aunt Patience had feared, of but short duration. She was soon again almost entirely confined to her bed; except that, in the afternoons for the sake of the change, she would recline for a short time upon the sofa in the parlor. But this was only for a few days, and then she was unable to leave her own apartment.

As I have said so little regarding my own feelings, in view of my mother's death, the reader may be led to think that I felt less keenly than I might have been supposed to do. If I have said little, it is for the reason that I have no words adequate to describe what my feelings were at the time. I felt stunned as by a heavy blow; and it seemed to me if my mother died I certainly could not live. I had yet to learn that grief does not kill — that is, not suddenly.

I have often since looked back to that time, and felt deeply humbled, while thinking how little I felt resigned to the will of heaven. I could not then, as I have since done, recognize the hand of a kind and loving Father in the stroke. I could only feel that my mother was leaving me, and all was darkness beyond. I now scarcely ever left my mother's room, except when Aunt Patience would almost compel me for a short time, to retire to my own apartment, that I might obtain a little rest. But the thought that soon I would have no mother was ever present to my mind, and I wished to remain with her as long as she might be spared to me.

About three weeks previous to my mother's death, Aunt Patience urgently requested me one afternoon to retire to my own room and seek some rest, saying I looked entirely worn out. After obtaining from her a promise that she would not allow me to sleep too long, I complied. My room seemed very cool and refreshing that sultry afternoon, and, lying down upon my bed, I soon sank into a profound slumber, which continued for three or four hours. Upon my going down stairs, I was surprised at the lateness of the hour, and enquired of Aunt Patience why she had not called me? She replied that as my mother had seemed quite comfortable, she thought it best to let me enjoy a sound sleep. I persuaded Aunt Patience to retire to rest soon after tea, as I intended watching that night by my mother. Thus far we had ourselves been able to attend to the wants of my mother, without assistance, as it pleased her better that either Aunt Patience or I should attend to her; but we had lately allowed a friend to sleep in the house, as we did not like to be left alone. That evening, after my mother had partaken of a little light refreshment, she seemed inclined to sleep. I took up a book and tried to become interested in its pages. As my mother now seemed to enjoy a peaceful slumber, I remember I thought her dreams must have been happy ones, for I often noticed a smile upon her countenance. I think she had slept nearly two hours, when she awoke, and requested me to give her a drink. I supported her upon my arm as I held to her lips a glass in which I had mixed some wine and water. Laying her gently back upon her pillows I enquired if I could do anything farther for her comfort? She replied that she felt quite comfortable; and, thinking that she might again fall asleep, I resumed my reading. After remaining quiet for sometime she softly called my name. As I stepped hastily to her bed-side, she said, —

"Come and sit near me, Clara, I have something to say to you."

Obedient to her request, I drew my chair near to her bedside, and seated myself. She clasped my hand in both hers, as she said, —

"My dear Clara, I have long wished to ask you if you are aware that I must soon leave you?"

As she said these words the grief of my overburdened heart defied control, and, burying my face in her pillows I sobbed convulsively. This sudden near approach to death sent an icy chill over my whole being.

"You must endeavor to compose yourself, my daughter," said my mother, "and listen to me."

I tried to restrain my tears as my mother continued.

"I have long wished to talk with you, but have deferred it from time to time, through fear of giving you pain; but I now feel it an imperative duty to converse with you upon the subject. Allow me to tell you a dream which visited me in the slumber from which I awoke a few minutes since. In my dream I seemed to be walking alone on a calm summer's evening, without any definite object in view. When I had walked for a considerable distance the scene suddenly changed, and I found myself walking by the banks of a placid river. Looking forward, I observed a person advancing to meet me, whom I at once knew to be your father. My joy was great at the prospect of meeting him; for in my dream I recollected that he had been long dead. I enquired of him how it happened that I met him there? He replied, 'I saw you coming when you were yet a long way off, and feared you might lose your way.' Turning back in the direction from whence he had come, he turned towards me, with a pleasant smile, and said, 'follow me.' As we walked onward, I observed that the river by which we walked seemed gradually to become more narrow the further we advanced. He continued to walk onward for some time, a little in advance of me, when suddenly stopping, he turned to me and said, 'My dear Alice, look across to the other side of the river, and behold the place which is now my home.' The breadth of the river had continued to lessen, till it was now only a narrow line of water which separated us from the opposite shore. I looked as he directed me, and, oh! Clara, I can find no words by which to describe to you what I saw. It so far surpassed anything pertaining to this world that I am unable to give you any description of it. I felt an intense desire to cross the narrow stream which separated me from the beautiful place. I enquired of your father if I could not with him cross the stream and enter those golden gates, which I could plainly see before me. He replied, 'No, my dear Alice, every one must cross this river *alone*. You must go back for a brief period, as you have yet a mission to perform before taking your final leave of earth. You must comfort the sorrowing heart of our child ere you leave her. Tell her of the home which I now inherit, where there is also a place prepared for you and for her, if you so live as to be found worthy to enter those gates which you see before you.' He then said, 'I must now leave you, and you must return to our Clara for a few brief days, when you will be summoned to rejoin me in yonder blissful abode.' I turned to make some further remark to him, but he had gone from my sight, and I awoke with my mind deeply impressed by my dream. But now," added my mother, to me, "the bitterness of death is already past. It is for you only that I grieve. I trust however, that instead of grieving immoderately for your mother you will endeavor to discharge your duty in whatever position it may please God to place you, and so live that whenever you may be called from this world it may be to meet your mother in Heaven. Since my illness my mind has been much exercised regarding my own state as a sinner; for be assured, Clara, that, in the near prospect of death, we find in ourselves much that is unworthy, which had before escaped our notice while in the enjoyment of health. But I am now happy while I tell you that all is peace with me. I now feel willing to depart whenever it is the will of my Heavenly Father to call me hence, and I feel confident that in a very few days I shall be summoned from earth. I am sorry to see you grieve," said my mother, for I was weeping bitterly; "endeavor to derive consolation from what I have said; and be thankful that when I leave you it will be to rejoin your dear father where there is neither sorrow nor sighing."

Seeing that my tears agitated my mother, I succeeded in checking them, and assumed an air of composure, which I was far from feeling. After the above conversation with me, my mother enjoyed a night of tranquil repose. I now felt the certainty of her death, and prayed for strength to meet the sorrow which that event would bring to me.

So calm and peaceful were the last days of my mother's life that we could hardly recognize the presence of the King of Terrors, till the damps of death were gathering upon her brow. She died at sunset on a mild evening in September. She had passed the day almost entirely free from pain. Toward evening she slept for an hour; on waking, she said to me, —

"My dear child, I think the hour of my departure has arrived. I feel that I am dying."

I now observed that look upon the countenance of my mother which tells us that a loved friend is no longer ours. She requested me to call Aunt Patience, which I instantly did. I also sent a hasty summons to her physician, although it was needless, for she was even then entering the dark valley. The physician soon arrived, and after one look at my mother, said to me, in a low voice, —

"My dear Miss Roscom, as a physician, I can be of no further use, but as a friend, I will remain with you."

The physician was an old and valued friend, being the same who had stood by the death-bed of my father, and he deeply sympathized with me in this, my second bereavement.

As I stood by my mother, my grief was not noisy; it was far too deep and powerful for that. Outwardly, I was quite calm. My mother had endeavored to prepare my mind for this hour. I had also prayed for strength to meet it with fortitude and resignation; but those who have stood by the dying bed of a fond mother may understand my sorrow. My mother was spared much of the suffering which attends the last moments of many. She seemed to be softly breathing her life away. After lying for some time tranquil and quiet, she suddenly opened her eyes and looked from one to the other of us. As they rested upon me, she made a sign that I should go nearer to her.

"Weep not, my dear child," said she, in a whisper; "be faithful, and you will yet meet me in heaven."

She also addressed a few words of like import to Aunt Patience. Suddenly, she raised her hands, and, as she looked upward, with a smile upon her countenance, we heard a sigh — and her spirit had returned unto God Who gave it.

I was borne from the apartment in a state of insensibility, and, when I awoke to consciousness, the doctor and Aunt Patience were standing at my bedside. After administering a quieting draught, the physician left us, saying to Aunt Patience that she must try and induce me to sleep, as that would help to restore my shattered nerves. Aunt Patience sat by me during the long hours of that night, but it was not until the day began to dawn that I sank into a heavy slumber, from which I did not awake until a late hour in the morning. On first awaking, it seemed to me that I had had a frightful dream; but, as my mind became more clear, I realized the sad truth that my mother was no more. I heard a footstep enter my room, and soon a familiar voice addressed me, saying, —

"My dear Clara, I have come to see if I can be of any assistance to you in your sorrow."

It was Mrs. Leighton who had thus entered my room, she having hastened to our dwelling as soon as she learned of my mother's death. I could not at first reply to her kind words; I could only weep. She did not force me to talk, but, gently as a mother could have done, did she bathe my fevered brow and throbbing temples. Telling me to remain quiet for a few moments, she left the room, and soon returned, bearing a cup of tea, which she insisted upon my drinking. She assisted me to dress, and opened a window to admit the cool morning air. I tearfully thanked her for those kind attentions. She insisted that I should lean upon her for support, as we descended the stairs, and indeed I felt scarcely able to walk without assistance.

On going below, I found several kind friends, who had remained with Aunt Patience to render their assistance in any office of friendship we might require. Mrs. Leighton accompanied me to the room where lay the lifeless remains of my mother. I folded back the snowy napkin which covered her face, and gazed long upon those dear features, now stamped with the seal of death. As I gazed upon her now peaceful countenance, I felt that to wish her back again would be almost a sin. I also derived much comfort from the consoling words of Mrs. Leighton. I cannot dwell longer upon these sorrows. When I stood at my mother's grave, and looked down upon her coffin, after it had been lowered into the earth, I almost wished that I too were resting by her side. Since that period I have experienced other sorrows; but the sharpest pang I have ever felt, was when I turned away from the graves where rested the remains of both father and mother.

As I have before mentioned, Aunt Patience had, in the course of her life, passed through many trying vicissitudes, and, previous to her death, my mother had considered that we could make no better return for the debt of gratitude we owed her than by making provision for her old age. I say, with good reason, that we owed her a debt of gratitude, for, during her residence with us, she had shown the utmost kindness to both my mother and myself. And when my mother's health failed her, the care and attentions of Aunt Patience were unceasing. With a view of making provision for Aunt Patience, my mother had made arrangements that our house should be sold, and the money deposited for her future benefit. In making this arrangement, my mother wished me to accept of a portion of the money which the sale of the house would bring; but I declined, saying that, as she had given me a good education, I was amply able to support myself, so long as I was blessed with health. My mother assented to the arrangement, saying that I could draw money from the deposit should I ever have occasion so to do.

We remained for two months in our lonely home, after the death of my mother; at the end of which time the new owner took possession of the dwelling. Aunt Patience had decided upon going to reside with a relative who lived in Massachusetts, and the interest of the money, deposited for her use, was to be regularly remitted to her. We disposed of the furniture, with the exception of a few cherished articles, which I reserved for myself; these the purchaser kindly allowed me to leave in one of the upper rooms till I might wish to remove them. The same day that Aunt Patience set out on her journey to Massachusetts, I returned to Mrs. Leighton.

CHAPTER IX.
Friendly Attentions.

It was well for me that my mind was actively employed; had it been otherwise I should have continually brooded over my sorrows. As it was, when engaged with my duties in the school-room, my thoughts would wander to those two graves in the churchyard, and my tears would fall upon the book from which I was listening to a recitation from my pupils. Georgania having left home, I had only Birdie and Lewis as pupils. Much pity did those affectionate children evince for me when they could not but observe my grief. Birdie would often say, —

"Please, Miss Roscom, do not grieve so much; we all love you dearly, and will be very kind to you."

And Lewis, who could never bear to see my tears, would say, —

"I will be a little brother to you, Miss Roscom, so please don't cry any more."

To please my pupils, I endeavored to appear cheerful; but truly the heart knoweth its own bitterness. One thought, however, afforded me some consolation, and that was, that I was obeying my mother's dying injunction, by striving to do my duty in the position in which I was placed. As days and months passed away, I, in some measure, regained my usual cheerfulness, although I was nowise inclined to forget my mother.

A year had now passed since I saw her laid in the grave. I often visited her resting-place, and there I renewed my resolve to follow her precepts; and many a time, kneeling by her grave did I implore wisdom from on high to enable me to follow the counsels I had so often received from those lips, now sealed in silence. It seemed to me, at such times, that I almost held communion with the spirit of my mother.

I experienced much kindness from every member of Mr. Leighton's family. I spent my leisure time mostly in my room. They did not, of course, invite me to join parties, but they would often urge me to join a few friends in their own parlor; but I always replied that my deep mourning must be my excuse. I had no taste for company or mirth.

One afternoon the Leightons had gone to join a picnic party some two miles from the city. They had invited me to accompany them, but as usual I declined. I felt sad and lonely that long afternoon, and, being left entirely alone, I could not prevent my thoughts from recurring to the past. I thought of all the happy, careless days of my childhood; then my memory ran back to the night, when, at ten years of age, I stood by the death-bed of my father. With the eye of memory, I again saw my mother, as she stood bowed with grief at the grave of my father; and now I was left alone to mourn for both father and mother. Memory also fondly turned to Miss Edmonds, my first teacher. I felt that to see her again would indeed be happiness; but I knew not where Miss Edmonds then resided. The last time I had heard from her she contemplated going South, as governess in a gentleman's family. Then came the memory of the happy years I passed in Mrs. Wentworth's school. Where now were the many friends I had then known and loved? As these thoughts passed in quick succession through my mind, I could not refrain from weeping; and, as I was under no restraint from the presence of others, my tears seemed almost a luxury. I know not how long my fit of weeping might have continued had not one of the domestics entered the room, and informed me that a poor woman was in the kitchen seeking charity.

"I thought," said the girl, "as the other ladies are all away, you might give her a trifle, for she seems very needy."

Hastily drying my tears, I went down to the kitchen, where I found a young woman, who would have been very pretty but for the look of want and suffering depicted upon her countenance. It was evident, from her appearance, that she was not an habitual beggar. As I approached her, she seemed much embarrassed, as she said, —

"Sure an' its mesilf that never expected to come to this at all, at all."

"My poor woman," said I, "you appear to have been unfortunate."

"An' its mesilf that has been misfortunate," she replied, as the tears gathered in her fine, dark eyes. She continued, —

"There was never a happier couple than Dinnis O'Flaherty an' I the day the praste made us one. But, after a while, the wages got low, and the times were hard wid us. 'Polly,' says Dinnis to me one day, 'will you be afther goin' to Ameriky wid me?' 'Dinnis,' says I, 'wherever it plases you to go its I, Polly McBrine, that's ready and willin' to follow.' We sailed in the *St. Pathrick*, and tin days afther I saw my darlin' Dinnis buried in the salt say. He fell sick wid a faver, and all me prayers for his life could not save him; an' here I am, a lone widdy, in a shtrange land, without a penny in me pocket, nor a place to lay me head."

Here the poor woman's grief choked her utterance, and, covering her face with her hands, she wept aloud. I requested the domestic to bring her some food, which she ate like one famishing. I placed in her hand money sufficient to secure her from want for two or three days at least. I did not in the least doubt her story, for her countenance bore the impress of sincerity. When she left, I requested her to call again in two or three days, as I felt certain that Mrs. Leighton would assist her in obtaining some employment. She left me with many thanks, and blessing me after the manner of her country.

CHAPTER X.
A Surprise.

After tea I felt that I must walk out in the air, as I was suffering from a severe headache. I made my way to the church-yard, and sought the graves of my parents; and, seating myself at the headstone of my mother's grave, I remained for a long time wrapped in profound meditation.

I know not how long I remained thus, for I took no note of time; but when I raised my head at the sound of approaching footsteps, the shades of evening were gathering around me. It was Willie Leighton whose footsteps had aroused me from my reverie.

"My dear Clara," he began.

But when I looked up with a little surprise at his familiar use of my christian name, it being the first time he had thus addressed me, he colored slightly, and said, —

"I beg pardon, Miss Roscom, for thus intruding upon your solitude, but, finding you absent on our return, I came to seek you and, with your permission, to escort you home. I think you do wrong to come to this lonely place to cherish a sorrow which seems to me to be almost unreasonable. I would not have you forget your parents; but, surely, if they are permitted to look down upon you from their home in heaven, they would not wish to see you thus debar yourself from society and all the innocent pleasures of youth. The dews of evening," said he, "are beginning to fall, and I must insist upon your return home."

On our way home I could not help a feeling of uneasiness lest Willie's attentions to me should displease the family. I had allowed him to accompany me home, as I could not have done otherwise without absolute rudeness; yet I feared that, in so doing, I should displease his friends. My uneasiness increased as, upon entering the house, I thought I detected a shade of displeasure in the manner of Mrs. Leighton toward me. If Willie noticed anything of the kind, he *seemed* unconscious of it, for he made several efforts to engage us in conversation; but, for some reason or other, no one, except himself, seemed inclined to be social that evening. I felt very much depressed in spirits, for I attributed their silence to displeasure because Willie had accompanied me home, and, at an early hour, I bade them good night, and retired to my own apartment. After reading, as was my custom, a chapter in my Bible, and commending myself to the care of Heaven, I sought my pillow; but hour after hour passed away and sleep refused to visit my eyes. Again and again I mentally asked myself what had I done to merit the coldness which Mrs. Leighton had shown in her manner to me? It was not my fault that Willie had sought me, and in a kind and gentlemanly manner escorted me home; and I only attributed his attention to that respect which the *real* gentleman ever accords to a lady, be she rich or poor. I, however, decided that in future I should receive no attentions from Willie. The Leightons were kind, but extremely proud, and I feared that the pleasure Willie had lately evinced in my society had displeased them, although his attentions had been nothing more than a person socially inclined might be expected to show to one dwelling beneath the same roof. Again did the remark made by Mrs. Kingsley occur to my mind, and I firmly decided that, if Mrs. Leighton was displeased, she should have no further cause for displeasure, for I too was possessed of a proud spirit. The dawn of the new day glimmered in the east 'ere sleep closed my eyes, and then my slumbers were disturbed by unpleasant dreams. One dream, in particular, I still remember. I seemed, in my dream, to be a homeless wanderer I know not whither. I had left the limits of the city and was walking in the open country, on a road that seemed strange and unfamiliar to me. At length such a feeling of loneliness and misery overpowered me that I felt unable to proceed further. Seating myself by the roadside, I burst into tears. Raising my eyes, I observed a female figure approaching me, which I soon recognized as my mother. She drew near, and, laying her hands upon my head, as if in blessing, said, —

"Fear not, my beloved daughter, only continue in the path of duty and all will yet be well."

With a cry of joy, I sprang forward to embrace her, and awoke to find the sun shining dimly through the partially closed blinds of my window. I felt fatigued and nervous, after passing such a restless night. I was startled by the pale and haggard countenance which my mirror reflected that morning. I had scarcely finished my toilet when the breakfast bell rang, and I hastened down stairs, where the family were already assembled around the breakfast table.

Whatever of displeasure Mrs. Leighton might have felt the previous evening seemed to have vanished with the light of morning. Perhaps, thought I, her displeasure existed only in my own imagination, after all. Noticing my pale countenance, she enquired if I was ill? I replied that I had a slight headache, owing to my not having slept well. She kindly offered to excuse me from attending to my pupils that morning, but I told her that I felt quite able to attend to my usual duties. In the course of the day I mentioned to her the case of the poor woman who had called the day previous. She replied that, after seeing her and making some enquiries regarding her capability, she would speak to a friend of hers, who was in want of a servant, and she had no doubt she could influence her friend to engage her, should she consider her a suitable person. Accordingly, when Mrs. O'Flaherty called, two or three days after, Mrs. Leighton questioned her in regard to her capability as a servant. She replied that she had had considerable experience as a servant in genteel families, previous to her marriage in the old country. Mrs. Leighton requested her to call again shortly, saying that she hoped to be able to find her a situation. Mrs. Leighton further informed her that, if the lady engaged her, it must be entirely on her own recommendation; and that she hoped she would prove herself faithful and trustworthy. She replied, —

"An' its mesilf that'll be afther doin' me best to plaze the leddy, mem."

And, with many thanks, she left the house. Mrs. Leighton was much interested by the intelligent countenance and honest, truthful manner of the woman, and she accordingly so strongly enlisted the sympathies of her friend, Mrs. Wallingford, that she agreed to give her a trial. Mrs. O'Flaherty seemed very thankful when she called, soon after, and Mrs. Leighton informed her that she had obtained a situation for her. Mrs. Leighton also furnished her with money sufficient to purchase some plain, but decent clothing, and a few days after she entered upon her duties in the dwelling of Mrs. Wallingford, who afterwards frequently remarked to Mrs. Leighton that she had much reason to thank her for providing her with the best servant she had ever engaged.

CHAPTER XI.
Embarrassing Interviews.

My time passed in the usual daily routine of duties. About this time Georgania returned to spend a few weeks at home. Though much improved in personal appearance, she was far from being a pleasant companion. Her manner, to me, was exceedingly haughty, almost contemptuous. She seemed to have entirely forgotten my unwearied pains in laying the foundation of her education. I could never understand the reason of her dislike to me. The feeling must always have existed, though kept in check during the time she had been my pupil. I think the rest of the family must have noticed her unpleasant manner to me; and, I have no doubt, remonstrated with her upon the subject. I was of a proud, sensitive nature, and the many slights, in an indirect way, which I suffered from her roused my indignation, and I was revolving the idea in my mind of seeking another home, when an event occurred which caused my departure from the home of the Leightons sooner than I anticipated. On the morning of the day of which I speak, Laura was unable to get out, as she was suffering from a cold. She was very anxious to execute some shopping that morning, and asked me if I would undertake to make her purchases, as I knew exactly what she wanted. I gladly assented, and, as I passed the sitting-room, on my way up stairs, I heard Willie say, —

"I too have business up town, and I will drive Miss Roscom to the store where she is to make her purchases, and call for her on my return."

Mrs. Leighton replied in a low, but changed voice, —

"Why not send James, the coachman; it is more proper."

I did not wait to hear Willie's reply, but, when I came down, prepared for going out, the coachman was in waiting with the carriage. I was glad that Willie was not to accompany me, for, since the evening he had escorted me home, I had carefully avoided his society.

I was sitting that evening in the garden, in a kind of arbor, covered with weeping-vines. I was deeply interested in the volume

I held in my hand, and was much surprised when Willie suddenly entered the arbor, and took a seat by my side. I made a hasty movement to rise and leave the arbor, when he addressed me saying, —

"Why is it, Miss Roscom, that you constantly avoid me, and treat me with such marked coolness? I am sure I have not merited such treatment. I have long sought an opportunity to speak with you alone, and now you must hear me. Allow me to tell you that I have long loved you, with a deep and true affection. Will you not become my wife, and thereby render me the happiest of mortals?"

I was so much surprised by this unexpected declaration that it was some moments before I could collect my thoughts sufficiently to reply. I at length said, —

"Although deeply sensible of the honor you have done me, I must say in reply, that I can never become your wife."

He regarded me with unfeigned surprise as he said, —

"Then you do not love me, Clara. I had hoped that I was not wholly indifferent to you."

I replied, —

"As I believe you have addressed me with candor, I will answer you in the same manner. I do love you; and, were I guided by my own heart in the matter, my reply to your honorable proposal would have been different. But there are insurmountable barriers to our union."

"Name them," was his reply.

"Mr. Leighton," I answered. "Whether or not you are aware of the fact, that I am unable to say; but I *know* that your family would never consent to your marriage with their governess. They may respect and treat me kindly in my present position, but would never be willing to receive me as a daughter. It will, therefore, be wiser for you to place your affections upon some one in your own position in life."

"Am I not," replied Willie, "free to follow my own wishes in the matter? What care I for those butterflies of fashion, whose highest enjoyment is to shine in the gay assembly or crowded ball room. My heart's devotion must be given to one who possesses true nobility of mind. Should my parents refuse their consent to our marriage, then shall I feel justified in following the dictates of my own heart. I have never disobeyed my parents, and have endeavored to be guided by their counsels, but in this matter I must act in accordance with my own affection and judgment. In everything except wealth you are my equal, and I have enough for us both. Allow me to tell my parents that my happiness rests upon their consent to our marriage; and, should they withhold their consent, I will marry you and abide the consequences, for I am certain they will soon be sensible of their error." Being anxious to terminate the interview, I replied, —

"I must answer you, Mr. Leighton, in the manner which I consider will be best for us both. Never will I consent to become the wife of any man, and, by so doing, alienate him from his parents. I have experienced nothing but kindness from all your family, and I cannot take a step which will bring sorrow and disquiet into your heretofore happy home. Be advised by me and never allude to this subject again. I can be your friend, but not your wife. I intend, as soon as circumstances permit, to seek another home. Remember me as a friend only, and whatever my own feelings may be, I shall at least have the satisfaction of knowing that I have acted wisely and for the best."

His countenance expressed extreme agitation, as, rising, he said, —

"You have made me very unhappy, Miss Roscom. I will remain silent for the present; but go not away from here, as that would destroy my only hope."

When I entered the house, I heard the excited voices of Mrs. Leighton, Laura, and Georgania in the parlor. I heard Mrs. Leighton say, as I passed the door of the parlor, —

"Are you sure, Georgania, that you understood aright?"

"Quite sure, mamma," she replied; "I plainly heard Willie ask her to become his wife; how I *hate* her; and the thought of Willie's loving her almost causes me to hate him."

"Hush!" exclaimed Mrs. Leighton; "I will investigate this matter myself."

I hurried up to my room. I knew there was trouble in store for me, and I felt strong to meet it; for my own conscience acquitted me of any wrong-doing. After some little time had passed, I heard the footsteps of Mrs. Leighton ascending the stairs; and a moment after she rapped at my door. I opened the door and invited her to enter, and be seated. She then seated herself, and sat for some moments in silence. Her countenance expressed both sorrow and anger, for, up to this time, I believed that Mrs. Leighton had loved me. I waited for Mrs. Leighton to open the subject, for I well knew what had brought her to my room, and I cared not how soon she made known the object of her visit. At length she said, —

"It seems to me, Miss Roscom, that you have rendered a very base return for my kindness."

As she seemed waiting my reply, I said, —

"Will you have the goodness, Mrs. Leighton, to explain your words, for I am unable to comprehend their meaning?"

Her voice expressed much displeasure as she answered:

"I was not aware that my words required any explanation; but, if they do, it shall be given in few words. How dare you so far forget your own position, and ours, as to entice my son into making a proposal of marriage to one so much his inferior as you must know yourself to be?"

Should I live a hundred years I can never forget the shock her words gave me. I fairly trembled with anger. Rising to my feet, I looked her steadily in the face, as I said, —

"That your words are false, as well as heartless, I need not tell you, as you are already aware of the fact. I appeal to you if I have ever in any way courted the society of Willie. If he has asked me to become his wife, is it through any fault of mine? But you need give yourself no uneasiness upon the subject, for I have already told Willie that I will never become the wife of any man whose friends would look upon me as their inferior. For, though poor, and obliged to labor for my bread, I possess a spirit equally proud with your own, and that spirit your insulting words have roused. When you accuse me of enticing Willie into making a proposal of marriage, you well know that your accusation is false and without foundation."

"I suppose," said Mrs. Leighton, after a short silence, "that you will see the propriety of seeking another home."

"You might," I replied, "have saved yourself the trouble of reminding me of this, as I intend, this night, to leave your house. I intend to show you that I shall prove no hindrance to your son's marrying in accordance with your wishes. Allow me to express my heart-felt thanks for your past kindness to me; but we must now part."

Mrs. Leighton's anger, by this time, was beginning to cool.

"I am perfectly willing," said she, "that you should remain here till you can obtain another situation. When I spoke of your seeking another home, I wished not that you should understand that I wished you to leave immediately."

I thanked her, but said "I preferred going at once."

She enquired whither I intended going? I replied that there were several families residing in the city who had known and loved my mother, who would gladly shelter her orphan daughter.

Mrs. Leighton owed me, at the time, one hundred dollars of my salary; as I had not required the money, I had left it in her hands. Leaving the room, she soon returned with the money in her hand, and pressed me to accept of fifty dollars over and above what was owing me. I thanked her, but said I wished to accept only of what was my just due. As she refused to receive back the money, I laid it upon the table, and began making my preparations for leaving her house. In less than an hour my trunks were packed, and I was ready to go. Laura and Georgania, I think purposely avoided me, for I did not see them before leaving. I felt grieved when I parted with Birdie and Lewis, for I had become strongly attached to them. Lewis used often to say that boys never ought to cry; crying, he said, was only for girls and babies; but he must have forgotten himself on this occasion, for he cried bitterly when I bade him good-bye. As I turned from my pupils, Mrs. Leighton came forward and extended her hand to me. I could not refuse the hand that had so often administered to the wants of my dying mother. Neither of us uttered a word. We shook hands in silence, and I passed from the house, and entered the carriage which was in waiting for me. There was a family by the name of Burnside, with whom I had been intimate from childhood; to them I intended going, and in a few minutes I was set down at their door.

It chanced to be Mrs. Burnside herself who answered my ring at the door. In a few brief words I informed her of the circumstances which had caused me to leave Mrs. Leighton so suddenly; at the same time, asking her if she was willing to afford me a home for a short time, till I could obtain another situation?

"My dear Clara," she replied, "to my home you are freely welcome for any length of time you may wish to remain. Tomorrow we will talk further of the matter, but not another word tonight, for you look very much fatigued."

The family consisted of Mr. and Mrs. Burnside, and an aunt of Mrs. Burnside's, who resided with them. They had two daughters, but they had both married and removed a long distance from their early home. Mrs. Burnside offered to conduct me to my room, which offer I gladly accepted, for I wished to be alone. The excitement which had sustained me through the events of the past few hours had now subsided; and, when left alone in my room, I sat down to reflect calmly upon my situation. I could not but feel justified in the step I had taken; but I could not avoid a feeling of uneasiness when I reflected that I was now homeless. I did not wish to remain long with Mrs. Burnside, as I well knew they would accept of no compensation from me; and, for that reason, I felt the necessity of obtaining another situation as soon as possible; but I could come to no decision till after conversing with Mrs. Burnside upon the subject. After kneeling and imploring the protection and guidance of my Heavenly Father, I retired to rest, and, as I was worn out by the exciting events of the evening, sleep soon furnished a welcome relief from all anxious thoughts.

I was greeted kindly by Mr. and Mrs. Burnside the next

morning, when we met at the breakfast table. The aunt, being somewhat of an invalid, did not usually take her morning meal with the family. The only allusion to my circumstances was made by Mr. Burnside, who said I had better defer any conversation upon the subject for the present, and that, in the meantime, he wished me to consider his house as my home.

About eleven o'clock that morning, as I was sitting in the room with Mrs. Russell, Mrs. Burnside's aunt, the servant came up to inform me that a young gentleman was in the parlor, who wished to see me. Looking at the card which the girl handed me, I read the name of Willie Leighton. I was sorry to wound his feelings; but, when I left their dwelling, I firmly resolved that I would never intentionally meet with Willie again. I therefore requested the servant to inform Mr. Leighton that I was engaged. It was no easy matter for me to send this message to *him*; but my pride sustained me.

Two or three weeks passed quietly away. During this time, Birdie and Lewis twice came to see me, but whether by permission or by stealth I could not determine, and I would not enquire. Willie called repeatedly, but I never granted him an interview, as I deemed it best for both that we should not meet.

I shall never cease to remember with gratitude the kindness I received from Mr. and Mrs. Burnside, and, as I wished not to abuse their hospitality, I thought it advisable, when some two months had passed away, to devise some means of earning my own support. They would have assisted me in obtaining a situation in Philadelphia; but I wished to leave my native city, and see if new scenes and new friends would not have a beneficial effect upon my mind. I had now no remaining tie to bind me to Philadelphia. I grieved, it is true, at the thought of leaving the place which contained the graves of my parents. Nevertheless, I felt myself to be in the path of duty, while preparing to leave my native city.

CHAPTER XII.
A New England Home.

I knew I had an uncle living in the State of New Hampshire, whom I had not seen since I was twelve years of age — he having visited us at that time. He was my mother's only brother, and to him I decided to go. I once thought of going to aunt Patience, but finally gave up the idea. I retained a very distinct recollection of my uncle. I remembered that he and my mother had strongly resembled each other, although he was ten years her senior. When quite young he had married a very worthy woman, and their union was blessed by two children, a son and daughter; but they had laid them both in the grave at an early age; therefore they were now childless. I had never seen my aunt, but my heart turned toward them, and my resolution was soon taken to visit them. They resided about three miles from the village of Littleton, in New Hampshire.

The only obstacle in the way of my wishes was the long journey from Philadelphia to New Hampshire. I felt reluctant to undertake so long a journey alone. This obstacle was unexpectedly removed by the arrival of a Mr. and Mrs. Egmont, from the State of Ohio; they were relatives of Mrs. Burnside, and were journeying to the Eastern States, to visit some friends who resided there. Mr. Burnside mentioned to them my desire to visit my uncle in New Hampshire, and they gladly consented that I should accompany them on their journey. As they intended remaining but a few days in Philadelphia, I was obliged to hasten the preparations for my departure.

I could not but observe the hand of a kind Providence in directing Mr. and Mrs. Egmont to visit Philadelphia at this particular time.

On the evening preceding my departure I paid a farewell visit to the graves of my parents, and I shed some very bitter tears when I reflected that I might never again stand by this loved spot. I exacted a promise from Mrs. Burnside that, should any of the Leightons make enquiries concerning me, she would not inform them of my destination.

We left Philadelphia at a very early hour the next morning, and, after a very long and somewhat tedious journey, arrived in safety at the busy village of Littleton. Mr. Egmont conducted me to an hotel till he could make the necessary enquiries for finding my uncle. I knew he resided about three miles from the village, but was unable to say in what direction. Mrs. Egmont invited me to accompany them to their friends, who lived in the village, and rest before seeking my uncle; but, as I had arrived so near the termination of my journey, I wished to reach the home of my uncle without further delay. After accompanying Mrs. Egmont to their friends, Mr. Egmont returned to the hotel, where I awaited him. I was seated near a window, in the sitting-room, and heard him making enquiries of one and another for Mr. Wayland my uncle. No one seemed to know anything of the person he sought. As the landlord passed that way, he turned to him and enquired if he knew a farmer in that vicinity by the name of Wayland? He replied that, having resided only for a short time in Littleton, his acquaintance did not, as yet, extend beyond the limits of the village, and that he knew of no such person. I was beginning to fear that my uncle had removed to some other place, as I had not heard anything from him for a considerable time, when a ragged-looking boy, apparently about twelve years of age, made his way up to Mr. Egmont, and said —

"I can tell you where Mr. Wayland lives. He lives about three miles from here, on the Waterford Road. I knows you see, for I worked for him this fall, pickin' pertaters."

Giving the boy a piece of silver as he thanked him for his information, Mr. Egmont came to inform me that, when I had partaken of the dinner he had ordered for me, he would accompany me to the home of my uncle.

The lad before mentioned had given Mr. Egmont so accurate a description of my uncle's residence that, when we came in view of the square, old-fashioned farm-house, described by the boy, we at once knew it to be my uncle's home. As we came in sight of the house, the question — how will they receive me? — arose in my mind; but the recollection which I retained of my uncle was of so pleasing a character that I had little doubt of meeting with a cordial welcome. As we drew near, I observed an elderly-looking man in the yard, engaged in mending some farming implement. From the appearance of the place, it seemed that the front entrance was but little used, the front door and blinds being closely shut. I was at that time wholly unacquainted with the habits and customs of country people. As we drove up to the gate, the man I had before observed, paused in his employment, and regarded us, as I thought, with no little surprise. Surely, thought I, this man cannot be my uncle Wayland. At the time of his visit to my mother he was a young and fine-looking man; but the man I now beheld was bowed as it were by age, and his hair was nearly white. I should have remembered that since I had seen him he had laid both of his loved children in the grave. True it is that sorrow causes premature old age; but, upon a second look at his countenance, I could clearly trace his resemblance to my mother. His eyes, when he raised them to look at us, so strongly resembled hers that my own filled with tears, which I hastily wiped away.

Alighting from the carriage, Mr. Egmont addressed my uncle, saying, —

"Have I the pleasure of speaking to Mr. Wayland?"

He replied in the affirmative, and added, —

"I know not whether or not I am addressing an old acquaintance; but your countenance is not familiar to me."

Mr. Egmont replied, —

"I am not aware that we have ever met before; but this young lady who is your niece, Miss Roscom, has travelled in company with myself and wife, and I wished to leave her in your home before resigning my care of her."

My uncle seemed overjoyed at seeing me. He assisted me to alight, and embraced me with true affection. He immediately conducted me into the house, and introduced me to my aunt. She was a middle-aged, kindly-looking woman; and I also received from her a cordial welcome to their home. They invited Mr. Egmont to remain till after tea, but he declined, saying that he had promised to return to their friends as soon as possible. After some conversation with my uncle and aunt, they advised me to retire to my room and seek rest, after the fatigues of my long journey; and I gladly followed my aunt up the stairs, to a neat bed-room, tastefully furnished. I was weary both in body and mind, and, lying down upon my bed, I soon sank into a sound sleep. When I awoke, daylight was rapidly fading before the shadows of evening. I hastened down stairs, fearful that I had kept my uncle and aunt waiting for their tea. I enquired of my aunt if such were the case? She replied saying, —

"I gave the hired men their supper at the usual hour, but your uncle and I have waited to take our tea with you."

Can it be possible, thought I, that they take their meals with their hired servants? I had yet to learn the different usages of life in the city of Philadelphia and in a farm-house in the New England States. I wisely said nothing to my aunt of what was passing in my mind. Tea being over, we passed the remainder of the evening in social conversation. We had much to say, mutually of family matters. I told them many particulars connected with the death of my mother, of which I had never informed them by letter. They also told me much concerning their deceased children. Their son had died at the age of fifteen. As he had a decided taste for books, my uncle intended giving him an education, instead of training him to the life of a farmer. For a year previous to his death he attended school in Massachusetts. Returning home to spend his vacation, his parents thought his health was impaired, but attributed it to hard study, for he was naturally studious. They were hopeful that relaxation from study, with exercise in the open air, would soon restore him to his usual health. But their hopes were not to be realized; even then had death marked him for his prey; and consumption, which was hereditary in his father's family, soon laid him in the grave. Three months after the grave had closed over their beloved son, Walter, their daughter, Caroline, fell a victim to a malignant fever, which at that time prevailed in the neighborhood, and they saw her too laid in the grave, at the early age of twelve years — thus leaving them childless and sorrowing. We shed many tears while conversing of our mutual sorrows; and it was quite a late hour for the simple habits of their household when we separated for the night.

CHAPTER XIII.
New Occupations.

When going down stairs the next morning I was surprised, the hour was so early, at finding my uncle and aunt, with their two farm servants, already seated at the breakfast table. I must confess that these two farm servants seemed to me strangely out of place, sitting thus familiarly at the same table with their master and mistress. My uncle introduced them to me, by the names of Mr. Barnes and Mr. Hawkins, their Christian names being Solomon and Obadiah, and by those names they were mostly called in my uncle's family. Solomon, was a good humored looking man of some thirty years of age; he had, I afterwards learned, been for some years in my uncle's employ. Obadiah was a youth of about seventeen years of age. His extreme bashfulness in the presence of strangers in general, and of ladies in particular, caused him to appear very awkward. Added to this, he was, to use a common term, very homely in his personal appearance. His hair was very light, almost white; his eyes too were of a very light color, and uncommonly large and prominent. He was also freckled, and very much sunburned. He seemed very much over-grown, and his general appearance suggested the idea that he must be in his own way — a position of which he seemed painfully conscious. He had a most unpleasant habit of keeping his eyes constantly in motion. As I was seated directly opposite to him at the breakfast table, I found it very difficult to restrain my inclination to laughter, for I could not raise my eyes without encountering one of those furtive glances. The idea occurred to me that he was meditating on some means of escape from the table, and it was with much difficulty that I maintained a becoming gravity. I was very glad, however, when my uncle made some remark which provoked a general laugh; but I am ashamed to acknowledge that I looked to see what effect a smile would have upon the countenance of Obadiah; but my curiosity, however, was not to be gratified, for, judging by his appearance, his thoughts were of too serious a nature to admit laughter. I was glad when breakfast was over, and I am certain that Obadiah was more than glad.

My aunt, like most of the farmers' wives in the vicinity, had no assistance in performing her household work, except in very busy seasons. I begged of her to allow me to assist her, although I feared that I should appear very awkward in the performance of duties to which I was so little accustomed. My aunt at first refused, saying I was not accustomed to kitchen-work. But when I begged to be allowed to try my hand in assisting her, she brought me one of her large, checked aprons, which she advised me to put on. Thus attired, I washed and wiped the breakfast dishes, and arranged them in her spotless cupboard, saying to her that, while I remained an inmate of her house, she must allow me to assist her to the best of my ability, adding that I should be much happier if allowed to assist in her labors, than otherwise. Seeing me so anxious, my aunt allowed me to take my own way in the matter. I succeeded much better than I had feared; and when the morning's work was finished, my aunt laughingly said that, with a little practice, she thought I should make a very useful kitchen-maid.

In the afternoon she invited me to accompany her to the room which had been her daughter's. The room was tastefully, though not richly furnished.

"This," said my aunt, "was Caroline's room from her childhood. I have never allowed anything to be disturbed in the room since her death, except that I occasionally air and dust it. I suppose I am somewhat childish and fanciful; but it would pain me to see this room occupied by another."

Over the mantel-piece — for almost every room in my uncle's house contained a fire-place — there hung a picture of my cousin Caroline, taken six months previous to her death. I drew nigh to look at the picture. One glance told me that she had indeed been a beautiful child. The picture was enclosed in a beautiful frame of leather-work, which had been the work of her own hands. I gazed long upon the fair picture, fondly hoping that the loss her friends had sustained, by her death, was her eternal gain, by being thus early removed from a world of sin and sorrow to her home in Heaven. Opening a drawer in a small bureau, my aunt told me to look at her school-books.

By examining the books I was convinced that she must have been a child of no ordinary capacity, for her age. I also examined some of her apparel, with many other articles, which had been presents to her from friends.

Seeing the tears, which I found impossible to repress, my aunt became so much affected that I made some pretext for hastening our departure from the room; and, when we went down stairs, I endeavored to turn our conversation to some cheerful subject, to divert her mind from her sorrow, which had been vividly recalled by our visit to that lonely room.

The view which my uncle's residence afforded of the surrounding country was very pleasing to the beholder. Whatever way the eye turned, it rested upon well-cultivated farms, on which were erected comfortable and, in many instances, handsome and commodious dwellings.

In the distance, the summits of the White Mountains were distinctly visible, they being about twenty miles distant from my uncle's residence.

Mr. and Mrs. Egmont, according to promise, paid us a visit before leaving Littleton. My uncle and aunt were much pleased by their friendly and social manner; and, when they took their leave, we parted from them with sincere regret. They left Littleton soon after, on their homeward journey.

Three weeks had now passed since my arrival at my uncle's home, and I found myself daily becoming more and more attached to my kind uncle and aunt. Obadiah appeared to feel much more at his ease in my presence than at the first. When I learned that he was an orphan-boy and had no home, I felt a deep sympathy for him; but still, when I encountered one of those glances, I often found it very difficult to avoid laughter. I learned from my aunt that he, being left an orphan, had been put to work at a very early age; and, consequently, had had but few advantages for study and improvement. He could read tolerably, and write a little. My aunt was of the opinion that notwithstanding his peculiarities, he was possessed of good common sense, and would make good progress in study if he had any one to render him the necessary assistance. I at once offered to assist him in his studies, and proposed to him that he should spend a portion of the long evenings in study. He seemed at the first to be somewhat startled by my proposition; but, seeing that I was in earnest, gladly consented, and forthwith commenced his studies. My aunt cautioned me about laughing, if he should chance to make comical blunders; and it was well that she did so, for some of his blunders were laughable in the extreme; but "forewarned is forearmed." After a time I learned that he really possessed an intellect of no mean order. He soon made rapid progress in study. He seemed fully to appreciate the pains I took in teaching him, and endeavored, by many little acts of kindness, to show his gratitude to me.

Soon after my arrival, my aunt, one day, said to me, —

"I hope you will feel happy with us; for I wish you to consider our house as your home for the future. You know not," she continued, "how glad I am of your company, and how your presence cheers us; we will gladly adopt you as our daughter, if you can be happy with us."

I thanked her with tears in my eyes, and added that I was very happy in receiving so warm a welcome to their home, and would gladly do my utmost to fill a daughter's place to them. I further informed my aunt that I should be very happy to consider her house as my home, but that I should prefer teaching, as soon as I could find a desirable situation, as such had been my intention when I left Philadelphia. But when I mentioned the subject to my uncle, he seemed much hurt that I should think of such a thing. I told him that the wish to teach did not proceed from any feeling of discontent in my home, but that I thought it wrong to remain idle, while possessing an education which qualified me for usefulness. He replied that if I felt anxious to teach, we would talk about it the following spring; but, said he, you must think no more about it for this winter, at any rate; and so the subject was suffered to drop.

We led a very quiet life at my uncle's that winter. We saw but little company, except that occasionally the wife of some neighboring farmer would drop in to take a social cup of tea with my aunt.

There was a maiden lady residing in the village of Littleton who was always a welcome visitor at my uncle's residence, — her name was Miss Priscilla Simmonds. She was somewhat advanced in years, and of a very mild and prepossessing appearance. Upon the death of her parents, which took place many years before, she was left the owner and sole tenant of the house in which she lived. She lived entirely alone, and was considered a very valuable person in the village. She seemed, upon all occasions, to adapt herself readily to surrounding circumstances. At merrymakings, no one was so lively or social as Miss Simmonds: in the chamber of sickness, no hand so gentle and no step so light as hers; and when death visited a household, her services were indispensible. Although occupying a humble position in life, she was very much respected by all who knew her. Very few there were in the vicinity but could recall some act of kindness from Miss Simmonds, rendered either to themselves or their friends; and many there were who could remember the time when her hands had prepared the form of some loved relative for its last resting-place in the grave. Thus was Miss Simmonds bound to the hearts of the people of Littleton, as by a strong cord. In person she was tall; she had fine dark eyes, and her hair was lightly sprinkled with grey. From the expression which her countenance wore at times, I gathered the idea that she had, at some period of her life, experienced some deep sorrow. I one day enquired of my aunt if such were not the case. She gave me an evasive reply, and, perceiving that she wished to avoid the subject, I made no further enquiries.

I trust the reader will pardon this digression from my story.

In the course of the winter my uncle gave a party, to afford me an opportunity of becoming acquainted with the young people of the place. If the party lacked some of the forms and ceremonies practised in the city drawing-rooms upon like occasions, it certainly was not wanting in real enjoyment.

CHAPTER XIV.
School at Mill Town.

I believe there is no season more favorable to sober reflection than when we find ourselves alone, after mingling for a time in a scene of mirth and gaiety. After the departure of our guests, and my uncle and aunt had retired to rest, I indulged in a long fit of musing, as I sat alone by the kitchen-fire. In the silence and loneliness of the hour, my thoughts turned to my former home, and to the circumstances which had caused me to leave it; and although I had resolved to think no more of Willie Leighton, somehow or other, on this occasion, I found my thoughts wandering to him and to the seeming fatality which had separated us. The only living relatives of whom I had any knowledge were my uncle and aunt, and the before-mentioned aunt of my mother.

But a circumstance which I had heard my father mention in my childhood had of late often recurred to my mind. I recollected often hearing my father speak of a twin-brother, and that they had been left orphans at the age of eight years; also, that he, my father, had been adopted by a gentleman residing about fifty miles from the city of Philadelphia, who had given him a very good business education, and had procured for him a situation in the city when he became of suitable age. But the case had been different with his brother Charles. He too had been adopted, but by a very different kind of man from the one who had received my father. He did not give him sufficient education to qualify him for mercantile business, and at the time that Mr. Williams procured a situation for my father in the city, his brother Charles was apprenticed to learn the art of printing. He had, it seemed, entertained a dislike to the employment from the first, which increased to such a degree that he ran away from his employer; and instead of returning to his former home, he left the city. He was then fifteen years of age. My father had never been able to gain any tidings from him, and at length came to the conclusion that he must be dead. I know not why it was, but of late this circumstance had haunted my mind continually. The idea seemed to fix itself in my mind that I should yet see this long-lost uncle. I tried to banish the thought as an absurdity, but was unable to do so. As the idea returned to my mind with such frequency, I ceased trying to banish it, and prayed that what I now thought to be an idle fancy might prove a happy reality.

How cheering to us is the return of spring, after the deep snows and severe frosts of winter.

I very much enjoyed the sugar-making season at my uncle's farm. I derived all the more pleasure from its being to me such a novelty.

Although quite happy in my uncle's home, I still wished to carry out my former design of teaching, and as the season advanced, I again spoke to my uncle and aunt upon the subject. They were at first very unwilling to yield their consent; but, as they perceived that I was really anxious about the matter, they yielded their assent to my wishes.

About five miles west of my uncle's farm was the small village of Mill Town, so called from the number of different mills erected on the fine water-privilege it contained. As the village was small, it contained but two schools; one a public school, and the other a select school, which had for three years been taught by a young lady from the State of Maine, who had relatives residing at Mill Town. But Miss Landon, for such was the lady's name, intended returning to her home in Maine in the month of June. I had formed a very pleasant acquaintance with this young lady during the winter, and she strongly advised me to secure her pupils, if I wished to teach, promising to use her influence to aid me in obtaining pupils; and, owing to her kindness, I had no difficulty in obtaining a sufficient number of pupils for opening a school. I was very glad to obtain a situation so near my home, that I might be able to visit my uncle and aunt at least once every week, and spend my Sabbaths with them.

"After all," said my uncle, "I don't know but you are right in wishing to teach, and I dare say, will be happier thus employed than otherwise."

Accordingly, I opened my school about the middle of June, with twenty-five pupils. I had made arrangements to board in the house of the minister, who resided in the village. His name was Mr. Northwood, or Parson Northwood, as he was usually called by the villagers. He was very much respected on account of his many excellent qualities both as pastor and friend. His family consisted of himself, his wife, and two little girls, who attended my school.

I was highly pleased with my school at Mill Town. My pupils were mostly girls between the ages of ten and fifteen years. I had one class of quite young boys, whose parents preferred a select to a public school.

Many years have passed since I was wont to summon those loved pupils around me in that little school-room. Since that period, when far removed from those scenes, and surrounded by circumstances widely different, memory oft recalled those pupils in that New England village.

About this time I received a letter from Aunt Patience. The letter informed me that her health was somewhat impaired, and that she sensibly felt the approaching infirmities of age. I knew not her exact age, but I was certain that she must be considerably advanced in years. She stated that she was quite happy in her home, but added, —

"My Dear Clara, I had thought to have ended my days with your dear mother; and when the thought comes home to my mind, that she is now no more, it makes me very sad."

I was happy to know that, owing to the provision made for her, Aunt Patience enjoyed all the comforts of life. Since her removal to Massachusetts we had not often corresponded; but, as often as I did write, I enclosed a small sum from my own earnings, lest the interest of the deposit should prove insufficient for all her wants.

My mother left with me the injunction that, should my own life be spared, never to forget Aunt Patience in her old age: and I would cheerfully have endured any privation myself, if, by so doing, I could have added to her happiness; for the injunction of my dying mother I regarded as most sacred.

I closed my school for the summer holidays, and I was, as well as my pupils, glad to be released from the school-room during the sultry weather which prevails in the month of August.

CHAPTER XV.
A Happy Re-Union.

Upon my return home, my uncle said he thought I should enjoy a change of air and scene for a time as he fancied I was looking pale and thin. I replied that I felt quite well, and felt no wish to leave my home during vacation.

However, about this time, a party was formed among my acquaintances for visiting the White Mountains, and they were anxious that I should make one of their number; and, as my uncle and aunt strongly advised me to go, I at length consented.

The sublime scenery of the White Mountains has been so often and so ably described by tourists, that any description from me would be superfluous. Upon our arrival at the Profile House, we found it so much crowded with guests that we had no little difficulty in obtaining accommodation. When one party left, the vacancy was almost immediately filled up by fresh arrivals of pleasure-seekers. Every one seemed highly to enjoy themselves, and time passed swiftly away.

I was one evening seated on the piazza, engaged in a very pleasant conversation with several ladies and gentlemen, who, like me, had sought the piazza to enjoy the refreshing coolness of the evening air, after an intensely hot day. I noticed a carriage approaching in which several persons were seated. I did not at first pay much attention, as the arrival of strangers was a matter of very frequent occurrence; but, as the carriage drew nigh, my attention was riveted by a lady seated therein. She made some smiling remark as one of the gentlemen stepped from the carriage and assisted her to alight. That smile was sufficient — it was the very smile of Miss Edmonds, the same happy smile which had so pleased my fancy years ago. The seven years which had passed since I had seen her had somewhat changed her countenance; but her smile was the same. As she took the arm of the gentleman who accompanied her, and ascended the steps of the piazza, I stepped forward and spoke to her as any stranger might accost another in a place of public resort. I wished to see if she would recognize me. She replied to me only as she might have done to any other stranger, but without the least sign of recognition. Perceiving that she did not recognize me, I went near to her and said, —

"Can it be possible, Miss Edmonds, that you have forgotten your old pupil, Clara Roscom?"

In a moment I was clasped in her arms and felt her kisses upon my cheek. Turning to the gentleman whose arm she had left, she said, —

"Allow me, Miss Roscom, to introduce to you Mr. Harringford, my husband."

I acknowledged the introduction as well as my feelings of joyful excitement would admit of, for I knew of no other friend whose presence would afford me so much happiness as she with whom I had so unexpectedly met. Seeing that she looked very much fatigued, I conducted her at once to my own apartment. She was very anxious to learn all that had befallen me since we parted in Philadelphia, but I insisted upon her resting before entering upon the long conversation which we anticipated enjoying together.

When Miss Edmonds, or Mrs. Harringford as I must now call her, had somewhat recovered from her fatigue, we derived mutual satisfaction from a long and confidential conversation. In giving me a brief sketch of her life during the time we had been separated, Mrs. Harringford said, —

"On going to New York, I obtained a situation as governess, which, for various reasons, I did not like, and I decided upon seeking another situation. I chanced about this time to meet with a lady whose home was in South Carolina. Her husband had business which required his presence in the City of New York, and he had prevailed upon her to accompany him. The lady had, some years before, formed a slight acquaintance with Mrs. Leonard, the lady in whose house I was employed as governess, and when she visited the city she sought out Mrs. Leonard, and their former acquaintance was resumed. During one of her visits I happened to hear her remark that a friend of hers, residing in Greenville, S. C., had commissioned her if possible to find her a governess for her three little daughters, who would be willing to remain for some years, and the salary she offered was very liberal. Instantly my resolution to go South was taken. As I had anticipated, I had some difficulty in obtaining the consent of my parents to my undertaking, but, when they found that my heart was really set on going, they at length consented. I felt no fears regarding the journey, as I was to accompany Mr. and Mrs. Carlton on their homeward journey, and they promised to see me safely at my new home. It is needless for me to dwell upon particulars. I spent more than four years in the family of Mr. Leslie, where I went as governess. I was kindly treated by them, and shall ever remember them with gratitude. During the last six months of my residence with the Leslies, I became acquainted with Mr. Harringford, who is now my husband. He was transacting some business in Greenville, which detained him for a considerable time. I often met him at parties. We were mutually pleased with each other, and, when he left Greenville, I was his promised wife. My home is now at Jackson, in Tennessee, where Mr. Harringford resided previous to our marriage.

"I felt a strong desire to visit my parents, at New York, this summer; and, as Mr. Harringford had heard much of the beautiful scenery of the White Mountains, he persuaded me to accompany him to New Hampshire for the purpose of visiting them, and to that circumstance I owe the happiness of again meeting with you. I have ever remembered you as the bashful school girl I left in Philadelphia, and when I found you so much changed you cannot wonder that I failed to recognize you."

In my turn I narrated to Mrs. Harringford the events of my life since we parted. Her tears flowed often as she listened to the particulars of my mother's death, for she had much loved any mother. I kept nothing back, not even the circumstance which had caused me to leave Mrs. Leighton. The intimate friendship existing between us made it easy for me to speak freely to Mrs. Harringford. She informed me that she intended visiting Philadelphia before returning South, as she had many old friends residing there. As she contemplated visiting the Leightons, I exacted from her a promise that she would conceal from them her knowledge of my residence. I had never once heard from them since leaving Philadelphia.

Mrs. Burnside was the only one with whom I had corresponded; and I had requested her to avoid mentioning the Leightons in her letters to me. But of late I had felt a strong desire to hear from them, and I requested Mrs. Harringford to give me some account of the family in the letter she proposed writing from Philadelphia.

The party of young friends who had accompanied me from Littleton were quite ready to return at the expiration of a week; but Mrs. Harringford intended remaining a week longer, and she was very anxious that I should remain with her. I therefore allowed my friends to return without me. I wished to enjoy the society of Mrs. Harringford as long as possible, for I thought it quite probable that we might never meet again.

We spent a happy week together after the return of my friends to Littleton. The only shadow upon our happiness was the thought — how soon we must be parted, perhaps for life. From all I observed of Mr. Harringford I thought him to be worthy, in every respect, of the bride he had won.

Happy days pass swiftly by, and the morning soon arrived when we must bid each other adieu. Before we parted, Mrs. Harringford drew a costly diamond ring from her finger, and, placing it upon mine, said, —

"Wear this, my dear Clara, for my sake; and, when you look upon it think of me, who will often think of you, and will pray for your happiness both here and here-after."

The moment of parting had arrived. We parted on the piazza of the Profile House; they to proceed on their journey, and I to return to my uncle and aunt.

I have never since met with Mrs. Harringford. The ring she gave me at parting still encircles my finger, and when I gaze upon it I often think of the loved friend who placed it there.

I received an affectionate welcome from my uncle and aunt upon my return, and I was truly glad to find myself once more at home. Mrs. Harringford had promised to take an early opportunity of writing to me, and I had requested her to give me some account of the Leightons. Separate from other causes, I felt anxious to hear from Birdie and Lewis, for I was strongly attached to those two affectionate children. A letter from her arrived in due time. After giving me information of many of my former friends, she said, —

"And now, Clara, it only remains for me to give you an account of my visit to Mrs. Leighton, although I fear I shall give you pain instead of pleasure by so doing. When I called on Mrs. Leighton, I was struck with surprise at her changed appearance. You doubtless remember, Clara, what beautiful hair Mrs. Leighton had. You will scarcely credit me when I inform you that it is now thickly sprinkled with grey. She appeared like one who struggled with some secret sorrow. An air of sadness seemed to reign in the home, where formerly all was joy and happiness. Mrs. Leighton so strongly urged us to spend the night with them that we could not refuse. Laura was absent, visiting some friends in the country. Georgania and Bertha were both absent, attending school. Lewis has not yet been sent from home, but attends school in the city. He has grown a fine, manly-looking boy. He made many enquiries of me, if I had seen or heard from you? I was sorry that I was not at liberty to tell him how lately I had seen you, for I am sure that it would have afforded him much pleasure. My enquiry for Willie caused a pained expression to cross the countenance of both Mr. and Mrs. Leighton. Mr. Leighton replied briefly by saying, 'Willie is at present in England.' Later in the evening, when the gentlemen had gone out, Mrs. Leighton said to me, — 'As you are an old friend, Mrs. Harringford, I will explain to you the cause of Willie's absence. You doubtless remember Clara Roscom who was a former pupil of yours. After you left Philadelphia, she completed her education at a distant boarding school, and soon after her return home I engaged her as governess in my family. We soon learned to love and respect Miss Roscom, on account of her many excellent qualities, and we treated her very kindly. She left us to attend to her mother during the illness which terminated in her death, and after that event she again returned to us. But, to tell you all in a few words, Willie fell in love with her, and asked her to become his wife. When I first learned the fact I suppose I made use of some rather strong language to Miss Roscom, so much so that she left my house that very night. She remained for a short time with a Mrs. Burnside, who resides in the city and then left Philadelphia, and we have never since been able to gain any knowledge of her residence. If Mrs. Burnside knows anything of her she gives no information upon the subject. I have no doubt that she is governed by Miss Roscom's direction, for she possessed a proud spirit. I regret some things I said to her, but the thought of Willie, our pride, uniting himself by marriage to our governess put me almost beside myself with indignation. But Willie was so blinded by his love for her that all considerations of family or wealth were as nothing to him. When he learned that Miss Roscom had left the city, and he found himself unable to learn anything of her, he became embittered towards us all. He soon after declared his intention of returning to England; but what grieves me most of all is, that he will hold no correspondence with us since leaving home. He has now been ten months absent. We have written to him again and again, but have received no reply.' As she concluded, Mrs. Leighton burst into a flood of tears, which, for some time, she was unable to check. You may believe me, Clara, when I tell you that you are happier today, while attending to the duties of your school, than is Mrs. Leighton, in her luxurious home."

Such was, in substance, the information which Mrs. Harringford's letter afforded me. I almost regretted having sought the information, for it made me very unhappy. It grieved me much to learn that Willie was self-exiled from his home and friends.

CHAPTER XVI.
Miss Simmonds' Story.

The fifteenth of September found me again installed in my position as teacher in my school at Mill Town. I still continued to board in the family of Parson Northwood. I retained all my former pupils, with the addition of several new ones.

Miss Simmonds had often invited me to pay her a visit in her home at Littleton, but I had as yet found no convenient opportunity for so doing. One Friday evening I decided to pay the long promised visit, and remain over the Sabbath with Miss Simmonds. She seemed very glad to see me, and gave me a friendly welcome to her humble home. But, humble as it was, it presented a picture of neatness and cozy comfort. After tea, and when her light household duties had all been carefully performed, we seated ourselves by a cheerful fire in her little sitting-room, and prepared to spend the long evening in social conversation. I had always been very fond of the company of Miss Simmonds. Her conversational powers were very good, and she was sufficiently well informed to render her a very agreeable companion. As the night closed in, one of those violent storms of wind and rain came on, which are so frequent in the Eastern States during the month of

November. The beating of the storm without caused our warm and well-lighted room to seem all the more cheerful. As the evening advanced I observed that Miss Simmonds grew thoughtful; and, although she endeavored to be social, it was evident that her mind was occupied by something else than the subject of conversation. After a short silence, she addressed me suddenly, saying, —

"I feel inclined, Clara, to relate a story to you, which at least has the merit of truth; for it is a chapter from my own life."

I gladly assented to listen to her story, for since I first met Miss Simmonds I had entertained an idea that there was something of romance attached to her life.

"Thirty years ago," began Miss Simmonds, "I was not the faded, care-worn woman which you now see before you. I was born in this village. My parents were poor but industrious people. They were blessed with two children, myself, and a brother, who was two years younger than I; but, ere he reached the age of ten, we were called to lay him in the grave, leaving me the sole comfort and joy of my bereaved parents. They had very much loved my little brother; and, when death claimed him, all the love which he would have shared with me, had he lived, was lavished upon me. There is little in my childhood and youth worthy of notice, as we occupied an humble sphere in life. I suppose you will hardly credit me, Clara, when I tell you that, at the age of sixteen I was called beautiful. It was something to which I had given but little thought; but the ear of youth is ever open to flattery, and I must confess that my vanity was flattered by being called beautiful by the residents of the then small village of Littleton.

"When I was about eighteen years of age," continued Miss Simmonds, "a young lawyer, by the name of Almont, opened an office in this village, for the practice of his profession. He came among us suddenly, and he informed those with whom he first made acquaintance, that he had formerly resided in Massachusetts. Many wondered at his locating himself here, as the village was then but small, and offered few inducements to professional men.

"He was very affable and pleasing in his address, and soon made the acquaintance of many of the young people of the village, and we soon found him to be a very agreeable addition to our picnic excursions and other parties for pleasure and amusement. He paid marked attention to me from the time when we first became acquainted; and, to shorten my story, after an acquaintance of six months, he asked me to become his wife. I am now an old woman, Clara, and need not blush to tell you that I had learned to love him with a deep affection, and I yielded a willing assent, provided that my parents approved. True, I had no knowledge of his connections or former life; but since his residence in our village, his conduct had been irreproachable, and he was fast gaining the respect and confidence of all who knew him. There was something very attractive in his personal appearance; he seemed to have seen much of the world, for so young a man, for he spoke in a familiar manner of many distant scenes and places. When he sought my hand in marriage, my parents did not object. He was gaining quite a lucrative practice both in Littleton and adjacent places, and he declared his intention of making Littleton his permanent home. Doubtless, this influenced my parents to favor his suit, as the thought of my settling in my native village was very pleasing to them. He was very much flattered by society, and I was all the more pleased to find myself the object of his choice. When our engagement became known, I had good reason for believing myself to be envied by many of my female acquaintances. Neither they nor I were aware how soon their envy was to be turned to pity. An early day was appointed for our marriage, and my poor parents exerted themselves to give me a suitable wedding outfit. About this time, Mr. Almont had business which obliged him to leave Littleton for a short time. When he bade me adieu I felt a foreboding of evil; and, after he had gone, I experienced a depression of spirits, for which I could not account. But, when he had been a week absent, and I received from him a cheerful letter, informing me of his return in a few days, I strove to banish my sad thoughts and busied myself in preparing my wedding outfit. Going one day to the Post Office, with the expectation of finding there a letter from Mr. Almont, I received this instead."

As she spoke, Miss Simmonds unfolded a letter, which I had observed her take from a drawer before commencing her story. It read thus: —

"Boston, June 4th, 18 —.

"To Miss Priscilla Simmonds:

Although you are, personally, a stranger to me, I nevertheless take the liberty of addressing you. By the merest chance I learned your name and residence, also, that you are shortly to be united in marriage to Mr. George Almont, a lawyer from the city of Boston.

"I felt it an imperative duty, before that event shall take place, to inform you that I am the wedded wife of the same George Almont, whom you are about to marry. He came to Boston about five years since, having, as he said, just completed his studies in the city of New York. He opened an office in this city for the practice of his profession; and, as his external appearance was pleasing, he soon gained an entrance into good society. I need not inform you that he was likely to make a favorable impression upon the mind of a young lady just entering society. He rose rapidly in his profession; and although my parents were wealthy, when they saw how deeply I was attached to him, they did not object to my receiving his addresses, as he bid fair to rise to a position of wealth and influence. It is needless, as well as painful, for me to dwell upon the subject. Two years after he first came to Boston we were married. We soon removed to our own dwelling, which was a wedding gift to me, from my father. For a time he treated me with the utmost kindness and affection. But you may believe me, Miss Simmonds, when I inform you that he has been a dissipated, unprincipled man from his youth. His seemingly correct habits had merely been put on, for the purpose of gaining him an entrance into respectable society. When he began to treat me with indifference and neglect, for a long time I bore it in silence; but I was at length forced to acquaint my parents of the matter. My father soon took measures to ascertain what manner of life he had led while pursuing his studies in New York; and the information he gained was very discreditable to Mr. Almont. But my parents advised me, as we were married, to try if, by kindness, I could not reclaim him from his evil ways. I willingly followed their advice, for I still loved him; but, I suppose the restraint which for a time he had imposed upon himself made him all the more reckless when he returned to his evil courses. He soon seemed to lose all respect for me as well as for himself; and his conduct became so vicious that my father recalled me to his home, and forbade Mr. Almont from ever again entering his dwelling. I could, I presume, have obtained a divorce from him with little difficulty, but I shrank from the publicity attached to such a course. I still reside with my father and mother. Mr. Almont left Boston soon after I returned to my parents. We heard nothing of him for some time; but we lately heard from a reliable source that he was residing in Littleton, in New Hampshire, and also of his approaching marriage. Nothing but a sense of duty would have induced me to make this communication to you. I would save another young life from being shadowed by the same cloud which has darkened mine. Should you doubt the truth of what I have written, you can easily satisfy yourself, by either visiting this city in person, or causing any of your relatives so to do. Enclosed you will find the street and number of my residence. I sincerely hope you will receive this communication in the spirit in which it is written, and that is, one of kindness, and a desire to save you from the sorrows which I have experienced.

"Yours truly,

"Malvina Almont."

Miss Simmonds continued, —

"You may be able to imagine, but I cannot describe the effect produced upon my mind by the perusal of this letter. I felt stupefied and bewildered. How I reached my home I could never tell. I entered the house just as my father and mother were sitting down to their noon-day meal. As soon as my mother caught sight of me she enquired of me what was the matter? I suppose the agony of my mind was depicted upon my countenance. Without a word, I placed the letter in her hand, which, after perusing, she handed to my father. The natural temper of my father was rash and impulsive, and the contents of that letter exasperated him beyond control. He used many bitter words, and threatened dire vengeance upon young Almont, should he ever again enter our dwelling. My mother begged of him to desist, saying that if he were indeed guilty, as the letter proved him to be, his sin would certainly bring its own punishment. When we had succeeded in quieting the anger of my father, we were able to converse upon the matter in a calm and rational manner. We finally decided that my father should read the letter to Mr. Almont upon his return, and see what effect it would produce upon him. Three days later he came. He entered our dwelling and accosted us with his usual bland and smiling manner. In a short time, my father turned and said, — 'During your absence, Mr. Almont, my daughter has received a most unaccountable letter which I wish to read to you, hoping you may be able to explain it.' The paleness which overspread his countenance on hearing my father's words put to flight the hope I had cherished that he would be able to prove the letter a falsehood. Without any further remark, my father read the letter to him, word for word. As he concluded he said, — 'And now, Mr. Almont, unless you are prepared to prove the information contained in this letter to be untrue, I wish you immediately to leave my dwelling, and, if you take my advice, you will also leave this village, for I cannot abide the sight of a wretch such as this letter proves you to be, and your silence be as testimony to its truth. Begone! I say, from the humble, but, heretofore, happy home, which your baseness has darkened by sorrow.' As my father uttered these words, he stamped with his foot, and pointed to the door. Without a word, Mr. Almont left the house, and on the day following, we learned that he had left Littleton, and gone no one knew whither. Many surmises arose concerning his sudden departure, for it was well known that we were engaged to be married, but no one had any knowledge of the facts of the matter. When the wonder had subsided, which any unusual event occasions in a small village, the subject was suffered to rest. I felt stricken as by a sudden blow. I felt no interest in life, but I endeavored, when in the presence of my parents, to assume a cheerfulness which was far from being the real state of my mind.

"To a few and tried friends only did we make known the real truth of the circumstances attending the departure of Mr. Almont from Littleton. Time passed on. Those who knew my sorrows respected them, and the name of George Almont ceased to be mentioned among our acquaintances. But it was something which I could never cease to remember. I had loved George Almont as one of my nature can love but once in her life, and, when I learned that I had been deceived in regard to his true character, the knowledge was very bitter to me. I loved him still — not as he really was, but I still loved the memory of what I had supposed him to be, when I gave him my affection. There are few lessons in life more bitter to either man or woman than to find themselves deceived by one to whom they have given their best affections. For a time I yielded to a bitter and desponding spirit. I excluded myself from all society, and brooded in solitude over my sorrow. I so far yielded to this unhealthy tone of mind that I gave up attending church, and I caused my parents much grief and anxiety by the sullen and apathetic state of mind in which I indulged.

"During the winter which succeeded the events of which I have spoken, there was a series of special meetings held in the Congregational Church in this village. A general interest was manifested in the subjects of religion by both old and young. Many of those who had been my former companions were hopefully converted. I had formerly been of a gay and lively disposition, fond of dress and amusement. The subject of religion was one to which I had scarcely ever given a thought. The world and its pleasures occupied my whole heart, and, when the world disappointed me, I knew not where to turn for comfort. True, I had, from a child, attended to the outward forms of religion, but my heart was untouched and I now see that it required a great earthly sorrow to turn my thoughts heavenward. I at first refused to attend the meetings of which I have spoken, though often strongly urged to do so, but, one evening, my parents so strongly urged me to accompany them to hear an aged minister from another State that I at length consented to go. It is a matter of thankfulness to me this day that I attended that meeting. As I have said, the minister was an old man, his hair was white as snow. There was something remarkably pleasant and venerable in his appearance. No one who heard his voice and gazed upon his mild countenance, could doubt that they listened to a good man. During the first prayer, on that evening, my heart became softened and subdued, and when he gave out his text, from Matthew xi. chap., 28, and two following verses, I listened to him with rapt attention. It seemed almost that he understood my individual case. In the course of his sermon, he said: — 'I presume there are few in this congregation who have not some burden of sorrow which they would gladly have removed. Shall I tell you how you may be released from this burden? Kneel humbly at the foot of the Cross; and while you pray for the forgiveness of your past sins, make a firm resolve, in the strength of the Lord, that your future life shall be given to His service; if you do this with sincerity, you shall surely find rest unto your souls. You need have no fears that you will be rejected, for hath not the Saviour said: — Him that cometh unto me I will in no wise cast out. You may, this very night, exchange your burden of sin and sorrow for the yoke which is easy and the burden which is light.'

"I have," said Miss Simmonds, "a distinct recollection of the look and manner of that aged man as he uttered these words, and it is a matter of heartfelt thankfulness to me the day that ever I heard his voice; for he it was who first guided my wandering feet into the paths of peace. When I returned to my home the words of that good man followed me. I thought much on the words of his text. Surely, thought I, if all are invited to come to the Saviour, I must be included in the number. Why may I not go now? With these thoughts in my mind, I kneeled in prayer. I prayed earnestly for the pardon of my sins and resolved, from that moment, to begin a new life. Before rising from my knees I experienced a sense of pardoning love, and I was happy.

"It was now that I became sensible of the wrong I had been guilty of, in allowing my sorrow to cause me to neglect my duties, for there is no one in any station of life but has claims of duty. I again engaged actively in the duties of life, with a feeling of thankfulness that I was privileged to cheer the declining years of my parents. Year after year passed away. I still remained with my father and mother; and I felt no wish to leave them, although I had more than one opportunity for so doing. My mother died at the age of sixty-five. I nursed her tenderly through a long and painful illness, and closed her eyes in death. My father and I were now left alone in our home. He was several years older than my mother. The infirmities of age were coming fast upon him."

CHAPTER XVII.
Penitent, and Forgiven.

On a stormy evening, like this, we were sitting together in this room when our attention was arrested by a timid knock at the door. My father opened the door, and I heard some one, in a feeble voice, ask permission to enter the house. My father conducted the stranger in, and gave him a seat by our cheerful fire. When the stranger entered the room, and I gained a view of his face, I at once knew that I stood face to face with George Almont. When I suddenly pronounced his name, my father made a hasty movement as if to speak with anger, but I gave him an imploring look and he remained silent. Although greatly changed, it was, nevertheless, George Almont who was now in our presence. After a few moments of silence, for after my exclamatory utterance of his name, neither of us had spoken, he turned his eyes, in which the light of disease painfully burned, and said, — 'You do well not to reproach me; the time for that is past, for I am, as you may see, on the verge of the grave. I have striven with disease, that I might reach this place, and if possible, obtain your forgiveness ere my eyes shall close in death. I know I have darkened a life, which, but for me, might have been bright and joyous. It is too much for me to expect your forgiveness, yet I would hear you pronounce that blessed word before I die. You may *now* believe me when I say, that it was my love for you which led me to deceive you. Knowing my wife's dread of any publicity being attached to her name, I thought the knowledge that I had a living wife would never reach you. Of the sinfulness of my conduct I did not at that time pause to think. I now sincerely thank my wife for preventing a marriage which in the sight of God, must have been but mockery. I now speak truly when I say to you, I never loved my wife; I married her for money. As I had no affection for her, my former habits of dissipation soon regained their hold on me. It will afford me some comfort to know that I have made strictly true confession to you. I have not, to my knowledge, a living relation in the wide world; and, till I met with you, I knew not the meaning of the word love; and I still believe that, had I met you earlier in life, your influence would have caused me to become a useful man and an ornament to my profession. But it is useless to talk now of what cannot be recalled. When I left this village, years ago, I was equally indifferent as to whither I went or what I did. I felt no wish to return to my wife; and, had I been then inclined, I well knew the just contempt and scorn I should meet with, although I believe she had once loved me. But I knew them to be a proud family, and I felt certain they would never overlook the disgrace and sorrow I had brought upon them. I have never since seen my wife, but I lately learned that she, with the rest of her family, removed to a western city some years ago. Since leaving this place I have wandered far and wide, never remaining long in one place. My mind has never been at rest, and, for that reason, I have been a lonely wanderer all these years. But my dissipated habits have done their work, and I feel that my earthly course is well nigh ended. I have dragged my feeble body to your dwelling, with the hope of obtaining your forgiveness ere I am summoned into eternity.'

"While listening to him, I had seated myself at my father's side. As he concluded, I said to my father, in a low voice, — 'If we forgive not our fellow-mortal, how can we expect the forgiveness of our Heavenly Father for our many sins?' I rose from my seat and extending to him hand, said, — 'You have, Mr. Almont, my entire forgiveness for all the sorrow you have caused me, and I hope you will also obtain the forgiveness of God.' My father also came forward, and, taking his hand, granted him his forgiveness. When he finished speaking he seemed entirely exhausted. My father led him into the adjoining room, and assisted him to lie down upon his own bed. He also gave him a little wine, which seemed somewhat to revive him. Observing that he rapidly grew worse, my father summoned our physician, who was an old friend, and knew all the circumstances connected with our former acquaintance with Mr. Almont. When the physician arrived, he expressed the opinion that death was fast approaching; said he, — 'I do not think he will see another sun rise,' — and he did not. He said but little, and suffered but little pain; but he sank rapidly. His mind was clear to the last. A short time before his death, he turned his eyes, over which the film of death was gathering, to my father, and, with much difficulty, said, — 'Pray — for — me.' My father knelt and implored the mercy of heaven on the soul that was departing. I could not bear that he should leave the world without one word in regard to what were his feelings in the near prospect of death. Going near, I said, — 'Do you feel willing to trust yourself to the Saviour's mercy to penitent sinners?' He gave a sign of assent, and a more peaceful expression settled on his countenance. 'I know,' said he in a whisper, 'that I have been a grievous sinner for many long years, yet the forgiveness guaranteed by you, whom I have so deeply injured, gives me a hope that God will also forgive the sins, for which I now trust I feel deeply penitent.' After this, he lay for a short time in a kind of stupor. Suddenly, he opened his eyes, and they rested upon my father, who stood by his bed-side. His lips moved slightly, and my father distinguished the words, — 'Pray for me.' He again knelt and prayed earnestly, in a subdued voice, for the spirit that was then entering the unknown future. A few moments after, and the soul of George Almont was summoned to leave its earthly tenement. When the small procession that had followed his remains to their last resting-place turned from the new-made grave, the two following lines from Gray's Elegy came unbidden to my mind: —

No further seek his merits to disclose,
Or draw his frailties from their dread abode.'

"Perhaps, Clara," continued Miss Simmonds, "you may, in your walks through what is now called 'The Old Burial-ground,' a short distance from the village, have observed a lonely grave, marked by a plain marble headstone, and shaded by the branches of an aged tree; you may have noticed this grave, and never given a thought to the poor mortal who sleeps there. That is the grave of George Almont. Three years later, my father died, and I was left alone. Since that period I have lived sometimes alone, and occasionally spending a short time with any family who happen to require my services, as I find it necessary to do something for my own support. I have been able to support myself in comfort and respectability, and even occasionally to bestow charity in a small way to those less favored than myself. I know not why I felt so much inclined to relate these circumstances to you this evening, for you are the first stranger to whom I ever related the story connected with my early life. I am no longer young, but the memory of my early sorrows time can never efface; although, aided by religion, I have learned resignation and cheerfulness. One thing more," continued Miss Simmonds, "and I have done."

Rising, she opened a drawer and, taking a locket therefrom, she placed it in my hand, saying, —

"You may, if you wish, Clara, look upon a picture of George Almont, taken when he was twenty-five years of age."

Opening the locket, I looked upon the picture of what must have been a very fine looking young man. I never beheld a more prepossessing countenance. No one who looked upon that picture would have dreamed of the sad story attached to the life of the original. Closing the locket, I gave it back to Miss Simmonds, who replaced it in the drawer without once looking upon the picture it contained. In conclusion, Miss Simmonds said, —

"I hope you are not wearied with an old woman's story."

I assured her that it had deeply interested me, although I feared the recital had been painful to her.

CHAPTER XVIII.
A New Joy.

I returned to my school, after having enjoyed a very pleasant visit with Miss Simmonds. I thought much of the story she had related to me. I endeavoured to learn a useful lesson from the cheerful resignation which Miss Simmonds evinced by her daily life.

Obadiah still pursued his studies with much zeal; and, upon my return home, each succeeding week, I gave him all the assistance in my power. The amount of knowledge he had derived, by devoting his leisure hours to study, was indeed wonderful. Awkward as he at first appeared to me, I found, as he progressed in his studies, that he possessed a powerful intellect, which only required proper culture to enable him to become a talented and useful man.

I now pass, with a few words, over a period of two years. During all this time I had continued the labors of my school at Mill Town, still considering my uncle's house as my home. Obadiah had, by the advice of my uncle, gone to pursue his studies in Massachusetts, having decided to obtain a thorough education. He intended fitting himself for college, and had saved money sufficient to defray his expenses while so doing, Miss Simmonds still resided in her home at Littleton, and the longer I enjoyed her friendship the more did I love and respect her. I had received several letters from Aunt Patience during the past two years. She had repeatedly urged me to visit her, but, for various reasons, I had been unable to do so; but at this time, I determined to pay her a visit. Accordingly, I prepared for my journey to Woodville a small village in Massachusetts, where she resided. She was very much pleased to see me. She was much changed since I had last seen her. Her once vigorous and active form was beginning to bow beneath the weight of years. She seemed to be very comfortably situated with her relatives; for, having but a small family, they were able to give her a quiet home. I enquired of her if she felt happy in her home?

"I feel quite happy and contented," she replied, "and have no wish to leave my present home, till you marry and possess a home of your own, when I should be very glad to make my home with you."

I replied that I had no intention of marrying at present but that if that event should take place during her lifetime, I should be most happy to receive her into my home.

The village of Woodville was not large; but its location was romantic and pleasant, being bounded on one side by a range of high hills, and on the other by a beautiful river. I was highly pleased with the place, and with the kind family with whom Aunt Patience resided. When I had spent about ten days at Woodville, I received a letter from my uncle, requesting my return home without delay. In a postscript he informed me that I need not be alarmed, as both he and my aunt were in good health; but that he did not wish to assign a reason for requesting my return. I could not imagine what had caused my uncle to summon me home, as he was aware that I had intended spending several weeks with my aunt; and I made all possible haste to set out on my homeward journey, and left Woodville the next morning after receiving my uncle's letter. When my uncle and aunt met me on my return, I knew by their manner that something unusual had taken place in my absence; but I judged from the countenance of both that, whatever the event might be, it was one of joy rather than sorrow. My uncle soon said, —

"Can you bear good news, Clara?"

I replied that I thought I could.

"Then," continued my uncle, "I have the happiness of informing you that the hopes you had so long cherished of seeing your uncle Charles will be realized, for he has arrived."

'Ere I could frame a reply, the door of the adjoining room opened, and my new-found uncle came hastily forward. He evinced much emotion as he tenderly embraced me, saying, —

"Your face strongly reminds me of the twin brother from whom I parted so many years ago. You know not how happy I am in finding the daughter of my dear brother."

I could trace in the features of my uncle Charles a resemblance to my dear father; but, as my father had died while quite a young man, the resemblance, at my uncle's time of life, was less striking than otherwise it might have been.

My uncle Charles was now sixty-five years old; but travel and exposure caused him to look much older than he really was. He informed me that he had first visited Philadelphia with the hope of finding my father; and, when he learned that my father and mother were both dead, he next enquired if they left any children? He learned that they left one daughter, who had resided for some time in the family of the Leightons, as governess; but had left Philadelphia three years since. He next sought out the Leightons, hoping to learn my residence; but they of course could give him no information upon the subject. They directed him to Mrs. Burnside, who at first was reluctant to give the information he sought; but, when he informed her of the relationship I bore to him, she directed him to my uncle Wayland, in New Hampshire, at whose residence he arrived one week previous to my return from Massachusetts. He soon after gave us the following brief account of his life, since he left Philadelphia, when a boy, which I reserve for the succeeding chapter of my story.

CHAPTER XIX.
Uncle Charles.

My uncle began his story as follows: —

"When I left Philadelphia, I had no definite object in view. I left without seeing my brother, to avoid the pain of parting, for we tenderly loved each other. His disposition and mine were widely different; he was quiet, industrious, and very persevering in whatever he undertook; while I, on the other hand, was rash, impulsive, and very impatient of restraint. My adopted father apprenticed me to learn the art of printing, without in the least consulting my wishes in the matter. It seemed to me that he might have granted me the privilege of choosing my employment; and, his failing to do so roused my indignation and doubled the dislike I already felt to the occupation of a printer. It was very hard for me to leave without seeing my brother; but I decided that, as he was very well contented in his situation, I had best go away quietly, so that, whatever might befall me, I should not be the means of bringing trouble to him. I had decided to leave my master the first opportunity that should offer for so doing. He one day gave me a sharp and, as I thought, unmerited rebuke, and ended by striking me a blow. That blow caused me to form the decision of leaving him at once, and that very night I left Philadelphia. I made my way to the city of New York, where I managed to live for a time by selling newspapers; but my profits were so small that I soon became disgusted with the employment, and I obtained the situation of waiter in a large hotel, where I remained for some time. I often thought of writing to my brother; but I was aware that the knowledge of my employment would be painful to him, for he was of a proud and sensitive nature. Time passed on, and I at length sailed as cabin-boy in a vessel bound for Liverpool, in England. I followed the sea for many years; and, in the bustle and turmoil of a sailor's life, I almost forgot my brother, from whom I had been so long separated. Yet sometimes, in the lonely hours of my night-watch on deck, when out in mid-ocean, would my thoughts turn to that once-loved brother, and tears would dim my eyes as memory recalled the days of our early childhood.

"I rose in my profession till I arrived at the position of second mate. It was at this time that, during a stay of some weeks duration in an English port, I met with one who won my affections; and, one year after, we were married. My wife resided with her friends in England, while I continued to follow the sea. My wife was to me an object of almost idolatrous attachment. Each time I visited England, I found it the harder to bid farewell to my wife, and again embark on the ocean. We had one child, a beautiful boy. I named him Henry, after my brother. When we had been two years married, I made a voyage to the Indies, and was absent nearly two years. When I returned, I learned that my wife and child had both been for some time dead. When I learned the sad truth I was like one bereft of reason. I could not reconcile myself to the thought that, in this world, I could never again behold my beloved wife and child. The very darkness of despair settled on my mind. I had not then, as I have since done, looked heavenward for consolation amid the sorrows of life.

"I can dwell no longer upon this dark period of my life, but hasten onward to the close of my story. I continued to follow the life of a sailor for some years after my bereavement. The hurry and bustle attendant upon my calling served in some measure to drive away thoughts of the past; but, after a time I even grew weary of the sea; and when I heard of the famous gold regions discovered in Australia, I felt a strong desire to visit the place. The desire of making money had less to do with my decision of going there than had the wish for change and excitement of some kind. Accordingly, I abandoned my sailor life, and made my way among the hundreds who were crowding to the gold regions of Australia.

"At that time I was poor, for I had never possessed the faculty for saving money. I was unaccustomed to the labors of mining, and in many instances, the knowing ones took me in, and for a long time I realized but little from my labors. But, as I persevered, against many discouragements, year after year, I at length began to be successful. I finally bought a claim, which, quite unexpectedly to me, yielded a golden harvest, and I soon found myself rich beyond my most sanguine expectations.

"Year after year I determined to re-visit Philadelphia; but, by this time my mind had become much engrossed by money-making, and each succeeding year brought fresh claims upon my time and attention.

"Time passed on, till I found myself fast growing old. I felt an intense longing to return to the land of my birth, and spend the few years which might remain to me of life in my native city. During my residence in Australia I met with a man who informed me that he was in Philadelphia at the time of my brother's marriage; and it was a severe trial when I found, upon my return, that my brother, and his wife had both been many years dead. During my homeward journey, I had formed the decision of spending my remaining days in the home of my brother, as I wished for quiet and repose. When I learned that they were both dead, all the affection of my worn and world-weary heart turned toward their orphan daughter."

Turning to me my uncle said, —

"Will you go, my dear child, and make bright the home of your aged uncle?"

I was about to give a joyful assent, when the thought of the kind uncle and aunt I must leave, caused me to hesitate. It seemed to me that they possessed a claim upon my affections superior to any other, and I was at a loss to decide as to what was my duty. I therefore remained silent, not knowing what reply to make. Observing my hesitation, my uncle Wayland said, —

"Lonely as we shall be without you, my dear Clara, I yet think it your duty to go with your uncle Charles, who is still more lonely than we. We must not be selfish; and I think we should feel willing to give you up."

I was much relieved to know that my uncle and aunt Wayland were willing that I should go, although I well knew their willingness was caused by what they considered my duty to my aged relative.

Till I prepared to leave my uncle and aunt, I knew not how tenderly I had learned to love them. I resigned my school at Mill Town, with much sorrow, for I had become strongly attached to my pupils. As my uncle and aunt tenderly embraced me at parting, my uncle said, while the tears coursed down his furrowed cheeks, —

"Remember, dear Clara, there will ever be for you a daughter's welcome, both in our hearts and home."

CHAPTER XX.
Lights and Shadows.

I was agitated by many contending emotions as I alighted from the train which had borne me to Philadelphia; but, along with many sad thoughts, came the consoling one, that I had not returned to my native city the friendless being I had left it.

We stayed for a short time with my old friends, the Burnsides, while my uncle attended to the business of buying and furnishing a suitable residence. Before removing to our home, my uncle engaged Mrs. Burnside to find a person suitable to occupy the position of housekeeper in his dwelling. It immediately occurred to Mrs. Burnside that my old friend, Mrs. O'Flaherty, would be well qualified for that position. She had remained in the service of Mrs. Wallingford since the time when I first introduced her to the reader; but, fortunately for us, Mr. Wallingford was about removing his family to a distant State, and they would no longer require her services. Mrs. O'Flaherty was overjoyed when she learned that she was to reside with me. When I, in company with Mrs. Burnside, called to make the necessary arrangements for her removal to her new home, I could hardly believe that the tidy, well dressed matron I saw could be the same poor woman to whom I had given food when hungry and destitute.

"Indade," exclaimed Mrs. O'Flaherty, "an' I niver expected to see the happy day whin I would live wid you in a home av yer own."

The matter was soon arranged, and an early day appointed for her to commence her duties as housekeeper in the dwelling of my uncle.

It was quite a change for me to find myself so suddenly removed from my position as teacher in a small school and installed as mistress in my uncle's elegant home in Walnut Street, Philadelphia. We found Mrs. O'Flaherty very trustworthy, and well qualified in every way for her position.

Soon after our return to Philadelphia, my uncle accompanied me to the graves of my parents. I cannot describe my feelings when I found myself, after so long an absence, again standing by the spot where reposed the dust of my loved father and mother. I seemed almost to feel their presence, and the tears I shed were gentle and refreshing. Seated by those graves, I, for the first time, spoke to my uncle of the circumstances which had caused me to leave Mrs. Leighton, and remove from Philadelphia. He expressed much sympathy for me and said, —

"You should endeavor to banish these circumstances from your mind. You are young, and, I trust, have yet many years of happy life before you."

I learned from Mrs. Burnside that Mr. Leighton had lately met with several heavy losses in business. William was still in England. He had written two or three letters to Birdie, but had corresponded with no other member of the family. Laura and Georgania had both married, and removed to a distant city. Birdie had finished her studies, and returned home. Lewis was attending school some two hundred miles from the city.

Mrs. Burnside further informed me that the health of Mrs. Leighton was very much impaired. According to the information I gained from Mrs. Burnside, there seemed to have been a great change in the family of Mr. Leighton since I left Philadelphia.

Time passed happily away in my new home. We often saw company, for all my old friends soon sought me out, when they learned of my return to the city; and my uncle, being of a social disposition, extended a kindly welcome to them all. Birdie Leighton called. I was truly glad to see her, and she seemed equally happy to meet me; but our meeting could not be otherwise than constrained and formal; and, owing to circumstances, anything like intimacy was, of course, out of the question. I had almost forgotten to mention that, among the first to call upon me in my new home, were Mrs. and Miss Kingsley, for she was *Miss* Kingsley still; the same who were so much shocked by meeting with a governess at a fashionable party. Surely, thought I, my uncle's money is working wonders, when I am already patronized by the exclusive Mrs. Kingsley. Their call I have never yet returned.

While walking one day, with a friend, I caught a glimpse of Mrs. Leighton, as she rode past in her carriage. She was so much changed that, at the first, I hardly recognized her; but, upon looking more closely, I saw that it was indeed Mrs. Leighton.

A year and a half had now glided by since my return to Philadelphia. Nothing worthy of note had taken place during this time.

The last letter from my friends in New Hampshire informed me that Obadiah was still pursuing his studies, with a view to the ministry. This afforded me but little surprise, as I had often heard him make remarks which led me to think he had an inclination to that calling.

One sultry evening in August, I retired early to my own room, as I was suffering from a severe head-ache. The usual remedies afforded me relief from pain; but I found myself unable to sleep. As the hour grew late, my nervous restlessness so much increased that, abandoning the idea of rest, I rose and lighted my lamp. I felt almost alarmed at my own agitation, which seemed so unaccountable, I seemed to feel the foreshadowing of some unusual event. After a time, I closed my window, and was about to extinguish my lamp and again seek repose, when I was startled by the sudden ringing of fire-bells. Hastily unclosing my window, I heard the sound of "Fire! fire!" echoed by many voices, and accompanied by the hasty tread of many feet upon the pavement. I observed the appearance of fire a few streets distant, but was unable to make out its exact location. I listened eagerly, hoping to gain from the many voices which reached my ears some account of the burning building. Presently the words — "Mr. Leighton's house is burning!" reached my excited ears. I saw that the fire was raging fearfully, as the adjacent streets were becoming lighter by the flames. I was about to call my uncle, when I heard his step approaching. A moment after he rapped at my door. Just then Mrs. O'Flaherty rushed up the stairs, breathless with terror.

"May the Saints defend us!" she exclaimed, as she burst into my apartment; "but is the city on fire? For wasn't it the light o' the flames shinin' on me windy that waked me out o' me sound slape."

My uncle endeavoured to allay her terrors, telling her that the city was certainly not on fire, although there was a burning building in our near vicinity. He soon declared his intention of visiting the scene of the fire.

I begged him to be careful and not expose himself to danger.

After my uncle left us, we stationed ourselves on the upper piazza, to watch the progress of the flames. From the confusion of voices in the street below I caught the words, —

"Poor Birdie Leighton is nowhere to be found, and it is feared she has perished in the flames."

I shuddered as I listened to these words. It was a terrible thought to me, that my once loved pupil had met with a death so dreadful. But I was unwilling to give up the hope that she would yet be, if not already, saved. We waited long in anxious suspense for the return of my uncle; but the day had begun to dawn before he came. I feared to ask what I longed to know. He must have read my anxiety in my countenance, for he soon said to me, —

"The Leightons are now all safe in the house of a neighbor; but Birdie came near meeting her death in the flames."

To my eager enquiries, he replied, —

"That before Mr. Leighton awoke, their sleeping apartment was filled with smoke, with which the flames were already beginning to mingle. He bore his wife from the apartment; and, with her in his arms, hastened to awake Birdie, whose room adjoined their own. She hastily threw on a portion of her clothing, and prepared to accompany her father and mother in their descent from the chambers. She had fainted from terror, while crossing the upper hall; and it was not till Mr. Leighton reached the open air with his wife in his arms, that he missed Birdie from his side. On leaving her apartment, he had besought her to keep close by him, as her mother required all his attention. The agony of Mr. and Mrs. Leighton, when, upon reaching the open air, they found Birdie to be not with them, may be better imagined than described. Mrs. Leighton became well-nigh frantic, and was almost forcibly conveyed to the house of a neighbor. As soon as Mr. Leighton was relieved from the care of his wife, he rushed toward the burning building, saying that he would either rescue Birdie or perish with her. But, ere he reached the entrance, a man issued from the house, bearing Birdie in his arms. The brave man had rushed up the burning staircase, and reached the spot where Birdie still lay, in a state of insensibility. Hastily enveloping her person in a thick, heavy shawl, which he had taken with him for the purpose, he rushed with her down the perilous staircase, and reached the open air in safety, his clothing only being singed by the flames. Never," said my uncle, "did I hear such a shout of joy as went up from the assembled multitude when the man who rescued Birdie came from the house, bearing her in safety to her father. Mr. Leighton fell on his knees and fervently thanked God for sparing the life of his child. 'Now,' said he, 'I am content that my dwelling should burn.' He grasped the hand of her rescuer, and said, with much emotion, — 'Words are too poor to express my gratitude; but, if my life is spared, you shall be rewarded.' 'I want no reward,' said the noble man, 'for having done my duty.' He was a laboring man, and had a large family dependent upon his daily earnings. Quite a large sum of money was soon raised among the assembled crowd, which he would not accept, till compelled to do so by the thankful multitude."

In conclusion, my uncle said, —

"Consciousness returned to Birdie soon after she was conveyed into the open air, and she was speedily conveyed to her anxious mother. The rescue of Birdie from so dreadful a death was to me a matter of deep and heartfelt thankfulness."

Previous to the burning of Mr. Leighton's dwelling his pecuniary affairs, according to common report, had become very much embarrassed; and this event seemed the finishing stroke to his ill-fortune. They were unable to save anything from their dwelling, being thankful to escape with their lives. He still continued his business; but, it was said, his liabilities were heavier than he was able to meet. He rented a moderate-sized house, and removed thither with his family. Those who visited them said it was but plainly furnished. Their servants, with one or two exceptions, had all been dismissed.

CHAPTER XXI.
Reconciled.

Lewis was recalled from school in the early autumn; and soon after, the news of Mr. Leighton's failure was eagerly discussed in the business world.

Lewis called to see me soon after his return. He was now a manly youth of fifteen. I was much pleased to see him; and, when he rose to go, after a lengthy call, I invited him to call often upon us. My uncle took a great fancy to the boy, and many evenings found Lewis our guest. I learned from Lewis, and others, that the health of Mrs. Leighton had so much failed that she was now entirely confined to the house.

Mr. Leighton had lately written to Willie, giving him an account of their misfortunes, and of the failing health of his mother; and concluded by earnestly requesting his return home, as he feared that it, was Willie's absence which was preying so heavily upon the mind of Mrs. Leighton as to cause, in a great measure, her failing health.

Lewis called one evening, and, upon entering the parlor, handed me a note. As I glanced at my name on the envelope, I at once recognized the hand-writing of Mrs. Leighton. Hastily breaking the seal, I read the following lines: —

"Elm Street, Nov. 25th, 18 — .

"To Miss Clara Roscom:

"I am extremely anxious for an interview with you; but my state of health will not allow of my leaving my own residence. I therefore earnestly request you to accompany Lewis upon his return home, for I *must* see you. I am sensible that I have no right to ask of you this favor; but I trust that the kindness of your heart will induce you to comply with my request.

"Yours truly,

"Cynthia Leighton."

When I had finished reading the note I could not forbear from questioning Lewis as to its meaning; but he refused to give me any information upon the subject, saying he was not at liberty to do so. All he would say of the matter was that his mother had requested him to give me the note, and await my reading of it. For a few moments I felt undecided as to going to the house of Mrs. Leighton; but, the thought that she was ill, and had sent for me, caused me to come to the decision that I would grant her request. I feared not to meet Mrs. Leighton, for I had done her no wrong. I therefore told Lewis that in a few moments I would be ready to accompany him. My uncle wished to send the carriage with me; but I told him it was quite unnecessary, as the distance was short and the evening was very fine, and Lewis had said he would accompany me when I wished to return home.

A few minutes' walk brought me to the dwelling of Mr. Leighton. Lewis conducted me at once to his mother's apartment. I saw as yet no other member of the family. After ushering me into the room, he withdrew, and left me alone with Mrs. Leighton. I quietly advanced into the room and paused before her. She was reclining in a large easy chair, and I was much surprised by her changed appearance. She was very thin and pale, and appeared to be weak and languid; and Mrs. Harringford's letter was recalled to my mind when I observed how gray was her once beautiful hair. She extended her hand to me; but, for some moments, was unable to utter a word. When she relinquished the hand I had given her, she motioned me to a seat. She seemed agitated by some painful emotion. I was the first to break the silence, which I did by saying, —

"Whatever may have been your object, Mrs. Leighton, in seeking this interview, you will see, by the readiness with which I have responded to your request, that I cherish no resentment toward you."

Becoming more composed, she replied to me in a low voice saying —

"As I was unable to go to you, I sent for you, that I may humbly ask your forgiveness for the injustice you have suffered from me. I now acknowledge, what you are probably already aware of, that it was a foolish and false pride which influenced my conduct toward you, when you left my house long ago. It requires reverses of fortune to convince us of the vanity of all earthly things; and reverses have overtaken me, and more than this; my failing health admonishes me that, unless a change for the better soon takes place, my days on earth will soon be numbered. During all the time that has passed since we have met, my mind has never been at rest; for though too proud to acknowledge it, I have ever been sensible that I treated you with cruelty and injustice. But my pride is now humbled and I beg of you to forgive me; for, believe me, I have suffered even more than you."

I extended my hand to her, saying, —

"I freely and fully forgive all the past, Mrs. Leighton, and I trust we may be friends for the future."

After sitting silent for a few moments, Mrs. Leighton again addressed me, saying, —

"Were it in your power, Clara, would you make me entirely happy?"

I replied that certainly I would. She regarded me earnestly as she said, —

"Will you become Willie's wife?"

I knew not what reply to make to a question so unexpected. At length I said, —

"Willie has been a long time absent. He may have changed his mind; or, he may be already married."

"I will answer for all that," replied Mrs. Leighton.

"Willie is here. He arrived two days since, and would have called to see you ere this, but I begged him to defer calling till I had seen you, and acknowledged my former injustice to you; for I am now sensible that I wronged a worthy and noble girl."

Remember, kind reader, that, although I had expected never again to meet with Willie Leighton, I still loved him with all the strength of a first love.

Before I could frame a reply to the last remark of Mrs. Leighton, the door opened, and Willie, accompanied by his father, entered the room.

I pass over our meeting. But Mr. Leighton, soon after, placing my hand in that of Willie, said, — "God bless you, my children; may you be happy."

When I returned home that evening, it was Willie not Lewis, who accompanied me.

CHAPTER XXII.
Clara's Marriage.

Willie was anxious that an early day should be appointed for our marriage; but I was unwilling that our marriage should take place until the ensuing spring. I wished not so suddenly to leave my uncle for the long wedding tour which Willie had in contemplation.

Laura and Georgania, accompanied by their husbands, came at Christmas to visit their parents. It was indeed a joyful family reunion. We accepted our present happiness, and made no unpleasant allusions to the past. If Georgania retained any of her old ways that were not agreeable, I was too much occupied by my own new-found happiness to be annoyed by them.

Willie generously urged his father to use a portion of the wealth he had inherited from his deceased relative in settling his deranged business affairs, and Mr. Leighton finally accepted the noble offer. Accordingly, he paid off the debts, and again started a business, which, if on a smaller scale than formerly, rested on a firmer basis.

During the winter, my uncle made a will bestowing the chief part of his wealth upon me. The house in which we resided, he intended as a wedding-gift, saying that we must accept of the gift encumbered by the giver, as he wished to reside with me during the remainder of his life.

"I have reserved enough," said my uncle, "for my own private use; and who has so rightful a claim to the wealth which a kind Providence has bestowed upon me, as the daughter of my twin brother?"

From the time of Willie's return the health of Mrs. Leighton slowly, but surely, improved; and, when winter softened into the balmy days of spring, her health became fully restored.

We were married on the twentieth of May; and, as Willie had decided upon England for our wedding tour, we sailed immediately after our marriage. We returned to our home, in Philadelphia, in October.

We soon found ourselves permanently settled in our own home, to the great joy of Mrs. O'Flaherty, who still retained her position as house-keeper.

"Indade, me daar misthress," said she, "an' it's good to see yees at home agin; for wasn't this the lonesom place whiles ye was absint."

Soon after our return, I mentioned the promise which I made long ago to Aunt Patience, that if I ever should possess a home of my own, I would receive her as an inmate of that home.

"I well remember," replied Willie, "the kind aunt who attended your mother during her last illness, and I will gladly do my utmost to render happy her declining years."

I had secretly felt some fears that my uncle might object to our receiving Aunt Patience to our home. A short time after, I mentioned the matter to my uncle, telling him of my mother's dying injunction to me, that I should not neglect Aunt Patience in her old age. His reply put all my fears to flight.

"I am glad, Clara," said my uncle, "to see that you respect the wishes of your deceased mother. Our dwelling is large, and we can surely find room for Aunt Patience. I will go for her myself, as I am at leisure, and would enjoy the journey."

With a light heart, I wrote to Aunt Patience, informing her of our intentions; and a few days later, my uncle set out on his journey to Massachusetts. When he returned, accompanied by my aged relative, tears mingled with my welcome, so vividly was my mother recalled to my mind by the meeting.

CHAPTER XXIII.
A Pleasing Incident.

Again it is the twentieth of May; and, this day five years ago, was my wedding-day. Two years since, and the fountain of a new love was stirred in my heart, namely, the love of a mother for her first-born son. One year since, I was called to stand by the dying-bed of Aunt Patience. Her end was peace; and her earthly remains rest beside those of my mother.

My uncle still lives with us, a hale and vigorous old man, over seventy years of age. The parents of Willie still reside in the city. Birdie and Lewis are both at home. Lewis assists his father in their business, which has again become very prosperous.

I bring my story to a close by relating an incident which took place the summer succeeding the date of this chapter. I had long wished to visit my friends in New Hampshire: but my own cares had hitherto prevented me; but this season I decided to pay the long-deferred visit. Willie was very glad to accompany me, having long wished to visit the Eastern States. Birdie and Lewis also bore us company. As our way lay through a portion of Massachusetts, I determined once more to visit the small village which formerly had been the home of Aunt Patience. We arrived at Woodville late on a Saturday evening, and on Sabbath morning were invited to hear a talented young preacher, who, we were informed, had lately been called as pastor to the Congregational Church in that village. As the young minister ascended the pulpit, his countenance struck me as being strangely familiar. As I was endeavoring to decide in my own mind where I could have before met him, it suddenly occurred to me that the young preacher was no other than my old friend, Obadiah Hawkins; and when, upon again raising my eyes I encountered one of those old-time furtive glances, I felt certain that I was right in my conjecture. The rough-looking youth, whom I had once thought so uncomely, had changed to a really fine looking man. When the services were closed, I at once made my way to him; and, as he had already recognized me, we soon renewed our former acquaintance. I introduced him to Willie, also to Birdie and Lewis. During the few days we remained at Woodville the young preacher called frequently. He soon evinced a marked partiality for the society of Birdie and, strange as it may seem, I observed that she was deeply interested in him. I know not how the matter may end, but I do know that, since our return home, Birdie receives frequent letters, addressed in a gentleman's hand, and post-marked "Woodville." Who knows but Obadiah Hawkins may yet be my brother-in-law?

In taking a retrospective view of the past, and contrasting it with the happy present, I feel that the consoling words which, in a dream, my mother uttered to me, years ago, have been more than verified, — "Fear not, my beloved daughter; only continue in the path of duty, and all will yet be well."

TERRY DOLAN

Some years since circumstances caused me to spend the summer months in a farming district, a few miles from the village of E., and it was there I met with Terry Dolan. He had a short time previous come over from Ireland, and was engaged as a sort of chore boy by Mr. L., in whose family I resided during my stay in the neighborhood. This Terry was the oddest being with whom I ever chanced to meet. Would that I could describe him! — but most of us, I believe, occasionally meet with people, whom we find to be indescribable, and Terry was one of those. He called himself sixteen years of age; but, excepting that he was low of stature, you would about as soon have taken him for sixty as sixteen. His countenance looked anything but youthful, and there was altogether a sort of queer, ancient look about him which caused him to appear very remarkable. When he first came to reside with Mr. L. the boys in the neighborhood nicknamed him "The Little Old Man," but they soon learned by experience that their wisest plan was to place a safe distance between Terry and themselves before applying that name to him, for the implied taunt regarding his peculiar appearance enraged him beyond measure. Whenever he entered the room, specially if he ventured a remark — and no matter how serious you might have been a moment before — the laugh would come, do your best to repress it. When I first became an inmate with the family, I was too often inclined to laugh at the oddities of Terry — and I believe a much graver person than I was at that time would have done the same — but after a time, when I learned something of his past life, I regarded him with a feeling of pity, although to avoid laughing at him, at times, were next to impossible.

One evening in midsummer I found him seated alone upon the piazza, with a most dejected countenance. Taking a seat by his side I enquired why he looked so sad; — his eyes filled with tears as he replied — "its of ould Ireland I'm thinkin' tonight, sure." I had never before seen Terry look sober, and I felt a deep sympathy for the homesick boy. I asked him how it happened that he left all his friends in Ireland and came to this country alone. From his reply I learned that his mother died when he was only ten years old, and, also, that his father soon after married a second wife, who, to use Terry's own words, "bate him unmarcifully." "It's a wonder," said he, "that iver I lived to grow up, at all, at all, wid all the batins I got from that cruel woman, and all the times she sint me to bed widout iver a bite uv supper, bad luck to her and the like uv her!" He did live, however, but he certainly did not grow up to be very tall. "Times grew worse an' worse for me at home," continued he, "and a quare time I had of it till I was fourteen years of age, when one day says I to mesilf, 'flesh and blood can bear it no longer,' and I ran away to the city uv Dublin where an aunt by me mother's side lived. Me aunt was a poor woman, but she gave a warm welcim to her sister's motherless boy; she trated me kindly, and allowed me to share her home, although she could ill afford it, till I got a place as sarvant in a gintleman's family. As for my father, he niver throubled his head about me any more; indade I think he was glad to be rid uv me, an' all by manes of that wicked woman. It was near two years afther I lift home that I took the notion of going to Ameriky; me aunt advised me against going, but, whin she saw that me mind was set on it, she consinted, and did her best, poor woman, to sind me away lookin' dacent and respectable. I niver saw me father or me stepmother agin. I had no wish to see her; but, although I knew me father no longer loved me, I had still some natral-like feelin's for him; but, as I had run away from home, I durst not go back, an' so I lift Ireland widout a sight uv him. But I *could* not lave it forivver, as it might be, widout one more sight uv me mother's grave. I rached the small village where me father lived about nightfall, and lodged in the house uv a kind neighbor who befrinded me, an' he promised, at my earnest wish, to say nothing to any one uv my wish. Early in the morning, before any one was astir in the village, I stole away to the churchyard where they buried me mother. I knelt down, I did, an' kissed the sods which covered her grave, an' prayed that the blessin' which she pronounced before she died, wid her hand restin' on me head, might follow me wheriver I might go." The boy took from his pocket a small parcel, carefully inclosed in a paper, which he handed to me, saying "I gathered these shamrocks from off me mother's grave, before I lift it forever." My own eyes grew moist as I gazed upon the now withered shamrock leaves which the poor boy prized so highly. Would that they had proved as a talisman to guard him from evil! I listened with much interest to Terry's story till our conversation was suddenly interrupted by Mr. — calling him, in no very gentle tones, to go and drive home the cows from the pasture. To reach this pasture he must needs pass through about a quarter of a mile of thick woods. He had a great dread of walking alone in the woods, which his imagination filled with wild animals. When he returned that evening he seemed very much terrified, and when questioned as to the cause, he replied that he "had met with a wild baste in the woods, and was kilt entirely wid the fright uv it."

We endeavoured to gain from him a description of the animal

he had seen, but for some time were unable. "What color was the animal?" enquired Mrs. — . "Indade Ma'am, an' its jist the color uv a dog he was," answered Terry. This reply was greeted with a burst of laughter from all present, at which he was highly offended. In order to pacify him I said, "we would not laugh at you, Terry, only that dogs are of so many different colors that we are as much in the dark as ever regarding the color of the animal you saw." "Well thin," replied he, "if you must know, he was a dirthy brown, the varmint, that he was." From what we could learn from him we were led to suppose that he had met with one of those harmless little creatures, called the "Woodchuck," which his nervous terror, aided by the deepening twilight, had magnified into a formidable wild beast.

A few evenings after, two or three friends of the family chanced to call; and in course of conversation some one mentioned an encampment of Indians, who had recently located themselves in our vicinity, for the purpose of gathering material for the manufacture of baskets, and other works of Indian handicraft. Terry had never seen an Indian, and curiosity, not unmixed with fear, was excited in his mind, when he learned that a number of those dark people were within three miles of us. He asked many questions regarding their personal appearance, habits, &c. It was evident that he entertained some very comical ideas upon the subject. After sitting for a time silent, he suddenly enquired, "Do they ate pratees like other people?" A lady, present, in order to impose upon his credulity, replied, "Indeed Terry they not only eat potatoes, but they sometimes eat people." His countenance expressed much alarm, as he replied, "Faix thin, but I'll kape out o' their way." After a short time he began to suspect they were making game of him, and applied to me for information, saying, "Tell me, sir, if what Mrs. — says is true?" "Do not be alarmed, Terry," I replied, "for if you live till the Indians eat you, you will look even older than you now do."

This allusion to his ancient appearance was very mischievous on my part, and I regretted it a moment after; but he was so much pleased to learn that he had nothing to fear from the Indians that he readily forgave me for alluding to a subject upon which he was usually very sensitive. I remember taking a walk one afternoon during the haymaking season to the field where Terry was at work. Mr. — had driven to the village with the farm horses, leaving Terry to draw in hay with a rheumatic old animal that was well nigh unfit for use. But as the hay was in good condition for getting in, and the sky betokened rain, he told Terry, upon leaving home, to accomplish as much as possible during his absence, and he would, if the rain kept off, draw in the remainder upon his return. As I drew nigh I spied Terry perched upon the top of a load of hay holding the reins, and urging forward the horse, in the ascent of a very steep hill. First he tried coaxing, and as that proved of little avail, he next tried the effect of a few vigorous strokes with a long switch which he carried in his hand. When the poor old horse had dragged the heavy load about half way up the hill, he seemed incapable of further exertion, and horse, cart, Terry and all began a rapid backward descent down the hill.

Here the boy's patience gave way entirely. "Musha thin, bad luck to ye for one harse," said he as he applied the switch with renewed energy. Just then I arrived within speaking distance and said, "Do you think, Terry you would be any better off if you had two of them." "Not if they were both like this one," answered he. I advised Terry to come down from his elevated position, and not add his weight to the load drawn by the overburdened animal. He followed my advice, and when with some difficulty we had checked the descending motion of the cart-wheels, we took a fair start, and the summit of the hill was finally gained.

"Its often," said Terry, "that I've seen a horse draw a cart, but I niver before saw a cart drawing a horse." There was one trait in the character of the boy which pleased me much; he was very grateful for any little act of kindness. He often got into difficulties with the family, owing to his rashness and want of consideration, and I often succeeded in smoothing down for him many rough places in his daily path; and when he observed that I interested myself in his behalf, his gratitude knew no bounds. I believe he would have made almost any sacrifice to please me. He surprised me one day by saying suddenly, "Don't I wish you'd only be tuck sick." "Why Terry," replied I, "I am surprised indeed that you should wish evil to me." "Indade thin," answered he, "its not for evil that I wish it, but for your good jist to let ye see how tinderly I would take care uv ye." I thanked him for his kind intentions, saying that I was very willing to take the will for the deed in this case, and had no wish to test his kindness by a fit of sickness.

He came in one evening fatigued with a hard day's work, and retired early to bed. His sleeping apartment adjoined the sitting-room. I had several letters to write which occupied me till a late hour; the family had all retired. I finished writing just as the clock struck twelve. At that moment, I was almost startled by Terry's voice singing in a very high key. My first thought was that he had gone suddenly crazy. With a light in my hand I stepped softly into the room, to find Terry sitting up in bed and singing at the top of his voice, a song in the "Native Irish Tongue." By this time he had roused every one in the house; and others of the family entered the room. By the pauses which he made, we knew when he reached the end of each verse. He sang several verses; at the time I knew how many, but am unable now to recall the exact number. He must surely have been a sound sleeper or the loud laughter which filled the room would have waked him, for the scene was ludicrous in the extreme: Terry sitting up in bed, sound asleep, at the hour of midnight, and singing with a loud voice and very earnest manner, to an audience who were unable to understand one word of the song. At the close of the last verse he lay quietly down, all unconscious of the Musical Entertainment he had given. The next morning some of the family began teasing him about the song he had sung in his sleep. He was loth to believe them, and as usual enquired of me if they were telling him the truth. "I'll believe whatever you say," said he, "for its you that niver toult me a lie yet." "You may believe them this time," said I, "for you certainly did sing a song. The air was very fine, and I have no doubt the words were equally so, if we could only have understood them."

"Well thin," replied he, "but I niver heard more than that; and if I raaly did sing, I may as well tell yee's how it happint. I dramed, ye see, that I was at a ball in Ireland, an' I thought that about twelve o'clock we got tired wid dancin and sated ourselves on the binches which were ranged round the walls uv the room, and ache one was to sing a song in their turn, an' its I that thought my turn had come for sure." "Well Terry," said I, "you hit upon the time exact at any rate, for it was just twelve o'clock when you favoured us with the song." Soon after this time I left the neighbourhood, and removed to some distance. Terry remained for a considerable time with the same family; after a time I learned that he had obtained employment in a distant village. The next tidings I heard of him was that he had been implicated in a petty robbery, and had run away. His impulsive disposition rendered him very easy of persuasion, for either good or evil; and he seldom paused to consider the consequences of any act. From what I could learn of the matter, it seemed he had been enticed into the affair by some designing fellows, who judged that, owing to his simplicity, he would be well adapted to carry out their wicked plans; and, when suspicion was excited, they managed in some way to throw all the blame upon Terry, who fearing an arrest, fled no one knew whither. Many years have passed since I saw or heard of Terry Dolan; but often, as memory recalls past scenes and those who participated in them, I think of him, and wonder if he is yet among the living, and, if so, in what quarter of the world he has fixed his abode.

THE FAITHFUL WIFE

It is a mild and beautiful evening in the early autumn. Mrs. Harland is alone in her home; she is seated by a table upon which burns a shaded lamp, and is busily occupied with her needle. She has been five years a wife; her countenance is still youthful, and might be termed beautiful, but for the look of care and anxiety so plainly depicted thereon. She had once been happy, but with her now, happiness is but a memory of the past. When quite young she had been united in marriage to Wm. Harland, and with him removed to the City of R., where they have since resided. He was employed as bookkeeper in a large mercantile house, and his salary was sufficient to afford them a comfortable support, — whence then the change that has thus blighted their bright prospects, and clouded the brow of that fair young wife with care? It is an unpleasant truth, but it must be told. Her husband has become addicted to the use of strong drink, not an occasional tippler, but a confirmed and habitual drunkard. His natural disposition was gay and social, and he began by taking an occasional glass with his friends — more for sociability than for any love of the beverage. His wife often admonished him of the danger of tampering with the deadly vice of intemperance; but he only laughed at what he termed her idle fears. Well had it been for them both had the fears of his wife proved groundless! It is needless for me to follow him in his downward path, till, we find him reduced to the level of the common drunkard. Some three months previous to the time when our story opens his employers were forced to dismiss him, as they could no longer employ him with any degree of safety to their business. It was fortunate for Mrs. Harland that the dwelling they occupied belonged to her in her own right — it had been given her by her father at the period of her marriage — so that notwithstanding the dissipated habits of the husband and father they still possessed a home, although many of the comforts of former days had disappeared before the blighting influence of the demon of intemperance. After being dismissed by his employers Mr. Harland seemed to lose all respect for himself, as well as for his wife and children, and, but for the unceasing toil of the patient mother, his children might have often asked for bread in vain.

So low had he now fallen that almost every evening found him in some low haunt of drunkenness and dissipation; and often upon returning to his home he would assail his gentle wife with harsh and unfeeling language.

Many there were who advised Mrs. Harland to return with her children to her parents, who were in affluent circumstances, but she still cherished the hope that he would yet reform. "I pray daily for my erring husband," she would often say, "and I feel an assurance that, sooner or later, my prayers will be answered; and I cannot feel it my duty to forsake him." But on this evening, as she sits thus alone, her mind is filled with thoughts of the past, which she cannot help contrasting with the miserable present, till her reverie is interrupted by the sound of approaching footsteps, which she soon recognizes as those of her husband: she is much surprised — for it is long, very long, since he has returned to his home at so early an hour — and, as he enters the room, her surprise increases when she perceives that he is perfectly sober. As he met her wondering gaze a kind expression rested upon his countenance, and he addressed her saying: "I do not wonder at your astonishment, dear Mary, when I call to mind my past misconduct. I have been a fiend in human shape thus to ill-treat and neglect the best of wives; but I have made a resolve, 'God helping' me, that it shall be so no longer." Seating himself by her side, he continued: "If you will listen to me, Mary, I will tell you what caused me to form this resolution. When I went out this evening I at once made my way to the public house, where I have spent so much of my time and money. Money, I had none, and, worse than this, was owing the landlord a heavy bill. Of late he had assailed me with duns every time I entered the house; but so craving was the appetite for drink that each returning evening still found me among the loungers in the bar-room trusting to my chance of meeting with some companion who would call for a treat. It so happened that tonight none of my cronies were present. When the landlord found that I was still unable to settle the 'old score,' as he termed it, he abused me in no measured terms; but I still lingered in sight of the coveted beverage; and knowing my inability to obtain it my appetite increased in proportion. At length I approached the bar, and begged him to trust me for one more glass of brandy. I will not wound your ears by repeating his reply; and he concluded by ordering me from the house, telling me also never to enter it again till I was able to settle the long score already against me. The fact that I had been turned from the door, together with his taunting language stung me almost to madness. I strolled along, scarce knowing or caring whither, till I found myself beyond the limits of the city; and seating myself by the roadside I gazed in silent abstraction over the moonlit landscape; and as I sat thus I fell into a deep reverie. Memory carried me back to my youthful days when everything was bright with joyous hope and youthful ambition. I recalled the time when I wooed you from your pleasant country home, and led you to the altar a fair young bride, and there pledged myself before God and man to love, honour and cherish you, till death should us part. Suddenly, as if uttered by an audible voice, I seemed to hear the words 'William Harland, how have you kept your vows?' At that moment I seemed to suddenly awake to a full sense of my fallen and degraded position. What madness, thought I, has possessed me all this time, thus to ruin myself and those dear to me? And for what? for the mere indulgence of a debasing appetite. I rose to my feet and my step grew light with my new-formed resolution, that I *would* break the slavish fetters that had so long held me captive; and now, my dear wife, if you can forgive the past and aid me in my resolutions for amendment there is hope for me yet." Mrs. Harland was only too happy to forgive her erring but now truly penitent husband; but she trembled for the future, knowing how often he had formerly made like resolutions, but to break them. She endeavoured, however, to be hopeful, and to encourage him by every means which affection could devise.

Through the influence of friends, his former employers were induced to give him another trial. He had many severe struggles with himself ere he could refrain from again joining his dissipated companions; but his watchful wife would almost every evening form some little plan of her own for his amusement, that he might learn to love his home. In a short time their prospects for the future grew brighter, his wife began to smile again; and his children, instead of fleeing from his approach as they had formerly done, now met him upon his return with loving caresses and lively prattle. Some six months after this happy change, Mrs. Harland one evening noticed that her husband seemed very much downcast and dejected. After tea, she tried vainly to interest him in conversation.

He had a certain nervous restlessness in his manner, which always troubled her, knowing, as she did, that it was caused by the cravings of that appetite for strong drink, which at times still returned with almost overwhelming force. About eight o'clock he took down his hat preparatory to going out. She questioned him as to where he was going, but could obtain no satisfactory reply; her heart sank within her; but she was aware that remonstrance would be useless. She remained for a few moments, after he left the house, in deep thought, then suddenly rising she exclaimed aloud, "I will at least make one effort to save him." She well knew that should he take but one glass, all his former resolves would be as nothing. As she gained the street she observed her husband a short distance in advance of her, and walking hastily she soon overtook him, being careful to keep on the opposite side of the street, that she might be unobserved by him. She had formed no definite purpose in her mind; she only felt that she must endeavor to save him by some means. As they drew nigh the turn of the street she saw two or three of his former associates join him, and one of them addressed him, saying, "Come on, Harland; I thought you would get enough of the cold water system. Come on, and I'll stand treat to welcome you back among your old friends." For a moment he paused as if irresolute; then his wife grew sick at heart, as she saw him follow his companions into a drinking saloon near at hand. Mrs. Harland was by nature a delicate and retiring woman; for a moment she paused: dare she go further! Her irresolution was but momentary, for the momentous consequences at stake gave her a fictitious courage. She quickly approached the door, which at that moment some one in the act of leaving the house threw wide open, and she gained a view of her husband in the act of raising a glass to his lips; but ere he had tasted its fiery contents it was dashed from his hand, and the shattered fragments scattered upon the floor. Mr. Harland, supposing it the act of one of his half-drunken companions, turned with an angry exclamation upon his lips; but the expression of anger upon his countenance suddenly gave place to one of shame and humiliation when he saw his wife standing before him, pale but resolute. In a subdued voice he addressed her, saying, "Mary, how came you here?" "Do not blame me, William," she replied; "for I could not see you again go astray without, at least, making an effort to save you. And now will you not return with me to your home?" The other occupants of the room had thus far remained silent since the entrance of Mrs. Harland; but when they saw that Mr. Harland was about to leave the house by her request, they began taunting him with his want of spirit in being thus ruled by a woman. One of them, who was already half drunk, staggered toward him, saying, "I'd just like to see my old woman follerin' me round in this way. I'll be bound I'd teach her a lesson she would'nt forget in a hurry." Many similar remarks were made by one and another present. The peculiar circumstances in which Mrs. Harland found herself placed gave her a degree of fortitude, of which upon ordinary occasions she would have found herself incapable. Raising her hand with an imperative gesture she said in a firm voice: "Back tempters, hinder not my husband from following the dictates of his better nature." For a few moments there was silence in the room, till one of the company, more drunken and insolent than the others, exclaimed in a loud, derisive voice: "Zounds, madam, but you would make a capital actress, specially on the tragedy parts; you should seek an engagement upon the stage." Mr.

Harland's eyes flashed angrily as his listened to the insulting words addressed to his wife, and, turning to the man who had spoken, he addressed him, saying, in a decided tone of voice: "I wish to have no harsh language in this room while my wife is present, but I warn each one of you to address no more insulting language to her." The manner in which Mr. Harland addressed them, together with the gentle and lady-like appearance of his wife, had the effect to shame them into silence. His voice was very tender as he again addressed his wife, saying, "Come Mary I wills accompany you home — this is no place for you." When they gained the street the unnatural courage which had sustained Mrs. Harland gave way, and she would have fallen to the earth, but for the supporting arm of her husband. For a few moments they walked on in silence, when Mr. Harland said, in a voice choked with emotion,

"You have been my good angel, Mary, for your hand it was which saved me from violating a solemn oath; but I now feel an assurance that I have broken the tempter's chains forever." I am happy to add that from this hour he gained a complete victory over the evil habit which well-nigh had proved his ruin; and in after years, when peace and prosperity again smiled upon them, he often called to mind the evening when his affectionate and devoted wife, by her watchful love, saved him from ruin, and perchance from the drunkard's grave.

EMMA ASHTON

It was a sad day for Emma Ashton, when, with her widowed mother, she turned from her father's new-made grave, and again entered their desolate home. None but those who have experienced a like sorrow can fully understand their grief as they entered their now lonely home, where a short time since they had been so happy. But the ways of Providence are, to our feeble vision, often dark and incomprehensible, and the only way by which we can reconcile ourselves to many trials which we are called to endure is by remembering that there is a "need be" for every sorrow which falls to our lot, in the journey of life. Emma was an only child and had been the idol of her father's heart, and no marvel if the world, to her, looked dark and dreary when he was removed by death. Added to the grief occasioned by their bereavement, the mother and daughter had yet another cause for anxiety and disquietude, for the home where they had dwelt for so many years in the enjoyment of uninterrupted happiness was now no longer theirs. Since quite a young man, Mr. Ashton had held the position of overseer, in a large manufactory in the village of W. Owing to his sober and industrious habits he had saved money sufficient to enable him, at the period of his marriage, to purchase a neat and tasteful home, to which he removed with his young wife. He still continued his industry, and began in a small way to accumulate money, when, unfortunately, he was persuaded by one whom he thought a friend to sign bank-notes with him to a large amount; but, ere the notes became due, the man he had obliged left the country, and he was unable to gain any trace of him, and was soon called upon to meet the claim. Bank-notes must be paid, and to raise money to meet the claim he was forced to mortgage his house for nearly its full value. His health failed; and for two years previous to his death he was unable to attend to his business. The term of the mortgage was five years, which time expired soon after his death. During the few last weeks of his life his mind was very much disturbed regarding the destitute condition in which he must leave his beloved wife and daughter; for he was too well acquainted with the man who held the claim to expect any lenity to his family when it should become due, and he was sensible that the hour of his own death was fast approaching. His wife tried to cheer him by hopeful words, saying: "Should it please our Heavenly Father to remove you, fear not that He will fail to care for the fatherless and widow." A short time before his death a sweet peace and hopeful trust settled over his spirit, and the religion he had sought in health afforded him a firm support in the hour of death. When all was over, and the mother and daughter found themselves left alone, their fortitude well-nigh forsook them, and they felt almost like yielding to a hopeless sorrow. Emma was at this time but fifteen years of age, possessed of much personal beauty, and also a very amiable and affectionate disposition. Since the age of six years she had attended school, and made rapid progress in her various studies till the sad period of her father's death. As Mr. Ashton had foreseen, Mr. Tompkins, the man who held the mortgage, soon called upon the widow, informing her that the time had already expired, and unless she found herself able to meet the claim, her dwelling was legally his property; but, as a great favor, he granted her permission to occupy the house till she could make some arrangement concerning the future, giving her, however, distinctly to understand, that he wished to take possession as soon as she could find another home. Mrs. Ashton thanked him for the consideration he had shown her, little as it was, telling him she would as soon as possible seek another home, however humble it might be; and Mr. Tompkins departed with a polite bow and a bland smile upon his countenance, well pleased that he had got the matter settled with so little difficulty. I presume he never once paused to think of the grief-stricken widow and her fatherless daughter, whom he was about to render homeless. Money had so long been his idol that tender and benevolent emotions were well-nigh extinguished in his world-hardened heart. For a long time after Mr. Tompkins left the house Mrs. Ashton remained in deep thought. There are, dear reader, dark periods in the lives of most of us, when, turn which way we will, we find ourselves surrounded, as by a thick hedge, with difficulties and troubles from which we see no escape.

At such periods it is good for us to call to mind the fact, that the darkest cloud often has a silver lining, and that if we discharged, to the best of our ability, our duties for the time being, the cloud, sooner or later, will be reversed, and display its bright side to our troubled view. The time had now arrived, when Mrs. Ashton must come to some decision regarding the future. She had no friends to whom she could turn for aid or counsel in this season of trial. When quite young she had emigrated from England with her parents and one sister, and settled in Eastern Canada. About the time of her marriage and removal to W. her parents, with her sister, removed to one of the Western States: and it may be the knowledge that she must rely solely upon herself enabled her to meet her trials with more fortitude than might have been expected. Some fifty miles from W. was the large and thriving village of Rockford, and thither Mrs. Ashton at length decided to remove. One reason for this decision was the excellent institution for the education of young ladies, which was there located. She was very anxious that her daughter should obtain a good education, but was sorely puzzled as to raising the money needful for defraying her expenses. There were a few debts due her husband at the time of his death; these she collected with little difficulty. Their dwelling had been handsomely furnished, and she decided to sell the furniture, as she could easily, upon their arrival at Rockford, purchase what articles were necessary for furnishing their new home, which must, of necessity, be humble. One article she felt they must retain if possible, and that was the piano given her by her father at the period of her marriage. She did at first entertain the idea of parting with it, thinking how far the money it would bring would go in defraying the expenses attendant upon Emma's education, but upon second consideration, she resolved that they would not part with her father's parting-gift to her, unless compelled to do so by actual want; and so when their old home was broken up the piano was carefully packed and forwarded to Rockford. The home where they had resided so long was very dear to them, and it would have grieved them to leave it at any time; but to leave at the glad season of spring, when the trees which shaded their dwelling were beginning to put forth their leaves, and the flowers which adorned their garden were bursting into bloom, seemed to them doubly sad. But their preparations for removal were finally completed; and they left their home followed by the good wishes of many who had long known and loved them. Upon their arrival at Rockford, Mrs. Ashton hired a cheap tenement in a respectable locality, which she furnished in a plain but decent manner. When they became settled in their new home they had still in hand money sufficient to secure them from immediate want, but as Mrs. Ashton wished Emma to enter at once upon her studies, she was very anxious to devise some means of earning money to meet necessary expenses. There was one family residing in Rockford with whom Mrs. Ashton had several years before been intimately acquainted: their name was Lebaron, and they at one time resided in the same village with the Ashtons. Mr. Lebaron had opened a store upon removing to Rockford; the world had smiled upon him, and he was now considered one of the most wealthy and influential men in the village.

It has been often said that "prosperity hardens the heart of man," but if such is the case in general, Mr. Lebaron proved an exception to the general rule. He had heard with much sorrow of the death of Mr. Ashton, and also of the other misfortunes which had overtaken the family; and no sooner did he learn of the arrival of the widow and daughter in Rockford, than, accompanied by his wife, he hastened to call upon them to renew their former acquaintance, and in a delicate and considerate manner to enquire if he could assist them in any way. Mrs. Ashton thanked them for their kindness, saying that although in no immediate need of assistance, yet she would be very thankful if they would assist her in obtaining employment. "If such is the case," replied Mrs. Lebaron, "I can easily secure you employment, as I am acquainted with many ladies who give, out work, and will gladly use my influence in your favor." "You will confer a favor upon me by so doing," replied Mrs. Ashton, "for I must rely upon my labor for a support for the future." Through the influence of these kind friends Mrs. Ashton soon obtained an abundant supply of work; and, when she became somewhat acquainted with the people of Rockford, her gentle and unobtrusive manner gained her many warm friends. Agreeable to her mother's wishes, Emma soon became a pupil in the seminary for young ladies, which was at that time under the direction of Miss Hinton, a lady who possessed uncommon abilities as a teacher, and was also aided by several competent assistants. Mrs. Lebaron had two daughters attending the institution at the time, and this circumstance, in a great measure, relieved Emma from the feeling of diffidence she might have experienced in entering a large school a stranger to both teachers and pupils; but her modest and unassuming manners, added to her diligence in study soon caused her to become a general favorite with her teachers. In schools, as well as other places, we often meet with those who are inclined to be jealous of merit superior to their own, and the seminary, at Rockford was no exception in this matter. Her teachers were guilty of no unjust partiality; true, they oftener commended her than some other members of her class, but not oftener than her punctual attendance, perfect recitations and correct deportment generally, justified them in doing. But it soon became evident that, if Emma was a favourite with her teachers, she was far from being such with many members of her class. At the time she entered school Miss Hinton found, after examining her in her various studies, that her attainments were already superior to those of several young ladies who had been for some time members of the school. Among the pupils who at the time attended the institution was a Miss Carlton, from the distant city of H. She was the petted and only child of wealthy parents; and, as is often the case, her disposition, which, under proper training, might have been amiable, had been spoiled by unwise indulgence on the part of her parents. Her capacity for learning was not good; she was also sadly wanting in application, and, at the time Emma entered the school, although Miss Carlton had attended for more than a year, her progress in study was far from being satisfactory to her teachers. She was at much pains to inform her classmates of her wealth and position, seeming to entertain the idea that this would cover every defect. Owing to Emma's superior attainments, compared with her own, she soon learned to regard her with a feeling of absolute dislike, which she took little pains to conceal; and many were the petty annoyances she endured from the vain and haughty Julia Carlton. She soon learned that Emma was poor; and that her mother toiled early and late to defray the expenses of her education; and more than once she threw out hints regarding this fact, among the other pupils, even in hearing of Emma; and, as often as opportunity offered, she slighted the unoffending girl, and treated her with all the rudeness of which she was capable. "Let those who wish associate with Miss Ashton," she would often say to her companions; "but I am thankful that I have been better taught at home than to make a companion of a girl whose mother is obliged to take in sewing to pay her school bills." These and other remarks equally malicious were daily made by Miss Carlton; and I am sorry that she soon found others in the school who were weak enough to be influenced by her also to treat Emma with coldness and contempt. Emma could not long fail to notice the many slights, both direct and indirect, which she endured from many members of the school, and she taxed her memory to recall any act by which she might have given offence; but, finding herself unable to recollect any thing on her part which could have offended any member of the school, she was not a little puzzled to account for the rudeness with which she was treated. It happened one day that during recess she remained at her desk in the school-room to complete an unfinished French exercise. Several of her companions soon after entered the adjoining recitation room, and, as they were not aware of her proximity, she became an unwilling listener to a conversation which pained her deeply. As Sarah Lebaron entered the room one of the girls addressed her, saying: — "When you first introduced Miss Ashton among us, I supposed her to be at least a companionable girl, but I have lately been informed that she resides in a cheap tenement, and, further, that her mother takes in sewing, and, if such is the case, I wish to cultivate no further acquaintance with her." "But then," added another girl, "Miss Hinton thinks her almost a saint, and sets her up as a model for us all; if there's any thing I do detest, it's these model girls, and I don't believe she's half as fond of study as she pretends; and, in my opinion, its only to hear the commendations of the teachers that she applies herself with such diligence; but Miss Hinton is so taken with her meek face and lady-like manners that she places her above us all, and, I suppose, we must submit, for as the old song says:

'What can't be cured must be endured.'"

"Well, I for one shall try some method of cure, before I put up with much more of her impudence and assumption," chimed in the amiable Miss Carlton; "pay attentions now, girls," continued she, "while I take my place in the class like Emma Ashton;" and separating herself from her companions, she crossed the room to one of the class-seats, with such a ludicrous air of meekness and decorum, that the girls were almost convulsed with laughter. Starting up and tossing her book from her hand she exclaimed, "It is so disgusting to see a girl in *her* position put on such airs." Miss Lebaron had not before spoken, but, when at length there was silence, she addressed her companions, saying, "if no other young lady present has any further remarks to make, I will myself say a few words if you will listen to me. I must say, I am surprised at the unkindness, even rudeness, which many of you have exhibited towards Miss Ashton. If she is poor it is death, and other misfortunes which have caused her to become so; and this circumstance should excite your sympathy, but surely not your contempt and ridicule. Poor as she is, she is my friend, and I am proud to claim her as such. As to her being companionable that is a matter of taste; I shall continue to follow mine, and each young lady present is at liberty to do the same; but be assured that unless you can furnish some more satisfactory reason for your disparaging remarks than you have yet done, they will bear no weight with me." With much irony in her voice Miss Carlton replied, "Really, Miss Lebaron, I am unable to reply to your very able defence of your charming friend, and will only say that I shall avail myself of the liberty you have kindly granted us, for each to follow her own taste in the choice of associates, and avoid Miss Ashton as much as possible." "As you please," replied Miss Lebaron, "it is a matter of perfect indifference to me;" and just then the school bell put an end to further conversation. As may be easily supposed, the delicate and sensitive spirit of Emma was deeply wounded by the above conversation; and it was with much difficulty that she maintained her composure for the remaining portion of the day. For once her lessons were imperfect; and with a heavy heart she returned to her home. That evening she, for the first time, mentioned to her mother the daily annoyances she suffered from her companions at school; and concluded by relating the conversation she had that day chanced to overhear. Mrs. Ashton could not feel otherwise than grieved; but as much as possible she concealed the feeling from her daughter. "My dear Emma," she replied, "their unkind words can do you no real harm, although they may render you unhappy for the time being. But keep the even tenor of your way; and they will, probably, after a time become ashamed of their folly. Should they make any further remarks regarding my laboring to give you an education, you may tell them that I esteem it as one of my chief blessings that I have health granted me so to do."

Time passed on; and the invariable kindness with which Emma treated her classmates finally gained her several warm friends; and some of them even apologized for their past unkindness. Miss Carlton still regarded her with a feeling of enmity and dislike; but as Emma seemed not to notice the many annoyances she experienced she was at length forced to desist, although the same resentful feeling remained in her heart.

When Emma left the seminary, after attending it for four years, her departure was deeply regretted by both teachers and pupils. As she had pursued her studies in a very systematic manner, she had acquired, before leaving school, a thoroughly good education, which she intended turning to account by teaching. Miss Carlton also left school at the same time to return to her elegant home in the city of H. It was fortunate for her that she was not obliged, as was Emma, to teach as a means of support; for, notwithstanding the unwearied pains of her teachers, her education, when she left school, was very superficial. Emma soon obtained a situation as teacher in a small village some twenty miles from Rockford, where she remained for two years. During her absence, her mother, to avoid being left alone, received as boarders two or three young ladies who attended school in the village. Emma's success as a teacher become so well known that she was at length offered a high salary to accept of the position of assistant teacher in an academy in the city of H., the same city where Miss Carlton resided. As the salary offered was very liberal, she decided to accept of the position, and as the situation was likely to prove a permanent one she was very anxious that her mother should accompany her; and after some deliberation upon the subject, Mrs. Ashton consented, thinking they would both be much happier together than otherwise. Emma proved quite as successful in thus her second situation as in the first; and owing to her position as teacher she soon formed acquaintance with several families of cultivated tastes and high respectability. She often received invitations to parties; but her tastes were quiet, and she usually preferred spending her evenings with her mother in the quiet of their own home, to mingling in scenes of mirth and gaiety; and it was only upon a few occasions that she attended parties, that her friends might not think her unsocial. At one of these parties she chanced to meet her former school mate, Miss Carlton, whose only sign of recognition was a very formal bow. This gave her no uneasiness; she cherished no malice towards Miss Carlton; but her ideas and tastes so widely differed from her own that she did not covet her friendship even had she been inclined to grant it her.

Meanwhile, with the widow and her daughter, time passed happily away. Emma's salary was more than sufficient for their support and they were happy in the society of each other. There was one family, by the name of Milford, who had treated them with much kindness since their residence in the city. Mrs. Milford at first placed two little girls under Emma's instruction, and thus began an acquaintance which soon ripened into intimate friendship; for, although occupying a high position of wealth and influence, Mrs. Milford was one of the few who place "mind above matter" and respected true worth wherever she met with it. Her eldest daughter, having finished her education at a distant boarding school, returned home about the same time her two sisters were placed in charge of Emma; and the little girls were so eloquent in their praise of their teacher, that their eldest sister became interested, and decided to call upon her at her home; and the lady-like appearance of both mother and daughter, together with the appearance of good taste which their home exhibited, strongly interested her in their favor.

Some six months previous to the period of which I am writing a young physician from the Upper Province located himself in the city of H. for the practice of his profession. According to common report, he was wealthy, and the study of a profession had with him been a matter not of necessity but of choice. Owing to his pleasing manners, as well as his reputed wealth, he soon became an object of much interest to many of the match-making mammas and marriageable young ladies of the city of H. He was soon favored with numerous invitations to attend parties, where he formed acquaintance with most of the young people in the fashionable circle of the city; and he soon became a general favorite in society. Among others, he attended a large party given by the Carltons, and by this means became acquainted with the family. He had called occasionally; and during one of those calls Mrs. Carlton very feelingly lamented that her daughter was often obliged to forego the pleasure of attending concerts, lectures and other places of public amusement for want of a suitable escort; and courtesy to the family would of course allow him to do no less than offer to become her attendant upon such occasions. Mrs. Carlton, however, put a very different construction upon these slight attentions, and already looked upon him as her future son-in-law.

When Dr. Winthrop had resided for about a year in the city, the Milfords also gave a large party, and Miss Ashton was included among their guests. The party was a brilliant affair, for the Milfords were a family of wealth and high social position. The young physician was among their guests; and Miss Carlton managed some way or other to claim his attention most of the evening. There was the usual amount of small talk, common to such occasions; about the usual number of young ladies were invited to sing and play, and, as usual, they were either out of practice or were afflicted with "bad colds." But it so happened that several young ladies who at the first begged to be excused, after much persuasion allowed themselves to be conducted to the piano, and played till it was evident from the manner of many that the music had become an infliction instead of a pleasure. When after a time Miss Ashton was invited to play, she took the vacant seat at the piano without any of the usual apologies; and began playing the prelude to a much admired song of the day; and before she reached the close of the first verse there was a hush through the room, and the countenance of each evinced the pleasure with which they listened to her performance. As she rose from the instrument Dr. Winthrop addressed Miss Carlton, saying: "Can you inform me who is that young lady? I never met her before; but she has favored us with the first real music I have listened to this evening." The young physician was not wanting in politeness, and he certainly must have forgotten that Miss Carlton occupied the seat at the piano a short time before. That young lady colored with anger as she replied: "Her name is Miss Ashton, and I understand she is engaged as an assistant teacher in one of the Academies in the city." "It is singular," replied Dr. Winthrop, "that I have never before met her at any of the numerous parties I have attended during the past year." "There is nothing very singular in that," replied Miss Carlton, "for I presume she is not often invited to fashionable parties, and I suppose it is owing to Mrs. Milford's two little girls being her pupils that we find her among their guests; but as you seem so much interested, I will tell you all I know of the *person* in question. When I attended school at Rockford, Miss Ashton was a pupil in the same institution; but, when I learned that her mother, who is a widow, took in sewing, to pay her school bills, I did not care to cultivate her acquaintance. She left school about the same time with myself, and I heard no more of her till she obtained a situation in this city." "Pardon me," replied the young physician; "but I see nothing in what you have stated that is in the least disparaging to the young lady; and I should be much pleased to make her acquaintance." "Our ideas slightly vary in these matters," replied Miss Carlton, with a haughty toss of her head; "but I will not detain you from seeking the introduction for which you seem so anxious. I am sorry I cannot oblige you by introducing you myself; but as I did not associate with her when at school, I am still less inclined to do so at the present time; I hope, however, you may find her an agreeable acquaintance;" and with a haughty manner she swept from his side in quest of companions whose tastes were more congenial. Dr. Winthrop obtained the desired introduction; and if Miss Carlton indulged the hope that he would find Miss Ashton an agreeable acquaintance, there was soon a fair prospect that her wishes would be realized; for the marked attention which Dr. Winthrop paid the lovely and engaging Miss Ashton soon formed the chief topic of conversation among the circle of their acquaintances. For once, public rumor was correct. Dr. Winthrop was very wealthy; but when a mere youth he had a decided taste for the study of medicine; and his parents allowed him to follow the bent of his own inclinations, in fitting himself for a profession for which he entertained so strong a liking. He had an uncle residing in a distant city, who was also a physician of high reputation, and, after passing through the necessary course of study, he had practiced his profession for two years under the direction of his uncle, before removing to the city of H. Up to the time when we introduced him to the reader matrimony was a subject to which he had never given a serious thought, and until he met with Miss Ashton he had never felt any personal interest in the matter. From what I have already said the reader will not be surprised to learn that the acquaintance begun at Mrs. Milford's party terminated in a matrimonial engagement; with the free consent of all who had a right to a voice in the matter. When the matter became known it caused quite a sensation in the circles in which Dr. Winthrop had moved since his residence in the city; but, happily for him, he was possessed of too independent a spirit to suffer any annoyance from any malicious remarks which chanced to reach his ears. When Miss Carlton first learned of the engagement, she indulged in a long fit of spiteful tears, to the imminent risk of appearing with red eyes at the forthcoming evening party. In due time the marriage took place; and the young physician and his lovely bride set out on their wedding tour amid the congratulations and good wishes of many true friends. After their departure

Mrs. Carlton remarked to several of her "dear friends" "that she had long since discovered that Dr. Winthrop was not possessed of refined tastes; and for her part she thought Miss Ashton much better suited to be his wife than many others which she could name." Had the doctor been present to express his sentiments regarding this matter, they would in all probability have exactly agreed with those already expressed by Mrs. Carlton. During their wedding tour, which occupied several weeks, they visited many places of note, both in Canada and the United States. Upon their return to the city Dr. Winthrop purchased an elegant house in a central location, which he furnished in a style justified by his abundant means; and with his wife and her mother removed thither.

In conclusion, we will again bestow a passing glance upon this happy family after the lapse of some twenty years. We find Dr. Winthrop now past the meridian of life surrounded by an interesting family of sons and daughters, whom he is endeavoring to train for spheres of usefulness in this life, as well as for happiness in the "life to come." His graceful and dignified wife still gladdens his heart and home. Time has dealt very gently with her; she is quite as good and almost as beautiful as when we last saw her twenty years ago. The two eldest of their family are boys, and this is their last year in College. Mrs. Winthrop has thus far attended herself to the education of her two daughters. Along with many other useful lessons, she often seeks to impress upon their minds the sin and folly of treating with contempt and scorn those who may be less favored than themselves in a worldly point of view; and to impress the lesson more strongly upon their young minds, she has more than once spoken to them of her own early history, and of the trials to which she was subject in her youthful days. But what of Mrs. Ashton? She still lives; although her once active form is beginning to bow beneath the weight of years, and her hair has grown silvery white. This year Dr. Winthrop has completed his preparations for leaving the city after more than twenty years close application to his profession. He resolved to remove with his family to some quiet country village, which would afford sufficient practice to prevent time from hanging heavily upon his hands; but he now felt quite willing to resign his fatiguing and extensive practice in the city. When he first formed the idea of seeking a country home, he enquired of his wife, if she had any choice regarding a location. "If it meets your wishes," replied she, "no other place would please me so well as the village of W, the home of my childhood and youth, and where my dear father is buried." He soon after made a journey to W, and was so much pleased with the thriving appearance of the village, and the industry and sobriety of the inhabitants, that he decided to seek there a home. Before he left his home, his wife requested him, should he decide upon removing to W, if possible to re-purchase their old home, knowing how much this would please her now aged mother. The purchase was soon completed, and ere he left the village the old house was in the hands of workmen, with his instructions as to improvements and repairs. Mrs. Ashton was very happy when she learned that they were to return to W. "I have been happy here," said she, "but I shall be still happier there." In a short time they removed from the city to take possession of the "dear old home" in W, now enlarged and adorned in various ways; but the same clear brook still flowed at the foot of the garden, and the same trees, only that they were older, and their branches had grown more wide-spreading, shaded the dwelling. As they passed beneath the shade of those well-remembered trees, Mrs. Winthrop addressed her mother, saying, "Do you remember, mamma, how sad we felt the morning we left our home so many years ago, and we little thought it would ever again be ours." Mrs. Ashton gazed fondly upon her daughter and the blooming children at her side, as she replied in the language of the Psalmist, "I have been young and now am old; yet have I not seen the righteous forsaken nor his seed begging bread."

THOUGHTS ON AUTUMN

Again has the season of Autumn arrived. The stated changes of the seasons serve as monitors to remind us of the flight of time; and upon such occasions the most unthinking can hardly avoid pausing to reflect upon the past, the present, and the probable future. Autumn has been properly styled the "Sabbath of the year." Its scenes are adapted to awaken sober and profitable reflection; and the voice with which it appeals to our reflective powers is deserving of regard. This season is suggestive of thoughts and feelings which are not called forth by any other; standing, as it were, a pause between life and death; holding in its lap the consummate fruits of the earth, which are culled by the hand of prudence and judgment, some to be garnered in the treasury of useful things, while others are allowed to return to their primitive elements. When spring comes smiling o'er the earth, she breathes on the icebound waters, and they flow anew. Frost and snow retreat before her advancing footsteps. The earth is clothed with verdure; and the trees put forth their leaves. Again, a few short months, and where has all this beauty fled? The trees stand firm as before; but, with every passing breeze, a portion of their once green leaves now fall to the ground. We behold the bright flowers, which beautify the earth, open their rich petals, shed their fragrance on the breeze, and then droop and perish. Sad emblem of the perishing nature of all things earthly. May we not behold in the fading vegetation, and the falling leaves of autumn, a true type of human life? Truly "we all do fade as a leaf." Life at the best is but a shadow that passes quickly away. Why then this love of gain, this thirst for fame and distinction? Let us approach yonder church-yard and there seek for distinction. There we may behold marble tablets cold as the clay which rests beneath them: their varied inscriptions of youth, beauty, age, ambition, pride and vanity, are all here brought to one common level, like the leaves which in autumn fall to the earth, not one pre-eminent over another. The inspired writers exhibit the frailty of man by comparing him to the grass and the flowers withering and dying under the progress and vicissitudes of the year; and with the return of autumn we may behold in the external appearance of nature the changes to which the sacred penman refers, when he says, "So is man. His days are as grass; as a flower of the field so he flourisheth. For the wind passeth over it and it is gone; and the place thereof shall know it no more." Autumn too, is the season of storms. Let this remind us of the storms of life. Scattered around us, are the wrecks of the tempests which have beaten upon others, and we cannot expect always ourselves to be exempt. Autumn is also the season of preparation for winter. Let us remember that the winter of death is at hand, and let us be impressed with the importance of making preparation for its approach. Let us then, as we look upon the changed face of nature, take home the lesson which it teaches; and, while we consider the perishable nature of all things pertaining to this life, may we learn to prepare for another and a happier state of being.

WANDERING DAVY

It was while I was spending a few days in the dwelling of Mr. C., a Scottish immigrant, that he received a long letter from his friends in Scotland. After perusing the letter he addressed his wife, saying: "So auld Davy's gone at last." "Puir man," replied Mrs. C. "If he's dead let us hope that he has found that rest and peace which has been so long denied him in this life." "And who was old Davy; may I enquire," said I, addressing Mr. C. "Ay, man," he replied, "'tis a sad story; but when my work is by for the night, I'll tell ye a' that I ken o' the life o' Davy Stuart." I was then young and very imaginative; and a story of any kind possessed much interest for me; and the thought that the story of Old Davy was to be a true one, rendered it doubly interesting; so I almost counted the hours of the remaining portion of the day; and when evening came I was not slow to remind Mr. C. of his promise. Accordingly he related to me the following particulars of the life of Davy Stuart; which I give, as nearly as possible, in his own words; for it seems to me that the story would lose half its interest were I to render it otherwise.

"Davy Stuart was an aul' man when I was a wee boy at the school. I had aye been used wi' him; for he often bided wi' us for days thegither; and while a boy I gave little heed to his odd ways an' wanderin' mode o' life; for he was very kind to mysel' an' a younger brither an' we thought muckle o' him; but when we had grown up to manhood my father tell'd us what had changed Davy Stuart from a usefu' an' active man to the puir demented body he then was. He was born in a small parish in the south of Scotland, o' respectable honest parents, who spared nae pains as he grew up to instruct him in his duty to baith God an' man. At quite an early age he was sent to the parish school: where he remained maist o' the time till he reached the age o' fourteen years. At that time he was apprenticed to learn the trade o' shoemaker, in a distant town. It wad seem that he served his time faithfully, an' gained a thorough knowledge o' his trade. Upon leaving his master, after paying a short visit to his native parish, he gie'd awa' to the city o' Glasgow, to begin the warld for himself. He continued steady and industrious, and was prospered accordingly; and at the age o' twenty-five he had saved considerable money. It was about this time, that he was married to a worthy young woman, to whom he had been long deeply attached. They had but one bairn, a fine boy, who was the delight o' his father's heart, and I hae heard it said by they who kenn'd them at the time, that a bonnier or mair winsome boy could 'na hae been found in the city, than wee Geordie Stuart.

Time gied on till Geordie was near twelve years aul', when it began to be talked o' among Mr. Stuart's friends that he was becoming owre fond o' drink. How the habit was first formed naebody could tell; but certain it was, that during the past year he had been often seen the war o' drink. His wife, puir body, admonished an' entreated him to break awa' fra the sinfu' habit, and he often, when moved by her tears, made resolutions o' amendment, which were broken maist as soon as made; an' it was during a longer season o' sobriety than was usual wi' him, that his wife, thinkin' if he was once awa' fra the great city he would be less in the way o' temptation, persuaded him to leave Glasgow an' remove to the sma' village o' Mill-Burn, a little way frae the farm which my father rented.

I well mind, said my father, o' the time when they first cam' among us, an' how kin' was a' the neebors to his pale sad-lookin' wife and the bonny light-hearted Geordie, who was owre young at the time, to realize to its fu' extent the sad habit into which his father had fa'n. When Mr. Stuart first came to our village he again took up his aul' habits o' industry, an' for a long time would'na taste drink ava; but when the excitement o' the sudden change had worn off, his aul' likin' for strong drink cam' back wi' fu' force, an' he, puir weak man — had'na the strength o' mind to withstand it. He soon became even war than before; his money was a' gane, he did'na work, so what was there but poverty for his wife an' child. But it is useless for me to linger o'er the sad story. When they had lived at Mill-Burn a little better than a twelve month, his wife died, the neebors said o' a broken heart. A wee while afore her death she ca'd Davie to her bedside, an' once mair talked lang an earnestly to him o' the evil habit which had gotten sic a hold o' him, an' begged him for the sake o' their dear' Geordie, who, she reminded him, would soon be left without a mither to care for him, to make still anither effort to free himself fra the deadly habit. I believe Davie was sincere when he promised the dyin' woman that he wad gie up drink. Wi' a' his faults, he had tenderly loved his wife, an' I hae nae doubt fully intended keepin' the promise he made her. For a lang time after her death, he was n'er seen to enter a public house ava', an' again he applied himsel' to his wark wi' much industry. After the death o' Mrs. Stuart, Geordie an' his father bided a' their lane. Their house was on the ither side o' the burn which crossed the high-road, a wee bit out o' the village. Time gie'd on for some time wi' them in this way. Davy continued sober and industrious, an' the neebors began to hae hopes that he had gotten the better o' his evil habit; he had n'er been kenned to taste strong drink o' ony kin' sin' the death o' his wife. One evening after he an' Geordie had ta'en their suppers, he made himsel' ready to gang out, saying to Geordie that he was gaun' doon to the village for a wee while, and that he was to bide i' the house an' he would'na be lang awa'. The hours wore awa' till ten o'clock, an' he had'na cam' hame. It was aye supposed that the boy, becoming uneasy at his father's lang stay, had set out to look for him, when by some mishap, it will n'er be kenned what way, he lost his footin', an' fell frae the end o' the narrow brig which crossed the burn. The burn was'na large, but a heavy rain had lately fa'n, an' there was aye a deep bit at one end o' the brig. He had fa'n head first into the water in sic a way that he could'na possibly won 'oot. It was a clear moonlicht night, an' when Davy reached the brig, the first thing he saw was his ain son lyin' i' the water. I hae often been told that a sudden shock o' ony kind will sober a drunken man. It was sae wi' Davy; for the first neebor who, hearin' his cries for assistance, ran to the spot, found him standin i' the middle o' the brig, perfectly sober, wi' the drooned boy in his arms; although it was weel kenned that he was quite drunk when he left the village. Every means was used for the recovery o' the boy, but it was a' useless, he was quite deed an' caul'. "Ah" said Davy, when tell'd by the doctor that the boy was indeed dead, "my punishment is greater than I can bear." Geordie had aye been as "the apple o' his een"; never had he been kenned to ill use the boy, even when under the influence o' drink; and the shock was too much for his reason. Many wondered at his calmness a' the while the body lay i' the house afore the burial; but it was the calmness o' despair; he just seemed to me like ane turned to stane. The first thing that roused him was the sound o' the first earth that fell on puir Geordie's coffin. He gie'd ae bitter groan, an' wad hae fa'n to the earth had'na a kind neebor supported him. His mind wandered fra that hour; he was aye harmless, but the light o' reason never cam' back to his tortured mind. Sometimes he wad sit for hours by Geordie's grave, an' fancy that he talked wi' him. On these occasions nothing wad induce him to leave the grave till some ither fancy attracted his mind. As I hae before said he was never outrageous, but seemed most o' the time, when silent, to be in deep thought; but his reason was quite gone, and the doctors allowed that his case was beyond cure. Many questioned them as to whether it were safe to allow him his liberty, lest he might do some deed o' violence; but they gave it as their opinion that his disease was'na a' ta' likely to tak' that turn wi' him, an' so was left to wander on. He never bided verra lang in a place, but wandered frae house to house through a' the country-side: and every one treated him wi' kindness. The sight o' a bonny fair-haired boy aye gave him muckle pleasure, an' he wad whiles hae the idea that Geordie had cam' back to him. From the day o' Geordie's death to that o' his ain', which took place a month sine, he was n'er kenned to taste strong drink; he could'na bear even the sight o' it. He lived to a verra great age, an' for many years they who did'na ken the story o' his early life ha'e ca'd him Wanderin' Davy. "I hae noo tell'd you his story," said Mr. C. addressing me; "an I hope it may prove a warnin' to you an' ithers o' the awfu' evils o' intemperance; an' I think it's high time my story was finished, for I see by the clock that it's growin' unco late." When the evening psalm had been sung, Mr. C. read a portion of the Scriptures and offered the usual nightly prayer, and soon after we all sought repose; but it was long ere I slept. The story I had listened to still floated through my mind, and when sleep at length closed my eyes it was to dream of "Wandering Davy," and the poor drowned boy.

LOOKING ON THE DARK SIDE

It is an old but true saying, that "troubles come soon enough without meeting them half way." But I think my friend Mrs. Talbot had never chanced to hear this saying, old as it is; for she was extremely prone at all times to look only upon the dark side, and this habit was a source of much trouble to herself as well as her family. Mr. Talbot might properly have been called a well-to-do farmer. They were surrounded by an intelligent and interesting family; and a stranger, in taking a passing view of their home and its surroundings, would have been strongly inclined to think that happiness and contentment might be found beneath their roof; but a short sojourn in the dwelling alluded to, would certainly have dispelled the illusion. This Mrs. Talbot was possessed of a most unhappy disposition. She seemed to entertain the idea that the whole world was in league to render her miserable. It has often struck me with surprise, that a person surrounded with so much to render life happy should indulge in so discontented and repining a temper as did Mrs. Talbot. She was famous for dwelling at length upon her trials, as often as she could obtain a listener; and when I first became acquainted with her I really regarded her with a feeling of pity; but after a time I mentally decided that the greater part of her grievances existed only in her own imagination. She spent a large portion of her time in deploring the sins of the whole world in general, and of her own family and immediate neighbors in particular; while she looked upon herself as having almost, if not quite, attained to perfection.

I recollect calling one day upon Mr. Talbot; he was of a very social disposition, and we engaged for a short time in a lively conversation. Mrs. Talbot was present, and, strange to tell, once actually laughed at some amusing remark made by her husband. He soon after left the room, and her countenance resumed its usual doleful expression as she addressed me, saying, "I wish I could have any hopes of Mr. Talbot; but I am afraid the last state of that man will be worse than the first." I questioned her as to her meaning; and she went on to tell me that her husband had once made a profession of religion; but she feared he was then in a "backslidden state," as she termed it. I know not how this matter might have been; but during my acquaintance with Mr. Talbot I never observed any thing in his conduct which to me seemed inconsistent with a profession of religion. He certainly excelled his wife in one thing, and that was christian charity; for he was seldom if ever heard to speak of the short-comings of others. It is quite possible that he thought his wife said enough upon the subject to suffice for both. Mrs. Talbot made a point of visiting her neighbors, if she chanced to hear of their meeting with any trouble or misfortune. The reason she gave for so doing was that she might sympathize with them; and if sickness invaded a household Mrs. Talbot was sure to be there; but I used often to think that her friends must look upon her as one of "Job's comforters," for no sickness was so severe, no misfortune so great, that she did not prophesy something worse still. According to her own ideas she was often favored with warnings of sickness and misfortune both to her own family and others. She was also a famous believer in dreams; and often entertained her friends at the breakfast table by relating her dreams of the previous night. I remember meeting with her upon one occasion, when it struck me that her countenance wore a look of unusual solemnity, even for her, so much so, that I enquired the cause. "Ah!" said she, "we are to have sickness, perhaps death, in our family very soon; for only last night I dreamed I saw a white horse coming toward the house upon the full galop; and to dream of a white horse is a sure sign of sickness, and the faster the horse seems in our dream to be approaching us the sooner the sickness will come." Her husband often remonstrated with her upon the folly of indulging in these idle fancies. I remember a reply he once made to some of her gloomy forebodings: "I think the best way is for each one to discharge their duty in the different relations of life; and leave the future in the hands of an All-wise Providence." "That is always the way with you," was her reply, "You have grown heedless and careless with your love of the world; but you will perhaps think of my warnings when too late." Before meeting with Mrs. Talbot I had often heard the remark that none were so cheerful as the true christian; but I soon saw that her views must be widely different. A hearty laugh she seemed to regard as almost a crime. A cheerful laugh upon any occasion would cause her to shake her head in a rueful manner, and denounce it as untimely mirth. Upon one occasion she went to hear a preacher that had lately arrived in the neighboring village. This same preacher was remarkable for drawing dismal pictures, and was very severe in his denunciations, while he quite forgot to offer a word of encouragement to the humble seeker after good. Upon the Sabbath in question Mrs. Talbot returned from church, and seated herself at the dinner table with a countenance of most woeful solemnity. Her husband at length enquired, how she had enjoyed the sermon. "Oh!" replied she, "he is a preacher after my own heart, and his sermon explained all my views clearly." "Indeed," replied Mr. Talbot, "he must have a wonderful flow of language to have handled so extensive a subject, in the usual time allotted to a sermon." His answer displeased her very much. Among her other gloomy forebodings she always seemed sure of the fact that Mr. Talbot would survive her; and she replied: "That is always the way. You make light of every thing I say; and I only hope you wont have all these things to repent of when I shall be no more." Mr. Talbot seemed sorry he had wounded her feelings, and replied: "We shall both live our appointed time, and it is not for us to decide which of us will be first removed." The last time I saw Mrs. Talbot she was indulging in her anticipation of some coming calamity. I have learned from various sources, that since I last saw her she has met with *real* afflictions of a very trying nature, even to the most hopeful; and it may be that the presence of real troubles, has put to flight many which were only imaginary; and she may by this time have learned to be thankful for whatever of blessings may yet be left her in her path through life.

EDWARD BARTON

My schoolmate Edward Barton, or 'Ned' as he was usually called by the boys, was such an odd character in his way, that I trust my readers will pardon me for introducing him to their notice. His father was a physician in a distant village, and was justly esteemed among the residents of the place. He had an extensive practice both in the village and surrounding country, and his time was very much occupied; and as Ned grew up he proved a source of constant anxiety to his father, who, being unable to keep him under his own eye, at length decided to send him to reside with some relatives in a farming district some twenty miles distant from his home. Ned's disposition was a singular compound of good and evil, and his conduct depended in a great measure, upon the companions he associated with. He was easily persuaded, and often during his father's frequent and lengthened absences from home he played truant from school, and associated with the worst boys in the village. I well remember the first morning he entered our school. He was then about twelve years of age; but, owing to his carelessness and inattention, he had made but slight progress in study. I learned afterwards that he had so long borne the names of "dunce" and "blockhead" in the school he attended in his own village, that he supposed himself to be really such, and made up his mind that it was useless for him to try to be anything else: and I think when our teacher first called him up for examination he was inclined to be of the same opinion. The teacher first addressed him by saying, "How far have you advanced in reading, my boy?" "Don't know sir, never thought anything about how far I've been." "Well, at least," replied the master, "you can tell me the names of the books you have studied, in reading and spelling." "Oh, yes," replied the boy, "I've been clean through 'Webster's Elementary and the Progressive Reader.'" "Can you tell me the subject of any of your lessons?" "I can just remember one story about a dog that was crossing a river on a plank with a piece of meat in his mouth, and when he saw his shadder in the water, made a spring at it and dropped the meat which he held in his mouth, and it was at once carried away by the current." "Well," said the teacher, "as you remember the story so well, you can perhaps tell me what lesson we can learn from this fable." "I thought," replied the boy, "when I read the story, that the best way is to hold on to what we are sure of, and not grab after a shadder and lose the whole." "Your idea is certainly a correct one," said the master, "and now we will turn to some other branch of study; can you cipher?" "Don't know, I never tried," replied the boy, with the greatest coolness imaginable. "Well," replied the teacher, "we will after a time see how you succeed, when you *do* try. Can you tell me what the study of Geography teaches us!" "O," said the boy, "geography tells all about the world, the folks who live in it, and 'most every thing else." The master then asked him some questions regarding the divisions of land and water, and for a short time he answered with some degree of correctness. At length, while referring to the divisions of water, the master said "can you tell me what is a strait?" This question seemed a "puzzler" to him, and for some moments he looked down as if studying the matter; when the question was repeated in rather a sharp tone, it seemed he thought it wiser to give an answer of some kind than none at all, and he replied: "When a river runs in a straight course, we call it straight, and when it twists and winds about, we call it crooked." "A river is not a strait," replied the teacher with the manner of one who prayed for patience. "Well! at any rate," said the boy, "straight is straight, and crooked is crooked, and that is all I know about it." It was evident from the teacher's manner that he was half inclined to think the boy was endeavoring to impose upon him by feigning ignorance; and he dismissed him to his seat for the time being, thinking, no doubt, that he had met with a case out of the common order of school experience. It seems that the boy had never before attended school with punctuality, and it required a long time to teach him to observe anything like system either in his conduct or studies. Our teacher though very firm, was mild and judicious in his government; and, thinking that possibly Ned's disposition had been injured by former harshness at school, resolved to avoid inflicting corporal punishment as long as possible; and try upon him the effect of kindness and mild persuasion. He had one very annoying habit, and that was he would very seldom give a satisfactory answer if suddenly asked a direct question, and often his reply would be very absurd, sometimes bordering on downright impudence. The master noticed one afternoon, after calling the boys from their play at recess, that Ned had not entered the school-room with the others. Stepping to the door, he found him seated very composedly in the yard, working busily upon a toy he was fashioning with a knife from a piece of wood. "Why do you remain outside, Edward, after the other boys are called in?" said the master. "Cos I did'nt come in, sir," replied Ned, without looking up, or even pausing in his employment. This was too much for the patience of any one; and seizing him by the arm the master drew him into a small room which adjoined the school-room; and bestowed upon him, what Ned afterwards confidentially informed us, was "a regular old-fashioned thrashing." I was not aware till then that the style of using the rod was liable to change, but it would seem that Ned thought otherwise; and if his screams upon this occasion were taken as proof in the matter, I should be inclined to think the old-fashioned method very effective. The whipping which Ned received created quite a sensation among us boys, for it was not often that Mr. S. used the rod. We began to have our fears that as he had got his "hand in," more of us might share the fate of poor Ned. In a very serious conversation which we held upon the matter, on our way home that evening, some of us asked Ned, why he screamed so loud. "I thought," said he, "if I hollered pretty well, he would think he'd licked me enough and stop; but I don't see what great harm I did any way. He asked why I stayed out; and I said, cos I did'nt go in, and I am sure I could'nt give a better reason than that." Time passed on, and by degrees Ned dropped many of his odd ways; and began to make tolerable progress in study; but still, much patience and forbearance was necessary on the part of the teacher. He had the same habit of frequently giving absurd answers in his class, as well as upon other occasions; but after a time his stupid answers were much less frequent, and Mr. S. began to indulge the hope that he would soon overcome the habit entirely. When he had attended school for about six months, as was the custom two or three times a year, we passed under what to the school boys was an "awful review" in presence of those awe-inspiring personages, termed in those days the school-trustees, and any other friends of the school who might chance to be present. We all, even to the teacher, had our fears lest Ned (who had not yet entirely discontinued the practice) should give some of his comical answers when questioned by our visitors; but the day came, and with it the school-trustees and a number of other friends. The classes were first examined in reading and spelling; and Ned acquitted himself much better than we had dared to hope; and we began to think he might pass the afternoon without making any serious blunder. After the reading and spelling lessons, the class was summoned for examination in Geography. Elated by his success in reading and spelling, Ned took his place with a pompous consequential manner, as if expecting to win countless laurels for his proficiency. He got along very well till some one put the question, "What may the Island of Australia properly be called on account of its vast size?" "One of the Pyramids," answered Ned in a loud confident voice. The gentleman who was questioning us looked astounded, and there fell an awkward silence, which was only broken by the half-smothered laughter of the others in the class. The teacher wishing to get over the matter in some way, at length said, "I am surprised, Edward, that you should give so senseless an answer to so simple a question." Now, one very striking peculiarity in Ned's character was his unwillingness to acknowledge himself in the wrong, however ridiculous his answer might be; and he was disposed to argue his point up on this occasion. "Any way," said he, "the Pyramids are large, and so is Australia; and I thought it might sometimes be called a pyramid for convenience of description." The idea of Ned entering into an argument with the trustees of the school, struck the rest of the boys as so extremely ludicrous, that our long pent-up mirth found vent in a burst of laughter through the whole class, and no one present had the heart to chide us; for it was with intense difficulty that the elderly gentlemen maintained their own gravity. The teacher was obliged to exercise his authority before Ned could be silenced; and the remaining part of the examination proved rather a failure. I know not how it happened, but from that day there was a marked improvement in Edward Barton, in every respect. He attended the school for two years; and when he left us it was to accompany his parents to one of the far Western States. His father had relatives residing in the West, and had received from them such glowing accounts of the country, that he decided upon removing thither. Any one who saw Ned when he left us would almost have failed to recognize him as the same boy who entered the school two years previous. Mr. S. was his friend as well as his teacher; and during the second year of his stay took a deep interest in him; he had thoroughly studied his disposition, and learned to bear with his faults, and under his judicious management Ned began really to make good progress in study. We had all become attached to him, and were all sorry when he left us. He was much elated with the prospect of his journey to the West; and talked much of the wonders he expected to behold on his way thither. He came one day at the noon-hour to collect his books and bid us good-bye, his father having come to take him home for a short time before setting out on their journey. The boys were all on the play ground when he entered the school-room to bid his teacher good-bye. When he came out he looked very sober, and there was a suspicious moisture in his eyes which very much resembled tears. Instead of the usual noisy mirth on the play ground there was almost complete silence, while Ned shook hands with us one by one, saying, "he would tell us all the wonders of the Western world when he came back." Years have rolled by with their various changes since that day; he has never yet returned; and I have only heard from him two or three times during the time. My last tidings were, that he was married and settled down to a life of industry upon a fine farm, in his western home; but I sometimes, when I think of him, even yet wonder, if he has learned the difference between the "Pyramids of Egypt" and the "Island Continent of Australia."

THE WEARY AT REST

The weary at rest. The idea was very strongly impressed upon my mind by a funeral which I once attended in the distant village of C. It was that of a very aged woman, whom I had often heard mentioned as one who had been subjected for many years to bodily suffering in no ordinary degree. I had never seen her, but was acquainted with many who visited her frequently; and I became interested from hearing her so often spoken of as a bright example of patience and resignation under affliction; and I was accustomed to enquire for her as often as I had opportunity. Owing to a rheumatic affection of her limbs, she had, as I was informed, been unable for several years to rise from her bed without assistance, and much of the time experienced severe pain. I was informed by her friends that through her protracted period of suffering she was never heard to utter a complaining or repining word, but was found daily in a calm even cheerful frame of mind. After a time I left the village and returned to my home. Returning thither to visit some relatives after the lapse of a few months, I met with a friend, soon after my arrival, who informed me of the death of old Mrs. H., which had taken place the day previous. Two days later I joined the large numbers who assembled to pay their last tribute of respect to one of the oldest residents of their village. As is usual upon funeral occasions, the coffin was placed in front of the pulpit, and a large number occupied the front pews which were appropriated to the friends of the deceased. In those pews were seated men in whose hair the silver threads were beginning to mingle, and women who were themselves mothers of families who all met around the coffin of their aged mother. Childhood, youth and middle age were all represented in that company of mourners. Their pastor, Mr. M., delivered a very appropriate discourse from the words, "Blessed are the dead who die in the Lord." In the course of his sermon he took occasion to remark, that a funeral discourse should apply to the living — not the dead. I had before listened to different sermons from this same text; but I never listened to a more searching application of the words than upon this occasion.

Near the close of his sermon, he said: "I presume many of you are aware that I deem it unnecessary as well as unwise, on occasions of this kind, for a minister to dwell at length upon the life and character of the deceased, for, as I have before said, our duty is with the living; but upon the present occasion, I think I may with propriety say, that we see before us the lifeless remains of one who has 'died in the Lord.' I have been for many years acquainted with our aged sister now departed, and have ever regarded her as an humble and earnest christian. I have frequently visited her during her lengthened period of suffering; and have felt deeply humbled for my own want of resignation to the ills of life, when I observed the exemplary manner with which this aged woman bore her sufferings, which at times were very severe; and more than this, I stood by her dying bed, which I can truly say presented a fore-taste of heavenly triumph."

At the close of the service permission was given for any one who was desirous of so doing to look upon the "corpse," and with many others I drew nigh the coffin. I had been told that the habitual expression of her countenance was one of pain, and I was surprised by the calm and peaceful expression which rested upon the face of the dead. There was no sign of past suffering visible; and the idea of perfect rest was conveyed to my mind, as I gazed upon her now lifeless features. When the strangers had all retired, the relatives and near friends drew nigh to take their last sad look of the aged one who in life had been so dear to them. It seemed that her age and utter helplessness had all the more endeared her to her children and other friends; and many of them wept audibly as they retired from the coffin. As the coffin was borne from the church, the choir sung in subdued tones, accompanied by the solemn notes of the organ, the beautiful hymn commencing with the lines,

> *"Thou art gone to the grave but we will not deplore thee,*
> *Though sorrows and darkness encompass the tomb;*
> *The Saviour hath passed through its portals before thee,*
> *And the lamp of his love is thy guide through the gloom."*

When the long procession reached the church yard, the coffin was lowered to its final resting place, and the Burial Service was read by their pastor, and most of the company departed to their homes. I know not how it was, but, although a stranger to the deceased, I was among the few who lingered till the grave was filled up. That funeral impressed me deeply; and has often since recurred to my mind, amid the cares and turmoil of after life.

THE RAINY AFTERNOON

"It's too bad," exclaimed Harry Knights, as he turned from the window, where for the last ten minutes he had been silently watching the heavy drops of rain as they pattered against the glass. "It's too bad," repeated he, "we can have no out-of-door play this afternoon;" and as he spoke his face wore a most rueful expression. I was one among a number of Harry's schoolmates who had gone to spend the day at the farm of Mr. Knights, Harry's father. The eldest of our number was not more than fourteen; and for a long time we had looked forward to this day with many bright anticipations of fun and enjoyment. The important day at length arrived, and so early did we set out upon our excursion that we reached Harry's home before eight o'clock in the morning. We spent the forenoon in rambling over the farm, searching out every nook and corner which possessed any interest to our boyish minds. Accompanied by Harry we visited all his favorite haunts — which included a fine stream of water, where there was an abundance of fish; also a ledge of rocks which contained a curious sort of cave, formed by a wide aperture in the rocks; and, last though "not least," a pond of water which, owing to its extreme beauty of appearance, Harry had named the "Enchanted Pond." He had said so much to us regarding the uncommon beauty of the spot that some of the boys, myself among the number, had often been inclined to ridicule him; but when we came within view of it, I for one ceased to wonder at his admiration; for before nor since, I never looked upon so lovely a scene. The pond was situated upon the back portion of the farm, in a clearing which had been made by a settler who had occupied the land for some years before it was purchased by Mr. Knights. The form of the pond was entirely circular, and it was surrounded by a green field, in which had been left standing, here and there, some fine old trees to add to the effect. I remember when I first gained a view of the spot, it reminded me of a surface of polished silver, bordered with emeralds. As we drew nigh we could see that its smooth waters were thickly dotted with the pure blossoms of the pond-lily. I have never since visited the spot, but the view I obtained of it that day, now so long ago, is still vividly present to my mind. By the time we again reached the farm-house, the dinner-hour had arrived; and our long continued exercise in the open air had so much improved our appetites that we did ample justice to the good things set before us. Dinner being over, we observed, what had before escaped our notice, that the sky was becoming overcast with dark clouds, and soon a heavy rain began to fall, which put an end to all our plans of out-of-door enjoyment for the afternoon. As I mentioned at the beginning, Harry was very much disappointed, for outside sports were his especial delight; and for a time his face looked almost as dark and forbidding as the sky itself. We tried to cheer him up, saying we would have some quiet games in the large dining-room, and we did succeed in getting him to join us; but somehow or other our games afforded us no enjoyment, and the question, "what shall we do with ourselves?" began to pass from one to the other among the group of eager, restless boys. "Would you like me to tell you a story, boys?" enquired Harry's mother, after observing for a time our vain attempts at enjoyment. Mrs. Knights was a lady of high culture, and possessed the happy faculty of rendering herself an agreeable companion to either the young or old; and more than one pair of eyes grew bright with pleased anticipation when she proposed telling us a story; and, of course, we all eagerly assented to her proposal. Seating herself in our midst, she took up a piece of needlework, saying, "I can always talk best when my hands are employed," and began as follows:

"I suppose none of you, perhaps not even my own Harry, is aware that my home has not always been in Canada; but I will now inform you that the days of my childhood and youth were passed in a pretty town near the base of the Alleghany Mountains in the State of Virginia. I will not pause at present to give you any further particulars regarding my own early years, as the story I am about to relate is concerning one of my schoolmates who was a few years older than myself. The pastor of the Church in the small village where my parents resided had but one son; and, when quite a little girl, I remember him as one of the elder pupils in the school I attended. I was too young at that time to pay much attention to passing events, but I afterward learned that, even then his conduct was a source of much anxiety and sorrow to his parents; his ready talent, great vivacity, and love of amusement continually led him into mischief and caused him to be disliked by many of their neighbors. It was in vain that the villagers complained, in vain that his father admonished and his mother wept; still the orchards were robbed, the turkeys chased into the woods, and the logs of wood in the fireplaces often burst into fragments by concealed powder. Time passed on, till he reached the age of sixteen years, when spurning the restraints of home, the erring boy left his father's house and became a wanderer, no one knew whither; but it was rumored that reaching a seaport town he had entered a merchant vessel bound upon a whaling voyage for three years. During the last year of his stay at home his conduct had been very rebellious, and his father almost looked upon him as given over to a reprobate mind. After his departure, his father was seldom heard to mention his name, but his friends observed that his hair fast grew white, and upon his brow rested an expression of constant grief and anxiety. He was a man that seldom spoke of his own troubles to any one; but it was plain to be seen that his erring boy was never absent from his thoughts, and there was a feeling and pathos in his voice when he addressed his congregation, especially the younger portion of it, which had never been noticed before. It was his custom upon the first Sabbath evening in each month to deliver an address to the youth of his flock, and it was noticed that his appeals had never been so earnest before, as after the departure of his son; but he seldom, if ever, mentioned his name, not even to his grief-stricken wife. Our pastor was not what could properly be styled an old man, but it was thought that his grief, like a canker-worm, sapped at the fountains of life; his bodily health became impaired, his vigor of mind departed, and, ere he had seen sixty years, death removed him from earth, to a home of happiness in Heaven. The widow was now bereft of both husband and child. She was comforted concerning her departed husband, knowing that it was well with him; but she sorrowed continually for her absent boy; and often, during the lonely hours of night, as the moaning of the winds fell upon her ear, she would start from her sleepless pillow and utter a prayer for her poor boy who might even then be tossing on the restless ocean, or perhaps wrecked upon a dangerous coast. She was a woman of good education, and much power of thought, and she at length found a partial relief from her sorrow by writing small works for publication. But how is it all this time with the wandering 'Prodigal?' Nine years have passed away since he left his home, when an agent for the sale of books for a large publishing house was spending a few days in one of the large cities of the West. During his stay in the place, his business as agent often led him into public places; and on several occasions he noticed a young man that attracted his attention. There was nothing prepossessing in his appearance; on the contrary, he bore the marks of dissipation in his countenance; his clothing was old and soiled, and once or twice he saw him when partially intoxicated. The agent was a middle-aged man, and was a close observer of those with whom he came in contact, and somehow or other he felt a strange interest in this young man for which he could not account; and meeting him so frequently, he determined to speak to him. As a pretext for accosting him he offered to sell him some books, although he had no hopes of success. The young man regarded him with visible surprise, when he enquired if he would not like to purchase a book. 'I have no money to spend for books,' replied the man, yet as if unable to resist the impulse, he leaned over the table, on which the agent had placed several books, and began looking them over; and finally selected one, inquired the price, and paid for it. They soon after parted, and the agent thought they should probably meet no more, as he expected soon to leave the city. He returned to the hotel where he boarded, and after tea seated himself on the piazza, to enjoy the cool evening air; when the same young man suddenly approached him, and grasping his hand said, in a voice choked with emotion: 'Tell me, sir, where, O! where did you get that book?' This young man was the erring but still loved son of the Virginian widow, who for these long dreary years had roamed over the earth, unfriended and unaided, vainly imagining his own arm sufficient to ward off the ills of life. He had wandered here from the coasts of the Pacific, where he had been wrecked; his money was nearly gone, and his health had become impaired by hardship and exposure as well as his dissipated course of life. As he afterwards said, he had no intention of reading the book when he purchased it merely out of civility to the stranger who accosted him so kindly; but after the agent left him he opened the book, and a cold dew broke out upon his forehead, for on the title-page he read the name of his *mother* as the author. Her thoughts were continually upon her lost son, and in her mind's eye she often traced his downward career. She imagined him worn and weary, his days spent in unsatisfying folly, and his moments of reflection embittered by remorse; unconsciously, in writing this little book she had drawn from her own feelings and addressed one in this situation. She pointed to him the falseness of the world, and bade him judge of the fidelity of the picture by his own experience; and she taught him the way of return to the paths of peace. And thus it was that the little book which the wretched young man had selected — some would say so accidentally, others, so providentially — proved the means of his return from the paths of sin and folly to those of sobriety and usefulness. He soon told his story to his attentive listener, and informed him of the relationship he bore to the author of the book he had purchased. As he concluded, he said, 'Oh, my mother, why did I leave you to become the hopeless being I am?' 'Not hopeless,' replied his companion in gentle tones. 'You have youth on your side, and may yet be a useful and happy man. I now understand the unaccountable interest which I felt in you when meeting you on several occasions before I spoke to you, and I feel that Providence directed me in the matter.' The agent stayed two days longer in the city, and then departed, the young man with him, for with the promptitude of his nature, to resolve was to act. He directed his course toward Virginia, the star of hope leading him on, and finally approached his native village. No words are adequate to describe the meeting between the lonely widow and her long lost, but now returning and penitent son. When informed that his father had been for some years dead, the shock to him was great, overpowering, but he uttered no repining word. 'I could not,' said he, 'expect the happiness of meeting both my parents again after causing them so much sorrow, and let me be humbly thankful that it is allowed me to cheer the declining years of my aged mother.' I well remember," said Mrs. Knights, "the return of the young man to his home, it was but a short time before I left Virginia; but I have been informed by friends still residing there that he was for several years the staff and support of his mother, of whom it might be said, 'her last days were her best days.' After the death of his mother, as he had no living tie to bind him to the spot, he removed to another section of country, where he married and is now a useful and respected member of society. And now boys," said Mrs. Knights, "allow me in conclusion to say to you all as one, as you value your own well-being in time and eternity, be sure that you honor and obey your parents; think of what the end of this young man might have been, and shun his example. But I see that the hour for tea is near at hand; and for a time I will leave you to amuse yourselves, while I assist in preparing your tea; and if you have been interested in my story, I may tell you another when you next pass a rainy afternoon at our house." We all thanked the kind lady for the interesting story, and I fear one very much hoped that the next day we chanced to pass at Mrs. Knights' farm would prove to be rainy in the afternoon.

THE STUDENT'S DREAM

Arthur Wilton had been for several years a student; but he was one of the plodding sort, who make but slow progress. The principal barrier to his improvement arose from one defect in his character; and that was the habit in which he constantly indulged, of deploring the past, without making any very strong efforts toward amendment in the future. He was one evening seated in his room; a ponderous volume lay open on his study-table, and for a time he vainly tried to fix his attention thereon, till finally he closed the book, and leaning back in his chair, his brows contracted, and the lines about his mouth grew tense, as if his thoughts were anything but pleasing. As usual he was bemoaning his misspent hours.

"Ah," said he, speaking in soliloquy, "they are gone, never more to return, the careless happy days of childhood, the sunny period of youth, and the aspiring dreams of mature manhood. I once indulged in many ambitious dreams of fame, and those dreams have never been realized. Many with whom I set out on equal ground have outstripped me in the race of life, and here am I alone. Many who were once my inferiors have nearly overtaken me, and doubtless they too will soon pass me by. What I very much prize is a true friend, and yet no friend approaches with a word of sympathy or encouragement; would that some would counsel me, as to how I may better my condition." Thus far had Arthur Wilton proceeded in his soliloquy, when his eyelids were weighed down by drowsiness, and he soon sank into a deep slumber. In his dream an aged man, with a most mild and venerable countenance stood before him, who, addressing him by name, said: "Thy heart is full of sorrow; but if you will listen to, and profit by my words, your sorrow shall be turned into joy. You have been grieving over the hours which have been run to waste, without pausing to reflect, that while you have been occupied with these unavailing regrets, another hour has glided away past your recall forever; and will be added to your already lengthened list of opportunities misimproved. You grieve that your name is not placed on the lists of fame. Cease from thy fruitless longings. Discharge faithfully your present duties, and if you merit fame it will certainly be awarded you. You also complain that no friend is near you. Have you ever truly sought a friend, by the unwearied exercise of those affections, and in the performance of those numberless offices of kindness by which alone friendship is secured and perpetuated?

'All like the purchase, few the price will pay;
And this makes friends such miracles below.'

Hast thou hoped for the society of the wise and good? Then with diligence and untiring zeal you should seek to fit yourself for such companionship. Have your early companions got before you in the race of life; and yet you remain at ease, dreaming over the past? Awake, young man, ere yet your day is done, and address yourself to your work with renewed energy; look forward to the future instead of brooding over the past, and be assured you will acquire wisdom, friends and every other needful blessing." With these words the aged man disappeared, and the student awoke. His fire had gone out and his lamp burned but dimly. He rose, replenished his fire, trimmed his lamp, and resumed his studies with ardor. This dream was not lost upon Arthur Wilton. Instead of now wasting his time in regrets for the past, he looked forward with a steady purpose of improvement, and from that period no harder student was to be found in the college; and he finally graduated with high honors. In after years he often related this dream to those of his acquaintances whom he thought in danger of falling into the same habit to which he himself had been so prone in his youthful days.

UNCLE EPHRAIM

For some years, when a child, I used daily to pass the dwelling of Uncle Ephraim, on my way to and from school. He was not my uncle; indeed he bore no relationship whatever to me, but Uncle Ephraim was the familiar appellation by which he was known by all the school-boys in the vicinity. He was among the oldest residents in the section, and although a very eccentric person, was much respected by all his neighbors. How plainly do I yet remember him, after the lapse of so many years! His tall figure, shoulders that slightly stooped, his florid complexion, clear blue eyes, and hair bleached by the frosts of time to snowy whiteness. The farm on which he resided had improved under the hand of industry, till since my earliest recollection, it was in a state of high cultivation. His dwelling was an old-fashioned structure, placed a little back from the main road, and almost hidden from view by thick trees. In an open space, a little to one side, was the draw-well with its long pole and sweep; and I have often thought that I have never since tasted such water as we used to draw from that well, as we used often to linger for a few moments in Uncle Ephraim's yard on our return from school during the hot summer afternoons. He must have been fond of children; for he was a great favorite among the boys; and he often gave us permission to gather fruit from the trees in the garden, provided we broke none of his prescribed rules. But the unlucky urchin who transgressed against a command, forfeited his good opinion from henceforth, and durst no more be seen upon his premises. I happened to be among the fortunate number who retained his approbation and good-will during all our acquaintance.

It was from Uncle Ephraim I received the first money I could call my own. In those days school-boys were not supplied very liberally with pocket-money, and when on one occasion I rendered him some slight service, for which he bestowed on me a piece of money, I felt myself rich indeed, and the possession of as many hundreds now would fail to afford me the same pleasure as did the few cents which made up the value of the coin.

Like all others, he had his failings and weak points; but he had also many very estimable traits of character. Among his failings very strong prejudices were most noticeable, and if for any reason he became prejudiced against one, he could never after see any good whatever in them. He also possessed rather an unforgiving temper when injured by any one. But on the other hand he was a friend to the poor; and seldom sent the beggar empty-handed from his door. He also gave largely to the support of the gospel, as well as to benevolent institutions. One very noticeable and oftentimes laughable peculiarity was his proneness to charge every thing that went wrong to the state of the weather. I think it was more from a habit of speech than from any wish to be unreasonable. I remember one day passing a field when he was trying to catch a horse that to all appearance had no idea of being captured. He tried various methods of coaxing him into the halter, and several times nearly succeeded, but just when he thought himself sure of him, the animal would gallop off in another direction. Out of all patience, he at length exclaimed, "What does possess that critter to act so today?" then glancing at the sky, which at the time happened to be overcast by dull murky clouds, he said: "It must be the weather." I chanced one day to be present when Uncle Ephraim was busily occupied in making some arithmetical calculations regarding his farm-products. The result not proving satisfactory he handed his slate to a friend for inspection, and it was soon discovered that he had made a very considerable error in his calculation. When the error was pointed out to him, he looked up with a perplexed countenance, saying; "It is the weather: nothing else would have caused me to make such a blunder." His son happened to marry against his wishes; so much so, that he had the ceremony performed without his father's knowledge; who afterwards, making a virtue of necessity, wisely made the best of the matter. On learning that his son was actually married without his knowledge, the only remark he made was this: "What could have induced Ben to cut up such a caper as to go and get married without my leave; it must have been the weather, nothing else," and as if he had settled the question to his own satisfaction he was never heard to allude to the matter again. Years passed away, till one day the tidings reached us that Uncle Ephraim was dangerously ill. He grew rapidly worse, and it was soon evident that his days on earth would soon be numbered. I have a very distinct recollection of stealing quietly in, to look upon him as he lay on his dying bed; of the tears I shed when I gazed upon his fearfully changed features. He was even then past speaking or recognizing one from another; and before another sun rose he had passed from among the living. I obtained permission to go in once more and look upon him as he lay shrouded for the grave. I was then a child of ten years, but even at that early age I had not that morbid terror of looking upon death, so common among children. With my own hands, I folded back the napkin which covered his face, and gazed upon his aged, but now serene, countenance. There was nothing in his appearance to inspire terror, and for a moment I placed my hand on his cold brow. He had ever been very kind to me, and I regarded him with much affection, and the tears coursed freely down my cheeks when I looked my last upon his familiar countenance now lifeless and sealed in death. I have forgotten his exact age, but I know it exceeded seventy years. It so happened that I did not attend his funeral; but he was followed to the grave by a large number of friends and neighbours, many of whom still live to cherish his memory.

STORY OF A LOG CABIN[1]

I lately came across this sketch in an old Magazine, bearing the date of 1842, and, thinking others might be as much interested by it as I was myself, I transcribe it in an abridged form to the pages of this volume.

It was a dreary day in autumn. Like the fate which attends us all, the foliage had assumed the paleness of death; and the winds, cold and damp, were sighing among the branches of the trees; and causing every other feeling rather than that of comfort. Four others and myself had been out hunting during the day, and we returned at nightfall tired and hungry to our camp. The shades of night were fast gathering around us; but, being protected by our camp, with a blazing fire in front, we soon succeeded in cooking some of the game we had shot during the day; and as we ate, the old hunters, who were my companions grew garrulous, and in turn related their numerous adventures. "You have lived in Dayton for some time," said an old hunter, addressing one of his companions. "Have you ever seen during your rambles the remains of a log cabin about two miles down the Miami Canal?" "I recollect it well, but there is a mystery attached to those ruins which no one living can solve. The oldest settlers found that cabin there; and it *then* appeared in such a dilapidated state as to justify the belief that it had been built many years previous." "Do you know any thing about it?" I eagerly asked. "I know all about it," replied the old hunter; "for I assisted in building it, and occupied it for several years, during the trapping season. That cabin," he continued, as a shade passed over his features, "has been the scene of carnage and bloodshed. But why wake up old feelings — let them sleep, let them sleep;" and the veteran drew his brawny hand over his eyes. All the curiosity of my nature was roused; and the old men seated by his side gazed upon him enquiringly, and put themselves in a listening attitude. The speaker, observing this, sat silent for a few moments, as if collecting his thoughts, and then related the following tale:

"There has come a mighty change over the face of this country since the time when I first emigrated here. The spot where now

1 I lately came across this sketch in an old Magazine, bearing the date of 1842, and, thinking others might be as much interested by it as I was myself, I transcribe it in an abridged form to the pages of this volume.

stand your prettiest towns and villages was then a howling wilderness. Instead of the tinkling of the cow-bells and the merry whistle of the farmer-boy as he calls his herd to the fold, might be heard the wild cry of the panther, the howl of the wolf, and the equally appalling yell of the aborigines. These were 'times to try men's souls'; and it was then the heart of oak and the sinews of iron which commanded respect. Let me describe to you some scenes in which such men were the actors; scenes which called forth all the energy of man's nature; and in the depths of this western wilderness, many hundreds of Alexanders and Caesars, who have never been heard of. At the time I emigrated to Ohio the deadly hatred of the red men toward the whites had reached its acme. The rifle, the tomahawk and the scalping knife were daily at work; and men, women and children daily fell victims to this sanguinary spirit. In this state I found things when I reached the small village opposite the mouth of Licking river, and now the great city of Cincinnati. Here in this great temple of nature man has taken up his abode, and all that he could wish responds to his touch; the fields and meadows yield their produce, and, unmolested by the red man whom he has usurped, he enjoys the bounties of a beneficent Creator. And where is the red man? Where is he! Like wax before the flame he has melted away from before the white man, leaving him no legacy save that courageous daring which will live in song long after their last remnant shall have passed away. At the time when I first stepped upon these grounds the red man still grasped the sceptre which has since been wrenched from his hand. They saw the throne of their father beginning to totter. Their realm had attracted the cupidity of a race of strangers, and with maddening despair, they grasped their falling power, and daily grew more desperate as they became more endangered. I among the rest had now a view of this exuberant west, this great valley of the Hesperides; and I determined to assist in extirpating the red man, and to usurp the land of his fathers. Among the men who were at the village, I found one who for magnanimity and undaunted courage merits a wreath which should hang high in the temple of fame, and yet, like hundreds of others, he has passed away unhonored, unsung. His name was Ralph Watts, a sturdy Virginian, with a heart surpassing all which has been said of Virginia's sons, in those qualities which ennoble the man; and possessing a courage indomitable, and a frame calculated in every way to fulfil whatever his daring spirit suggested. Such was Ralph Watts. I had only been in the town a few days, when Ralph and I contracted an intimacy which ended only with his death. I was passing the small inn of the town, when a tall man, with a hunting shirt and leggings on, stepped out and, laying his hand on my shoulder, said: 'Stranger, they say you have just come among us, and that you are poor; come along. I have got just five dollars, no man shall ever say that Ralph Watts passed a moneyless man without sharing with him the contents of his pocket — come along.' Ralph and I soon became inseparable friends. His joys as well as his sorrows were mine; in a word, we shared each other's sympathies; and this leads me to the scene of the log cabin. We often hunted together, and while on our last expedition, took an oath of friendship which should end only with death — and how soon was it to end! We left the infant Cincinnati one summer morning at the rising of the sun, and with our guns on our shoulders, and our pouches well supplied with ammunition, we struck into the deep wilderness, trusting to our own stout hearts and woodscraft for our food and safety. We journeyed merrily along, whiling away the hours in recounting to each other those trivial incidents of our lives which might be interesting, or in singing snatches of song, and listening to its solemn echo as it reverberated among the tall trees of the forest. Towards evening we reached our first camping ground — a spot near where the town of Sharon now stands. Here we pitched our tent, built our fire, cooked our suppers, and prepared to pass away the evening as comfortably as two hunters possibly could. All at once the deep stillness which reigned around us was broken by a low cry similar to that of a panther. We both ceased speaking and listened attentively, when the cry was repeated still nearer, as if the arrival was rapidly advancing upon us; and thus the cry was repeated, again and again, till its shrillness seemed not more than a hundred yards distant, when the voice changed to that of a yell, whose tones were so familiar to the ear of my companion as to exert quite a visible effect upon his actions. We both sprang to our feet and, seizing our guns, stood ready to fire at a moment's warning. "Halloo!" cried a deep voice, just outside our camp, but instead of answering it we nerved ourselves for a desperate encounter, feeling assured that several Indians were lurking outside our tent. "Halloo, white brudder, come out," cried the same voice in broken English. We consulted for a moment and finally decided to trust, for once, to Indian faith. Ralph first stepped forth and demanded in no very amiable voice, what was wanting. "Come out white brudder," was the answer. After assuring ourselves that there was but one person near we walked forward and found a large Indian sitting by the fire, both hands spread before the flame to protect his eyes from the light, that his keen gaze might rest unmolested upon us. As soon as he saw us a writhing grin spread over his painted features, and rising he offered us each his hand in a very friendly manner. The Indian drew from his belt a large pipe, gaudily painted, and from which depended a profusion of wampum, beads, and eagles' feathers. He lighted the pipe, and after taking a whiff, passed it to Ralph, who, following his example, passed it to me. After taking a puff I handed it to the Indian, who replaced it in his belt. This very important ceremony being finished, the Indian made known his business. After bestowing a thousand anathemas upon his red brethren, he informed us that he had left the red man forever, and was willing to join his white brothers, and to wage an exterminating warfare against his own kindred. We strove to extort from him the cause of this ebullition of passion, but he only shook his head in reply to our questions, and uttered a guttural "ough." We at first suspected him of some treacherous plot; but there was such an air of candor and earnestness in the communication he now made, that we threw aside all suspicion and confided in him. He stated that there was a large party of Indians in our rear, who had been tracking us for several hours; and that it was their intention early in the morning to surround us, and take us prisoners for victims at the stake; "but," said he, "if my white brudder will follow his red brudder he will lead him safe." We instantly signified our willingness to trust ourselves to his guidance, and, shouldering our blankets and guns, we left our camp, and followed our guide due north at a rapid gait. For several miles we strode through the thick woods, every moment scratching our faces and tearing our clothing, with the thick tangled brush through which we had to pass, but considering this of minor importance we hurried on in silence, save when we intruded too near the nest of the nocturnal king of the forest, when a wild hoot made us start and involuntarily grasp our rifles. "Sit on this log and eat," said our red guide. Finding our appetites sharpened by vigorous exercise, we sat on the log and commenced our repast, when our guide suddenly sprang from his seat, and with a hideous yell bolted into the forest and was soon lost to our sight. This conduct instantly roused our fear; and with one accord we sprang to our feet. We gazed around. Turn which way we would, the grim visage of a painted warrior met our terrified gaze, with his tomahawk in one hand, and his rifle in the other. "Perfidious villain," exclaimed Ralph, "and this is an Indian's faith." An Indian of gigantic size, dressed in all the gaudy trappings of a chief, now strode towards us. Ralph raised his gun, and closed his eye as the sight of the weapon sought the warrior's breast. "Don't shoot, and you will be treated friendly," cried the savage in good English. "So long as I live," said Ralph, "I'll never put faith again in an Indian's word." The gun went off, and the savage, with an unearthly cry, bounded high in the air, and fell upon his face a corpse. A scream, as if ten thousand furies had been suddenly turned loose upon the earth, rang around us; and ere we could start ten steps on our flight, we were seized by our savage foes, and, like the light barque when borne on the surface of the angry waves, were we borne, equally endangered, upon the shoulders of these maddened men. We were thrown upon the earth, our hands and feet were bound till the cords were almost hidden in the flesh; and then, with the fury of madmen, they commenced beating us with clubs, when another chief, who appeared to be of higher standing than the one who had just lost his life, rushed into the crowd, hurling the excited warriors to the right and left in his progress, and mounting upon a log he harangued them for a few moments with a loud voice. They at once desisted, perhaps reconciled by the prospect of soon seeing us burnt at the stake. We were carried to their encampment, where we were still left bound, with two sentinels stationed to guard us. In this painful state we remained all day; when towards evening another company of warriors arrived, and then vigorous preparations were made for burning us. A stake was planted in the ground, and painted a variety of fantastic colors; the brush was piled around it at a proper distance; and every other necessary arrangement made; while we sat looking on, subject to the continual epithets of an old squaw, whose most consoling remarks were: "How will white man like to eat fire," and then she would break into a screeching laugh, which sounded perfectly hideous. A cold chill pervaded my frame as I gazed upon these ominous signs of death; but how often is our misery but the prelude of joy. At the moment that these horrid preparations were finished, a bright flash of lightning shattered a tall hickory, near by; and then the earth was deluged with rain. The Indians sought the shelter, but left us beneath the fury of the storm, where we remained for several hours; but seeing that it increased rather than diminished, they forced us into a small log hut and leaving a man to guard us, bolted the door firmly and left us for the night. What were our reflections when left alone? Your imagination must supply an answer. But we did not entirely gave way to despondency. We were young and robust, and our spirits were not easily subdued. Instead of becoming disheartened our approaching fate emboldened us, and by looks, whose expression made known our minds to each other, we resolved to effect our escape or be slain in striving for it. Anything was preferable to the fiery torture which awaited us. Our guard proved just the man we wanted, for, having during the evening indulged rather freely in drinking whiskey, he soon sank into a profound slumber. Long and anxiously had we watched the man, and now our wishes were consummated. I contrived with much exertion to draw my knife from my pocket, and commenced sawing at the tough thong which confined my wrist. My heart beat high with joy, and already we felt that we were free, when the guard sneezed, opened his eyes, rolled them round the room, and discovered that he had been asleep. I slipped the knife into my pocket without his notice, and he discovered nothing to rouse his suspicions, although he regarded us closely for a long time. He finally sat down, lit his pipe and commenced smoking. After puffing away for half an hour, which seemed to drag by with the tediousness of a week, he laid his tomahawk (which contains the pipe) by his side, and after nodding for some time he again stretched himself upon the rough floor, and soon his deep snoring fell upon our ears. O! what music was that sound to us. I again drew the knife from my pocket, and with desperation freed my hands, and in one minute more Ralph stood like myself a free man. With the stealthy tread of a cat we reached the door, softly slid back the bolt, and once more we stood in the open air. The rain had ceased, the clouds had swept by, and the full moon pale and high in the heavens threw her light upon the tree tops, bathing them in liquid silver. Silently but rapidly we bounded through the forest, our fears of pursuit urging us onward; and by daylight were within twelve miles of the log cabin whose history I am telling. At that time there dwelt in that cabin, with his family, a trapper by the name of Daniel Roe. When we reached there we found Roe at home, to whom we recounted our adventure. He only laughed at our fears that the Indians might track us thus far, and we finally listened to his laughing remarks and concluded to rest in his cabin for several days. We heaped folly upon folly; for instead of putting the house in a state of defence, and preserving as much silence as possible we commenced trying our skill by shooting at a mark. We continued this exercise through the afternoon, partook of a hearty supper, chatted till bed-time, and then retired. Ralph soon fell sound asleep, but I could not; I felt a presentiment of approaching danger; still there was no visible signs of it, yet I could not shake off a peculiar nervousness which agitated me. I lay still for some time listening to the deep and regular breathing of Ralph, and ever and anon as an owl screamed I would start, despite the familiarity of the cry. Just as I turned in my bed, and was trying to compose myself for sleep, I heard a cry very similar to the hoot of an owl; still there was something about the sound which did not sound right. My heart commenced beating rapidly and a sweat started from my brow. I rose softly and looked through the chinks of the logs, but there was nothing to be seen. I listened attentively for at least an hour; but heard no sound to confirm my fears; and finally ashamed of my own nervousness, I could not call it *cowardice*, I slipped into bed, determined to sleep if possible. But soon I heard that same sound on the still air. I rose, dressed myself, but still I could see no form like that of an Indian. Just as I was on the point of abandoning my fears as idle and childish, I cast my eyes through an aperture between the logs; and saw the dusky forms of several Indians moving about the yard. I sprang to the bedside, and awoke Ralph, and in a few moments more, Roe, Ralph, and myself, stood with ready guns, waiting for a chance to shoot. A shot passing through one of the savages, told the rest they were discovered; and now a regular firing began. The Indians simultaneously uttered a fiendish shout, such as no person can imagine who has not heard the Indian war-scream; and then brandishing their tomahawks rushed upon the house and began hewing at the door. In a moment we were all down stairs, and our fire became so fatal that they were forced to retire several times; but with desperate courage they returned to the attack. I never experienced the feeling of utter despair but once in my life; and that was then. Roe came running down stairs (whither he had gone for more ammunition) and with a face white from terror, informed us that the ammunition was expended. Here we were, surrounded by a host of savages, fastened in a small house, with nothing to defend ourselves, and the helpless women and children under the roof. 'Let us open the door, and decide the contest hand to hand,' said Ralph Watts. 'O! my family, my wife and children,' groaned Daniel Roe, 'let us defend the house to the last.' And with nerves strung like iron, and hearts swelled to desperation, we waited in silence for the savages to hew their way through the door. The work was soon over, the savages uttered one deafening yell as the door gave way; and clubbing our guns we wielded them with giant energy. The dark forms of the savages crowded the door-way, their eyes glared madly at us, and their painted features working into a hundred malignant and fiendish expressions, which, together with their horrid yells, and the more heart-rending cries of women and children, all formed a scene of the most harrowing description. The battle was soon over. By some mishap I was hurled head foremost out the door; but so intent were the savages upon the battle within, that they did not once notice me, as they rushed forward to the scene of action.

Seeing that all was lost, and that to remain would only be throwing away my life uselessly, I sprang to my feet and slipping around the corner of the house I made my way over the old fortification[2] and soon left the noise far behind me. Much has been written and said of grief, but how little do we know of its poignant nature, till we suffer the loss of some dear friend. 'Tis when we behold an object of deep affection lying passive and dead — but a thing of clay unconscious of the pain it gives, that we feel *that* sorrow, which language is too feeble to express. I found it so, when upon returning to the cabin a few hours afterward, I found the dead bodies of all my friends mutilated and weltering in their blood. Around the body of poor Ralph lay six Indians, with their skulls beat in; his gun furnishing evidence, by its mutilated state, of the force with which he had used it. My story is soon finished. As the tears streamed from my eyes, I dug a grave where I deposited the remains of my friends, and after placing a large stone above their resting place, I departed, wishing never to return to the spot again, and I never have."

2 Near the spot where the cabin stands are the remains of immense works, but by whom and when built will forever remain hidden.

HAZEL-BROOK FARM.

Robert Ainslie, with his family, emigrated from Scotland about the year of 1843, and settled upon a new farm in the back-woods, in the township of R. in Eastern Canada. I can say but little regarding his early life, but have been informed that he was the eldest of quite a large family of sons and daughters; and also that he was a dutiful son as well as a kind and affectionate brother. It seems that he married quite early in life, and at that period he tended a small farm adjoining the one occupied by his father. The utmost harmony existed between the two families, and they lived in the daily interchange of those little offices of love and kindness which render friends so dear to each other. Several years glided by in this happy manner, but reverses at length came; and Robert formed the plan of emigrating to America. But when he saw how much his parents were grieved by the thought of his seeking a home on the other side of the Atlantic, he forbore to talk farther of the matter, and decided to remain at home for another year at least. That year, however, proved a very unfortunate one; his crops were scanty; and toward the spring he met with some severe losses, by a distemper which broke out among his farm stock. As the season advanced, he became so disheartened by his gloomy prospects, that he decided to carry out his former plan of emigrating to Canada; where he hoped by persevering industry to secure a comfortable home for himself and those dear to him. He had little difficulty in persuading his wife to accompany him, as her parents with her two brothers and one sister had emigrated some two years previous. It was more difficult, however, for him to persuade his father and mother that his decision was a wise one. "If ye maun leave us," said his mother, "can ye no seek anither hame nearer han', an' no gang awa across the water to yon' wild place they ca' Canada?" "We maun try to be reasonable, woman," said his father, "but I canna deny that the thought o' our first born son gaun sae far awa gie's me a sair heart." It was equally hard for the son to bid farewell to the land of his birth, and of a thousand endearing ties; but prudence whispered that now was his time to go, while he had youth and health, to meet the hard-ships that often fall to the lot of the emigrant. When his parents saw how much his mind was set upon it they ceased to oppose his wishes, and with his wife and children, he soon joined the large numbers who, at that period, were leaving the British, for the Canadian shores.

As may be readily supposed, the parting between the two families was a very sad one; but the last adieus were finally exchanged, and the poor emigrants were borne away on the billows of the Atlantic. During the first few days of their voyage they all, with the exception of their youngest child, suffered much from seasickness. This child was a little girl about three years old; and it seemed singular to them, that she should escape the sickness from which nearly all the passengers suffered, more or less. They soon recovered; the weather was fine, and many of their fellow passengers were very agreeable companions, and they began really to enjoy the voyage. But this happy state of things was but of short duration. Their little girl, wee Susie, as they called her, was seized with illness. They felt but little anxiety at the first, thinking it but a slight indisposition from which she would soon recover; but when day after day passed away with no visible change for the better they became alarmed, and summoned the physician, who pronounced her disease a slow kind of fever, which he said often attacked those who escaped the seasickness. He told the anxious parents not to be alarmed, as he hoped soon to succeed in checking the disease. But with all the physician's skill, aided by the unceasing attention of her fond parents, the sad truth that wee Susie was to die soon became evident. When the sorrowing parents became sensible that their child must die, they prayed earnestly that her life might be prolonged till they should reach the land. But for some wise reason their prayer was not granted; and when their voyage was but little more than half accomplished she died, and they were forced to consign her loved form to a watery grave. The lovely prattling child had been a general favourite with all on board, and her sudden death cast a gloom over the minds of all. Words would fail me to describe the grief of the parents and the two affectionate little brothers when they realized that "wee Susie" was indeed gone, and that they could never enjoy even the melancholy satisfaction of beholding her resting-place. Mr. Ainslie's domestic affections were very strong, and to him the blow was terrible. He now deeply regretted removing his family from their Scottish home, entertaining the idea, that had they not undertaken this journey their child might have been spared; and he wrote bitter things against himself for the step he had taken. Deep as was the mother's grief, she was forced to place a restraint upon it that she might comfort her almost heart-broken husband. Upon one occasion, in reply to some of his self upbraidings, she said, "I think, Robert, you're ow're hard on yoursel' now, when ye tak the blame o' puir Susie's death; ye surely canna think itherwise than the dear bairn's time had come; an' had we bided at hame it would ha' been a' the same; for we dinna leeve an' dee by chance, and the bounds o' our lives are set by Him who kens a' things."

These consoling words from his sympathising wife tended to lighten, in some measure, the burden of sorrow which oppressed his heart. The weather during the latter part of their voyage was stormy and uncomfortable, and they were truly glad when they at length reached the Canadian port. At the city of Montreal they parted with all those who had been their fellow passengers, as all except themselves were bound for the Upper Province, while they intended joining their friends in Lower Canada.

In the days of which I am speaking the emigrant's journey from the city of Montreal to the townships was toilsome in the extreme; and the same journey, which is now accomplished in a few hours by railway, was then the work of several days; and the only mode of conveyance for themselves and their luggage, were the horse-carts hired for the occasion. But their fatiguing journey was at length terminated; and they arrived safely at the bush settlement in R., where the friends of Mrs. Ainslie resided. That now thriving and prosperous settlement was then in its infancy, and possessed but few external attractions to the new comer; for at the period when Mrs. Ainslie's parents settled there it was an unbroken wilderness. It is needless for me to add that the wayworn travellers met with a joyous welcome from the friends who had been long anxiously looking for their arrival. Mr. and Mrs. Miller were overjoyed to meet again their daughter from whom they had been so long separated by the deep roll of the ocean; and almost their first enquiry was for the "wee lassie," who when they left Scotland was less than a twelve month old. Mr. Ainslie was unable to reply, and looked toward his wife as if beseeching her to answer to their enquiry. She understood the mute appeal, and composing herself by a strong effort said: "My dear father an' mither, a great grief has o'erta'en us sin' we left hame', an' our hearts are well-nigh broken; we buried wee Susie in the caul waters o' the ocean." She endeavoured to relate to them the particulars of the child's death; but her feelings overcame her, and for some moments they could only weep together. When Mr. Miller was able to command his voice he said, "God is good, my children, an' overrules a' things for our good, let us bow before Him in prayer;" and when they rose from their knees, they felt calmed and comforted, by the soothing influence of prayer. With the two boys, Geordie and Willie, fatigue soon got the better of their joy at meeting with their friends, and they were soon enjoying the sound sleep of healthful childhood; but with the elder members of the family, so much was there to hear and to tell that the hour was very late when they separated to seek repose. Mr. Ainslie decided upon purchasing a lot of land, lying some two miles north of the farm occupied by Mr. Miller. Although it was covered with a dense forest, its location pleased him, and the soil was excellent, and he looked forward to the time when he might there provide a pleasant home. They arrived at R. on the first of July. There were beside Mr. Miller but three other families in the settlement; but they were all very kind to the newly arrived strangers, and they assisted Mr. Ainslie in various ways while he effected a small clearing upon his newly purchased farm. They also lent him a willing hand in the erection of a small log house, to which he removed his family in the fall, Mrs. Ainslie and the children having remained with her parents during the summer; and kind as their friends had been, they were truly glad when they found themselves again settled in a home of their own, however humble. They were people of devoted piety, and they did not neglect to erect the family altar the first night they rested beneath the lowly roof of their forest home. I could not, were I desirous of so doing, give a detailed account of the trials and hardships they endured during the first few years of their residence in the bush; but they doubtless experienced their share of the privations and discouragements which fell to the lot of the first settlers of a new section of country. The first winter they passed in their new home was one of unusual severity for even the rigorous climate of Eastern Canada, and poor Mrs. Ainslie often during that winter regretted the willingness with which she bade adieu to her early home, to take up her abode in the dreary wilderness. They found the winter season very trying indeed, living as they did two miles from any neighbour; and the only road to the dwelling of a neighbour was a foot-track through the blazed trees, and the road, such as it was, was too seldom trodden during the deep snows of winter, to render the foot-marks discernible for any length of time. Their stores had all to be purchased at the nearest village, which was distant some seven miles, and Mr. Ainslie often found it very difficult to make his way through the deep snows which blocked up the roads, and to endure the biting frost and piercing winds on his journeys to and from the village. In after years when they had learned to feel a deep interest in the growth of the settlement, they often looked back with a smile to the "home-sickness" which oppressed their hearts, while struggling with the first hardships of life in the bush. Mr. Ainslie and his family, notwithstanding their many privations, enjoyed uninterrupted health through the winter, and before the arrival of spring they already felt a growing interest in their new home. Mrs. Ainslie regarded the labours of the workmen with much attention during the winter, while they felled the trees which had covered nearly ten acres of their farm. As each tree fell to the ground it opened a wider space in the forest and afforded a broader view of the blue sky. A stream of water, which in many places would have been termed a river, but which there only bore the name of Hazel-Brook, flowed near their dwelling, and as the spring advanced, the belt of forest which concealed it from view having been felled, she gained a view of its sparkling waters when the warm showers and genial rays of the sun loosened them from their icy fetters; and she often afterwards remarked that the view of those clear waters was the first thing which tended to reconcile her to a home in the forest. With the coming of spring their "life in the woods" began in earnest. When the earth was relieved of its snowy mantle, the fallen trunks of the trees, with piles of brush-wood, were scattered in every direction about their dwelling. But the fallow was burned as soon as it was considered sufficiently dry, the blackened logs were piled in heaps, and the ground was prepared for its first crop of grain. The green blades soon sprang up and covered the ground, where a short time before was only to be seen the unsightly fallow or the remains of the partially consumed logs.

It was a long time before Mr. and Mrs. Ainslie became reconciled to the change in their circumstances, when they exchanged the comforts and conveniences of their home beyond the sea, for the log cabin in the wilderness. Cut off as they were from the privileges of society to which they had been accustomed from childhood, they felt keenly the want of a place of worship, with each returning Sabbath, and next to this, the want of a school for their two boys; for taken as a people the Scotch are intelligent; and we rarely meet with a Scotchman, even among the poorer classes, who has not obtained a tolerable education. And the careful parents felt much anxiety when they beheld their children debarred from the advantages of education; but to remedy the want as much as lay in their power, they devoted the greater part of what little leisure time they could command to the instruction of their boys. They had been regular attendants at their own parish church in the old country; and very sensibly they felt the want, as Sabbath after Sabbath passed away, with no service to mark it from other days. "It just seems," said Mr. Ainslie, "that sin' we cam' to America we ha'e nae Sabbath ava." In order to meet the want in some measure, he proposed to the few neighbours which there formed the settlement, that they should assemble at one house, on each Sabbath afternoon, and listen to the reading of a sermon by some one present. "I think it our duty," said he, "to show our respect to the Sabbath-day by assembling ourselves together, and uniting in worship to the best o' our ability. I ha'e among my books a collection o' sermons by different divines, an' I am verra willin' to tak' my turn in the readin' o' ane, an' I'm sure you should a' be agreeable to do the same." His proposal met with the hearty approval of all his neighbours, and for some years each Sabbath afternoon saw most of the neighbours collected together for the best mode of worship within their reach. The bush settlements at this period were much infected by bears, and they often proved very destructive to the crops of the early settler, and also a cause of no little fear. I believe the instances have been rare when a bear has been known to attack a person, although it has happened in some cases; but the immigrant has so often listened to exaggerated accounts regarding the wild animals of America, that those who settle in a new section of country find it difficult to get rid of their fears. On one occasion when the Sabbath meeting met at Mr. Ainslie's house, Mrs. Ainslie urged her mother to remain and partake of some refreshment before setting out on her walk homeward. "Na, na," replied the old lady. "I maun e'en gang while I ha'e company, I dinna expec' to leeve muckle longer at ony rate, but wouldna' like to be eaten by the bears;" and for several years the one who ventured alone to the house of a neighbour after dark was looked upon as possessing more courage than prudence. But although the settlers often came across these animals, on the bush-road, I never heard of one being attacked by them. An old man, upon one occasion, returning in the evening from the house of friends, and carrying in his hand a torchlight composed of bark from the cedar tree, met a large bear in the thick woods. Being asked if he was not frightened, he replied, "Deed I think the bear was 'maist frightened o' the twa', for he just stood up on his twa hind legs, and glowered at me for a wee while till I waved the torch light toward him, when he gi' an awfu' snort, and ran into the woods as fast's ever he was able, an' I cam awa' hame no a bit the war, an' I think I'll never be sae' muckle feared about bears again." But these early settlers certainly found these animals very troublesome from their frequent depredations upon their fields of grain, and they often spent a large portion of the night watching for them, prepared to give them battle, but it was not often they saw one on these occasions, for these animals are very cunning, and seem at once to know when they are watched. It sometimes also happened that during the early period of this settlement people lost their way in the bush while going from one house to another. A woman once set out to go to the house of a neighbour who lived about a mile distant. Supposing herself on the right path she walked onward, till thinking the way rather long she stopped and gazed earnestly around her, and became terrified as she noticed that the trees and rocks, and every other surrounding object had a strange unfamiliar look; and she knew at once that she had taken a wrong path.

Becoming much alarmed, she endeavoured to retrace her steps, but after walking a long time would often return to the spot from which she set out. She left home about ten o'clock in the forenoon, and her friends, alarmed at her long stay, called together some of their neighbours and set out to look for her, knowing that she must have lost her way in the forest. They continued their search through the afternoon, sounding horns, hallooing, and calling her name, as they hurried through the tangled underbrush, and other obstructions, and at sunset they returned to procure torches with which to continue their search through the night; her friends were almost beside themselves with terror, and all the stories they had heard or read of people being devoured by wild animals rushed across their minds. But just when they had collected nearly every settler in the vicinity, and were preparing their torches to continue the search, the woman arrived safely at home, with no further injury than being thoroughly frightened and very much fatigued. She stated that she had walked constantly, from the time when she became aware she was lost, and that she was so much bewildered that she at the first did not know their own clearing, till some familiar object attracted her attention. As the neighbours were going to their homes, after the woman's return, they were, naturally enough, talking of the matter, regarding it as a cause of deep thankfulness that no harm had befallen her. Mr. G., one of the number, although a very kind-hearted man, had an odd dry manner of speaking which often provoked a laugh. It so happened that the woman who was lost was very small, her stature being much below the medium height. Laughter was far enough from the mind of any one, till old Mr. G., who had not before made a remark, suddenly said, "sic a wee body as you should never attemp' to gang awa' her lane through the bush without a bell hanged aboot her neck to let people ken where to find her in case she should gang off the richt road." This was too much for the gravity of any one; and the stillness of the summer night was broken by a burst of hearty laughter from the whole company; and the old man made the matter little better, when the laugh had subsided by saying in a very grave manner, "Well, after a' I think is would be a verra wise-like precaution wi' sic a wee bit body as her." Time passed on; other settlers located themselves in the vicinity, and the settlement soon began to wear a prosperous appearance. As soon as circumstances allowed, a school-house was erected, which, if rude in structure, answered the purpose very well. For some time the school was only kept open during the summer and autumn, as the long distance and deep snows forbade the attendance of young children during the winter season. They had as yet no public worship, except the Sabbath meetings before mentioned, which were now held in the schoolhouse for the greater convenience of the settlers. Mr. Ainslie was a man of much industry; and although his home was for some years two miles from any neighbour, it soon wore a pleasing appearance. The most pleasing feature in the scene was the beautiful stream of water which ran near his dwelling, and after which he named his farm. In five years from the time when he first settled in the bush, he exchanged his rude log house for a comfortable and convenient framed dwelling, with a well-kept garden in front, and near his house were left standing some fine shade-trees which added much to the beauty of the place. In process of time, the excellent quality of the soil in that range of lots attracted others to locate themselves in the vicinity; and Hazel-Brook farm soon formed the centre of a fast growing neighbourhood. Two sons and another daughter had been added to Mr. Ainslie's family during this time; and the birth of the little girl was an occasion of much joy to all the family. They had never forgotten "wee Susie," and all the love which they bore to her memory was lavished upon this second daughter in the family. The elder brothers were anxious to bestow the name of their lost favourite upon their infant sister, but the parents objected, having rather a dislike to the practice, so common, of bestowing upon a child a name that had belonged to the dead; and so the little girl was named Jennette, after her grandmother, Mrs. Miller. About this time old Mr. Miller died. He was an old man, "full of days," having seen nearly eighty years of life. He had ever been a man of strong constitution and robust health, and his last illness was very short; and from the first he was confident that he should never recover. When he first addressed his family upon the subject they were overwhelmed with grief. "Dinna greet for me," said he in a calm and hopeful voice, "I ha'e already leeved ayont the period allotted to the life o' man. I ha'e striven in my ain imperfect way to do my duty in this life, an' I am thankfu' that I am able to say that I dinna fear death; and I feel that when I dee I shall gang hame to the house o' a mercifu' Father." So peaceful was his departure, that, although surrounded by his mourning friends, they were unable to tell the exact moment of his death. Like a wearied child that sleeps, he quietly passed away. They had no burial ground in the settlement, and he was laid to rest several miles from his home. His family, with the exception of one son, had all married and removed to homes of their own some time previous to his death; and to this son was assigned the happy task of watching over the declining years of his widowed mother. Mr. Miller, as a dying injunction, charged this son never to neglect his mother in her old age, and most sacredly did he observe the dying wishes of his father. Mrs. Miller was also of advanced age. For three years longer she lingered, and was then laid to rest beside her departed husband.

Twenty years have passed away since we introduced Robert Ainsley with his family to the reader. Let us pay a parting visit to Hazel-Brook farm, and note the changes which these twenty years have effected. The forest has melted away before the hand of steady industry, and we pass by cultivated fields on our way to the farm of Mr. Ainslie. The clearings have extended till very few trees obstruct our view as we gaze over the farms of the numerous settlers, which are now separated by fences instead of forest trees. But the loveliest spot of all is Hazel-Brook farm. The farm-house of Robert Ainslie, enlarged and remodelled according to his increased means, is painted a pure white, and very pleasant it looks to the eye, through the branches of the shade-trees which nearly surround it. The clear waters of Hazel-Brook are as bright and sparkling as ever. The banks near the dwelling are still fringed with trees and various kinds of shrubs; but farther up the stream all obstructions have been cleared away, and the sound of a saw-mill falls upon the ear. Let us enter the dwelling. Mr. and Mrs. Ainslie, although now no longer young, evince by their cheerful countenance that they yet retain both mental and bodily vigour. As yet their children all remain at home, as the boys find ample employment upon the farm, and at the mill; While Jennette assists her mother in the labours of the household. For many years the setting sun has rested upon the gleaming spire of the neat and substantial church erected by the settlers; and now upon the Sabbath day, instead of listening to a sermon read by a neighbour, they listen to the regular preaching of the gospel, and each one according to his means contributes to the support of their minister. It was Mr. Ainslie who first incited the settlers to exert themselves in the erection of a suitable place for worship. Some of his neighbours at the first were not inclined to favour the idea, thinking the neighbourhood too poor for the undertaking. But he did not suffer himself to become discouraged, and after considerable delay the frame of the building was erected. When the building was once begun, they all seemed to work with a will, and to the utmost of their ability. Those who were unable to give money brought contributions of lumber, boards, shingles, &c., besides giving their own labour freely to the work; and in a short time the work had so far advanced that they were able to occupy the building as a place of worship, although in an unfinished state. But the contributions were continued year after year, till at length they were privileged to worship in a church which they could call their own. Mr. Ainslie was a man of talents and education, superior to most of the early settlers in that section, and it was his counsel, administered in a spirit of friendship and brotherly kindness, which worked many improvements and effected many changes for the better as the years rolled by. As we turn away with a parting glance at the pleasing scene, we cannot help mentally saying, — surely the residents in this vicinity owe much to Robert Ainslie for the interest he has ever taken in the prosperity and improvements of the place, and long may both he and they live to enjoy the fruit of their united labours.

OLD RUFUS

The memory of Old Rufus is so closely connected with the days of my childhood that I cannot refrain from indulging in a few recollections of him. The name of Old Rufus was not applied to him from any want of respect; but it was owing to his advanced age, and long residence in our vicinity, that he received this appellation. His name was Rufus Dudley. I remember him as an old man when I was a very young child; and his residence in the neighbourhood dated back to a period many years previous to the time of which I speak. He was born in the state of New York, where he resided during the early portion of his life, and where he married. His wife died before his removal to Canada. When he first came to the Province he located himself in a town a few miles from the village of C., where he married a second time. When first he removed to R. he was for some years employed in a saw-mill and earned a comfortable support for his family. My knowledge of his early residence in R. is indefinite, as he had lived there for many years previous to my recollection, and all I know concerning the matter is what I have heard spoken of at different times by my parents and other old residents of the place. It would seem, however, that his second marriage was, for him, very unfortunate, for to use his own words, "he never afterward had any peace of his life." I have been informed that his wife was possessed of a pleasing person and manners, but added to this she also possessed a most dreadful temper; which when roused sometimes rendered her insane for the time being; and finally some trouble arose between them which ended in a separation for life. They had two grown-up daughters at the time of their separation who accompanied their mother to a town at a considerable distance from their former home. In a short time the daughters married and removed to homes of their own. Their mother removed to one of the Eastern States. She survived her husband for several years, but she is now also dead. Soon after he became separated from his family Old Rufus gave up the saw-mill and removed to a small log house, upon a piece of land to which he possessed some kind of claim, and from that time till his death, lived entirely alone. He managed to cultivate a small portion of the land, which supplied him with provisions, and he at times followed the trade of a cooper, to eke out his slender means. His family troubles had broken his spirit, and destroyed his ambition, and for years he lived a lonely dispirited man. He was possessed of sound common sense and had also received a tolerable education, to which was added a large stock of what might be properly termed general information; and I have often since wondered how he could have reconciled himself to the seemingly aimless and useless life which he led for so many years. But in our intercourse with men, we often meet with characters who are a sore puzzle to us; and Old Rufus was one of those. When quite young I have often laughed at a circumstance I have heard related regarding the violent temper of his wife; but indeed it was no laughing matter. It seems that in some instances she gave vent to her anger by something more weighty than words. Old Rufus one day entered the house of a neighbor with marks of blows on his face, and was asked the cause. He never spoke of his wife's faults if he could avoid it; but on this occasion he sat for a moment as though considering what reply to make, and finally said: "O! there is not much the matter with my face any way, only Polly and I had a little brush this morning." I know not how serious the matter was, but Old Rufus certainly came off second in the encounter. This aged man is so deeply connected with the early scenes of my home life that I yet cherish a tender regard for his memory; although the flowers of many summers have scattered their blossoms, and the snows of many winters have descended upon his grave. He was upon familiar terms with almost every family in the neighbourhood, and every one made him welcome to a place at their table, or a night's lodging as the case might be; and I well remember the attention with which I used to listen to his conversation during the long winter evenings, when, as was often the case, he passed a night in our dwelling. I recollect one time when the sight of Old Rufus was very welcome to me. When about nine years of age, I accompanied my brothers to the Sugar bush one afternoon in Spring; and during a long continued run of the sap from the maple trees it was often necessary to keep the sugar kettles boiling through the night to prevent waste. On the afternoon in question, my brothers intended remaining over night in the bush, and I obtained permission to stay with them, thinking it would be something funny to sleep in a shanty in the woods. The sugar-bush was about two miles from our dwelling, and I was much elated by the prospect of being allowed to assist in the labors of sugar-making. My brothers laughingly remarked that I would probably have enough of the woods, and be willing to return home when night came, but I thought otherwise. During the afternoon I assisted in tending the huge fires, and the singing of the birds, and the chippering of the squirrels as they hopped in the branches of the tall trees, delighted me, and the hours passed swiftly by, till the sun went down behind the trees and the shades of evening began to gather about us. As the darkness increased, I began to think the sugar-bush not the most desirable place in the world, in which to pass the night, and all the stories I had ever heard of bears, wolves and other wild animals rushed across my mind, and filled me with terror. I would have given the world, had it been at my disposal, to have been safely at home; and it was only the dread of being laughed at, which prevented me from begging my brothers to take me there. And when darkness had entirely settled over the earth, and the night-owls set up their discordant screams, my fears reached a climax. I had never before listened to their hideous noise, and had not the slightest idea of what it was. I had often heard old hunters speak of a wild animal, called the catamount, which they allowed had been seen in the Canadian forests during the early settlement of the country. I had heard this animal described as being of large size, and possessing such strength and agility, as enabled them to spring from the boughs of one tree to those of another without touching the ground, and at such times their savage cries were such as to fill the heart of the boldest hunter with terror. I shall never forget the laugh which my grown-up brothers enjoyed at my expense when trembling with terror, I enquired if they thought a catamount was not approaching among the tree-tops. "Do not be alarmed," said they, "for the noises which frighten you so much proceeds from nothing more formidable than owls." Their answer, however, did not satisfy me, and I kept a sharp look-out among the branches of the surrounding trees lest the dreaded monster should descend upon us unawares. Old Rufus was boiling sap, half a mile from us, and it was a joyful moment to me, when he suddenly approached us, out of the darkness, saying, "Well boys don't you want company? I have got my sap all boiled in, and as I felt kinder lonesome, I thought I would come across, and sleep by your shanty fire." The old man enquired why I seemed so much terrified, and my brothers told him that I would persist in calling a screech-owl, a catamount. Old Rufus did not often laugh, but he laughed heartily on this occasion, and truly it was no wonder and when he corroborated what my brothers had already told me, I decided that what he said must be true. His presence at once gave me a feeling of protection and security and creeping close to his side on the cedar boughs which formed our bed, while the immense fire blazed in front of our tent, I soon forgot my childish fears, in a sound sleep which remained unbroken till the morning sun was shining brightly above the trees. But it was long before I heard the last of the night I spent in the bush; and as often as my brothers wished to tease me, they would enquire if I had lately heard the cries of a catamount? Time passed on till I grew up, and leaving the paternal home went forth to make my own way in the world. Old Rufus still resided in R. When a child I used to fancy that he would never seem older than he had appeared since my earliest recollection of him; but about the time I left home there was a very observable change in his appearance. I noticed that his walk was slow and feeble, and his form was bending beneath the weight of years and his hair was becoming white by the frosts of time. I occasionally visited my parents, and during these visits I frequently met with my old friend; and it was evident that he was fast losing his hold of life. He still resided alone much against the wishes of his neighbours, but his old habits still clung to him. I removed to a longer distance and visited my early home less frequently. Returning to R., after a longer absence than usual, I learned that the health of Old Rufus had so much failed, that the neighbours, deeming it unsafe for him to remain longer alone, at length persuaded him to remove to the house of a neighbour, where each one contributed toward his support. His mind had become weak as well as his body; indeed he had become almost a child again, and it was but a short time that he required the kind attentions which all his old neighbours bestowed upon him. I remained at home for several weeks, and ere I left, I followed the remains of Old Rufus to the grave. I have stood by many a grave of both kindred and stranger; never before or since have I seen one laid in the grave without the presence of some relative; but no one stood by his grave who bore to him the least relationship. It was on a mild Sabbath afternoon in midsummer that we laid him to rest in the burial ground of R.; and if none of his kindred stood by to shed the tear of natural affection, there was many a cheek wet with the tear of sensibility when the coffin was lowered to its silent abode. I am unable to state his exact age, but I am certain that it considerably exceeded eighty years; and from what I can recollect of his life, I have a strong hope, that death opened to him a blessed immortality beyond the grave.

THE DIAMOND RING

"And has it indeed come to this," said Mrs. Harris, addressing her daughter Ellen, "must I part with my mother's last gift to obtain bread?" Mrs. Harris, as she spoke, held in her hand a costly diamond ring, and the tears gathered in her eyes, as the rays of light falling upon the brilliants caused them to glow like liquid fire. This costly ornament would have struck the beholder as strangely out of place in the possession of this poor widow, in that scantily furnished room; but a few words regarding the past history of Mrs. Harris and her daughter will explain their present circumstances. Mrs. Harris was born and educated in England, and when quite young was employed as governess in a gentleman's family. Circumstances at length caused the family with whom she resided to cross the Atlantic and take up their abode in the ancient city of Quebec. The young governess had no remaining ties to bind her to England. Her parents had been dead for many years; she had no sisters, and her only brother, soon after the death of their parents, went to seek his fortune in the gold regions of California. Some years had passed since she heard any tidings from him, and she feared he was no longer among the living, and when the family with whom she had so long resided left England for America, they persuaded her to accompany them. In process of time she was married to a wealthy merchant, and removed to Western Canada. Their union was a very happy one, and for some years, they lived in the enjoyment of worldly prosperity and happiness. But it often happens that sad and unlooked-for reverses succeed a season of long continued prosperity; and it was so in this case. I am not aware that Mr. Harris's failure in business was brought about through any imprudence on his part; but was owing to severe and unexpected losses. He had entered into various speculations, which bid fair to prove profitable, but which proved a complete failure, and one stroke of ill fortune followed another in rapid succession, till the day of utter ruin came. He gave up every thing; even his house and furniture was sacrificed to meet the clamorous demands of his hard-hearted creditors; and his family was thus suddenly reduced from a state of ease and affluence to absolute poverty. Mr. Harris possessed a very proud spirit, and his nature was sensitive, and he could not endure the humiliation of remaining where they had formerly been so happy. He knew the world sufficiently well to be aware that they would now meet with coldness and neglect even from those who had formerly been proud of their notice, and shrank from the trial, and with the small amount he had been able to secure out of the general wreck, he removed to the city of Toronto, some three hundred miles from their former home. They had but little money remaining when they reached the city, and Mr. Harris felt the necessity of at once seeking some employment, for a stranger destitute of money in a large city is in no enviable position. For some time he was unsuccessful in every application he made for employment, and he was glad at length to accept the situation of copyist in a Lawyer's Office, till something better might offer. His salary barely sufficed for their support, yet they were thankful even for that. His constitution had never been robust, and the anxiety of mind under which he labored told severely upon his health. He exerted himself to the utmost, but his health failed rapidly; he was soon obliged to give up work, and in a little more than a year from the time of their removal to Toronto, he died, leaving his wife and daughter friendless and destitute. Their situation was extremely sad, when thus left alone; they had made no acquaintances during the year they had resided in the city, and had no friend to whom they could apply for aid. After paying her husband's funeral expenses, Mrs. Harris found herself well-nigh destitute of money, and she felt the urgent necessity of exerting herself to obtain employment by which they at least might earn a subsistence. The widow and her daughter found much difficulty at first in obtaining employment. Some to whom they applied had no work; others did not give out work to strangers; and for several days Mrs. Harris returned weary and desponding to her home, after spending a large portion of the day in the disagreeable task of seeking employment from strangers; but after a time she succeeded in obtaining employment, and as their work proved satisfactory they had soon an ample supply; but just when their prospects were beginning to brighten Mrs. Harris was visited by a severe illness. They had been able to lay by a small sum previous to her illness, and it was well they had done so, for during her sickness she required almost the constant attention of her daughter, which deprived them of any means of support; but after several weeks of severe illness she began slowly to recover, and this brings us to the time where our story opens. The ring which Mrs. Harris held in her hand had been for many, many years an heir-loom in the English family to which she belonged. To her it was the dying gift of her mother, and the thoughts of parting with it cost her a bitter pang. But she had no friends to whom she might apply for aid; and to a refined and sensitive nature, almost anything else is preferable to seeking charity from strangers. The ring was the only article of value which she retained, and sore as was the trial, she saw no other way of meeting their present wants, than by disposing of this her only relic of former affluence and happiness; and she trusted, that by the time the money which the sale of the ring would bring should be expended, they would be again able to resume their employment. With a heavy heart Ellen Harris set out to dispose of this cherished memento. She remembered an extensive jewelry shop, which she had often passed, as she carried home parcels of work, and thither she made her way. The shop-keeper was an elderly man with daughters of his own, and he had so often noticed this pale sad-looking young girl as she passed his window, that he recognized her countenance the moment she entered the shop; and when in a low timid voice she enquired if he would purchase the ring, he was satisfied that he was correct in his former conjecture, that she belonged to a family of former wealth and respectability. But young as she was there was a certain reserve and dignity in her manner, which forbade any questions on his part. The man had for many years carried on a lucrative business in his line and he was now wealthy; and knowing that he could afford to wait till the ring should find a purchaser he had no fears of losing money on so valuable an article; and, as is not often the case in such transactions, he paid her a fair price for the ring, although less than its real value. Ellen returned, much elated by her success; the money she had received for the ring seemed to them in their present circumstances a small fortune. "Little did once I think," said the widow, as she carefully counted the bank-notes, "that a few paltry pounds would ever seem of so much value to me; but perhaps it is well that we should sometimes experience the want of money, that we may learn how to make a proper use of it; and be more helpful to those less favored than ourselves." The money they obtained more than sufficed for their support, till Mrs. Harris so far recovered, as to allow them again to resume their employment. They now had no difficulty in obtaining work, and although obliged to toil early and late, they became cheerful and contented; although they could not but feel the change in their circumstances, and often contrast the happy past, with their present lot of labor and toil.

The shopkeeper burnished up the setting of the diamonds and placed the ring among many others in the show-case upon his counter. But so expensive an ornament as this does not always find a ready purchaser, and for some months it remained unsold. One afternoon a gentleman entered the shop to make some trifling purchase, and, as the shopkeeper happened to be engaged with a customer, he remained standing at the counter, till he should be at leisure, and his eye wandered carelessly over the articles in the show-case. Suddenly he started, changed countenance, and when the shopkeeper came forward to attend to him he said in voice of suppressed eagerness, "will you allow me to examine that ring," pointing as he spoke to the diamond ring sold by Ellen Harris. "Certainly, Sir, certainly," said the obliging shop-keeper, who, hoping that the ring had at last found a purchaser, immediately placed it in his hand for inspection. The gentleman turned the ring in his hand, and carefully examined the sparkling diamonds as well as the antique setting; and when he observed the initials, engraved upon the inside, he grew pale as marble, and hurriedly addressed the astonished shopkeeper saying, "In the name of pity, tell me where you obtained this ring?" "I am very willing to inform you," said the man "how this ring came into my possession. Several months ago a young girl, of very delicate and lady-like appearance, brought this ring here and desired me to purchase it. She seemed very anxious to dispose of the ornament, and, thinking I could easily sell it again, I paid her a fair price and took the ring, and that is all I can tell you about the matter." "You do not know the lady's name?" said the gentleman anxiously. "I do not," replied the man, "but I have frequently seen her pass in the street. The circumstance of her selling me this valuable ring caused me to notice her particularly, and I recognized her countenance ever after." "Name your price for the ring," said the gentleman, — "I must purchase it at any price; and the next thing, I must, if possible, find the young lady who brought it here, I have seen this ring before, and that is all I wish to say of the matter at present; but is there no way in which you can assist me in obtaining an interview with this young lady?" "I have no knowledge of her name or residence; but if you were in my shop when she chanced to pass here I could easily point her out to you in the street." "You may think my conduct somewhat strange," said the gentleman, "but believe me my reasons for seeking an interview with this young lady are most important and if you can point her out to me in the street I will endeavour to learn her residence, as that will be something gained." Before the gentleman left the shop he paid for the ring, and placed it in his pocket. For several days, he frequented the shop of the jeweller with the hope of gaining a view of the lady. At length one morning the shop-keeper suddenly directed his attention to a lady passing in the street, saying, "there, Sir, is the young lady from whom I purchased the ring." He waited to hear no more, but, stepping hastily into the street, followed the lady at a respectful distance; but never losing sight of her for a moment till she entered her home two streets distant from the shop of the jeweller. He approached the door and rang the bell. The door was opened by the same young lady, whose manner exhibited not a little embarrassment, when she beheld a total stranger; and he began to feel himself in an awkward position. He was at a loss how to address her till, recollecting that he must explain his visit in some way, he said: "Pardon the intrusion of a stranger; but, by your permission, I would like to enter the house, and have a word of conversation with you." The young girl regarded the man earnestly for a moment; but his manner was so gentlemanly and deferential that she could do no less than invite him to enter the little sitting-room where her mother was at work, and ask him to be seated. He bowed to Mrs. Harris on entering the room, then seating himself he addressed the young lady, saying: "The peculiar circumstances in which I am placed must serve as my apology for asking you a question which you may consider impertinent. Are you the young lady who, some months since, sold a diamond ring to a jeweller on Grafton street?" Mrs. Harris raised her eyes to the stranger's face, and the proud English blood which flowed in her veins mantled her cheek as she replied, "before I permit my daughter to answer the questions of a stranger, you will be so kind as to explain your right to question." The stranger sprang from his seat at the sound of her voice, and exclaimed, in a voice tremulous from emotion, "don't you know me Eliza, I am your long lost brother George." The reader will, doubtless, be better able to imagine the scene which followed, than I am to describe it. Everything was soon explained, many letters had been sent which never reached their destination; he knew not that his sister had left England, and after writing again and again, and receiving no reply, he ceased altogether from writing. During the first years of his sojourn in California, he was unfortunate, and was several times brought to the brink of the grave by sickness. After a time fortune smiled upon his efforts, till he at length grew immensely rich, and finally left the burning skies of California to return to England. He landed at New York and intended, after visiting the Canadas, to sail for England. The brother and sister had parted in their early youth, and it is no wonder that they failed to recognize each other when each had passed middle age. The brother was most changed of the two. His complexion had grown very dark, and he had such a foreign look that, when convinced of the fact, Mrs. Harris could hardly believe him to be one and the same with the stripling brother from whom she parted in England so many years ago. He was, of course, not aware of his sister's marriage, and he listened with sorrow to the story of her bereavement and other misfortunes. "You must now place a double value upon our family ring," said he, as he replaced the lost treasure upon his sister's hand; "for it is this diamond ring which has restored to each other the brother and sister who otherwise might never have met again on earth. And now, both you and your daughter must prepare for a voyage to dear old England. You need have no anxiety for the future; I have enough for us all and you shall want no more." Before leaving the City, accompanied by her brother, Mrs. Harris visited the grave of her husband; and the generous brother attended to the erection of a suitable tombstone, as the widow had before been unable to meet the expenses of it. Passing through the Upper Province they reached Montreal, whence they sailed for England. After a prosperous voyage they found themselves amid the familiar scenes of their childhood, where they still live in the enjoyment of as much happiness as usually falls to the lot of mortals.

THE UNFORTUNATE MAN

On a sultry afternoon in midsummer I was walking on a lonely unfrequented road in the Township of S. My mind was busily occupied, and I paid little attention to surrounding objects till a hollow, unnatural voice addressed me, saying: "Look up my friend, and behold the unfortunate man." I raised my eyes suddenly, and, verily, the appearance of the being before me justified his self-bestowed appellation — the unfortunate man. I will do my best to describe him, although I am satisfied that my description will fall far short of the reality. He was uncommonly tall, and one thing which added much to the oddity of his appearance was the inequality of length in his legs, one being shorter by several inches than the other, and, to make up for the deficiency, he wore on the short leg a boot with a very high heel. He seemed to be past middle age, his complexion was sallow and unhealthy, he was squint-eyed, and his hair, which had once been of a reddish hue, was then a grizzly gray. Taken all together he was a strange looking object, and I soon perceived that his mind wandered. At first I felt inclined to hurry onward as quickly as possible, but, as he seemed harmless and inclined to talk to me, I lingered for a few moments to listen to him. "I do not wonder," said he, "that you look upon me with pity, for it is a sad thing for one to be crazy." Surprised to find him so sensible of his own situation I said: "As you seem so well aware that you are crazy, perhaps you can inform me what caused you to become so." "Oh yes," replied he, "I can soon tell you that: first my father died, then my mother, and soon after my only sister hung herself to the limb of a tree with a skein of worsted yarn; and last, and worst of all, my wife, Dorcas Jane, drowned herself in Otter Creek." Wondering if there was any truth in this horrible story, or if it was only the creation of his own diseased mind, I said, merely to see what he would say next, "What caused your wife to drown herself; was she crazy too?" "Oh no," replied he, "she was not crazy, but she was worse than that; for she was jealous of me, although I am sure she had no cause." The idea of any one being jealous of the being before me was so ridiculous that it was with the utmost difficulty that I refrained from laughter; but, fearing to offend the crazy man, I maintained my gravity by a strong effort. When he had finished the story of his misfortunes, he came close to me and said, in slow measured tones: "And now do you think it any wonder that I went raving distracted crazy?" "Indeed I do not," said I; "many a one has gone crazy for less cause." Thinking he might be hungry, I told him I would direct him to a farm-house, where he would be sure to obtain his supper. "No," replied he, "this is not one of my hungry days; I find so many who will give me nothing to eat that when I get the offer of a meal I always eat whether I am hungry or not, and I have been in luck today, for I have eaten five meals since morning; and now I must lose no more time, for I have important business with the Governor of Canada and must reach Quebec to-morrow." I regarded the poor crazy being with a feeling of pity, as he walked wearily onward, and even the high-heeled boot did not conceal a painful limp in his gait. But I had not seen the last of him yet. Some six months after, as I was visiting a friend who lived several miles distant, who should walk in, about eight o'clock in the evening, but the "unfortunate man." There had been a slight shower of rain, but not enough to account for the drenched state of his clothing. "How did you get so wet?" enquired Mr. — . "O," replied he, "I was crossing a brook upon a log, and I slipped off into the water; and it rained on me at the same time, and between the two, I got a pretty smart ducking." They brought him some dry clothing, and dried his wet garments by the kitchen fire, and kindly allowed him to remain for the night. For several years, this man passed through S. as often as two or three times during each year. He became so well known in the vicinity, that any one freely gave him a meal or a night's lodging as often as he sought it. Every time he came along his mind was occupied by some new fancy, which seemed to him to be of the utmost importance, and to require prompt attention. He arrived in S. one bitter cold night in the depth of winter, and remained for the night with a family who had ever treated him kindly, and with whom he had often lodged before. He set out early the next morning to proceed (as he said) on his way to Nova Scotia. Years have passed away; but the "unfortunate man" has never since been seen in the vicinity. It was feared by some that he had perished in the snow; as there were some very severe storms soon after he left S.; but nothing was ever learned to confirm the suspicion. According to his own statement he belonged to the state of Vermont, but, from his speech, he was evidently not an American. Several years have passed away since his last visit to S., and it is more than probable that he is no longer among the living.

THE OLD SCHOOLHOUSE

I lately visited the time-worn building, where for a lengthened period, during my early years, I studied the rudiments of education; and what a host of almost forgotten memories of the past came thronging back upon my mind as I stood alone — in that well remembered room. I seemed again to hear the hum of youthful voices as they conned or recited their daily tasks, and, as memory recalled the years that had passed since we used there to assemble, I could not avoid saying mentally: "My schoolmates, where are they?" Even that thought called to mind an amusing story related by a much loved companion who for a time formed one of our number.

He was older than most of the other boys, and was a general favourite with all. He was famous for relating funny stories, of which he had a never-failing supply; and when the day was too stormy to allow of out-of-door sports, during the noon hour, we used to gather around the large stove which stood in the centre of the room and coax H. M. to tell us stories. The story which recurred to my mind was of a poor Irishman, who, in describing a visit which he paid to the home of his childhood after a long absence, said: "At the sober hour of twilight, I entered the lonely and desarted home uv me forefathers, an' as I gazed about the silent walls, I said, 'me fathers, where are they?' an' did not echo answer, 'Is that you Pathrick O'Flannigan, sure?'"

I was in no mood for laughter, and yet I could not repress a smile, as memory recalled the comical voice and inimitable gestures with which young H. M. related the story. He was beloved by us all, and when he left school we parted from him with real sorrow. As I walked around, and looked upon the worn and defaced desks, I observed the initials of many once familiar names which many years before had been formed with a knife, which were not so much obliterated but I could easily decipher the well known letters. That desk in the corner was occupied by two brothers who when they grew up removed to one of the Eastern States, where they enlisted as soldiers in the war between the North and South. One of the brothers received his death-wound on the battlefield. In a foreign hospital he lingered in much suffering for a brief period, when he died and was buried, far from his home and kindred. The younger brother was naturally of a tender constitution and was unable to endure the hardships and privations of a soldier's life. His health failed him, and he returned to his friends, who had left their Canadian home, and removed to the State of Massachusetts; but all that the most skilful physicians could do, aided by the most watchful care of his tender mother, failed to check the ravages of disease. Consumption had marked him for its prey, and he died a few months after leaving the army; and, as his friends wept over his grave, they could see with their mind's eye another nameless grave in a far-away Southern State, where slept the other son and brother. The desk on my left hand was occupied by a youth, who has been for many years toiling for gold in California; and I have learned that he has grown very rich. I often wonder if, in his eager pursuit after riches, in that far-off clime, he ever thinks of the little brown school-house by the butternut trees, and of the smiling eager group who used daily to meet there. One large family of brothers and sisters, who attended this school for several years, afterward removed with their parents to one of the Western States, and years have passed away since I heard of them; but along with many others they were recalled to mind by my visit to the old School-House.

On the opposite side of the room is the range of desks which were occupied by the girls, and I could almost fancy that I again saw the same lively, restless group who filled those desks in the days of long-ago. Again I saw the bright smile which was often hidden from the searching eye of our teacher, behind the covers of the well-worn spelling-book, again I saw the mischievous glances, and heard the smothered laughter when the attention of the teacher was required in some other part of the room. But these happy careless days of childhood are gone never to return. Were I inclined, I could trace the after-history of most of the companions whom I used daily to meet in this school-room. With many of them "life's history" is done, and they sleep peacefully in the grave. Others have gone forth to the duties of life; some far distant, others near their paternal homes. Many of the number have been successful in life, and prospered in their undertakings, while others have met with disappointment and misfortune. It seemed somewhat singular to me that, as I stood alone in that room (after the lapse of so many years), I could recollect, by the name, each companion I used to meet there; yet so it was, and it seemed but as yesterday since we used daily to assemble there; and, when I reflected for a moment on the many changes to which I have been subjected since that period, I could hardly realize that I was one and the same. I lingered long at the old School-House, for I expected never to behold it again, having been informed that it was shortly to give place to a building of a larger size, and of more modern structure.

ARTHUR SINCLAIR

For several hours we had endured the jolting of the lumbering stage-coach over a rough hilly road which led through a portion of the State of New Hampshire; and, as the darkness of night gathered around us, I, as well as my fellow-travellers, began to manifest impatience to arrive at our stopping-place for the night; and we felt strongly inclined to find fault with the slow motion of the tired horses, which drew the heavily-loaded vehicle. Thinking it as well to know the worst at once, I asked the driver "what time we might expect to reach our destination for the night?" "It will be midnight at the least, perhaps later," replied he. This news was not very cheering to the weary travellers who filled the coach; and I almost regretted having asked the question. The roughness of the roads, together with the crowded state of the vehicle, made it impossible for any one to sleep, and it became an important question how we should pass away the tedious hours. A proposition was at length made, that some one of the passengers should relate a story for the entertainment of the others. This proposal met with the hearty approval of all, as a means of making our toilsome journey seem shorter; and the question of who should relate the story was very soon agitated. There was among the passengers one old gentleman of a very pleasant and venerable appearance, and judging from his countenance that he possessed intelligence, as well as experience, we respectfully invited him to relate a story for our entertainment. "I am not at all skilled in story-telling," replied the old gentleman, "but, as a means of passing away the tedious hours of the uncomfortable ride, I will relate some circumstances which took place many years since, and which also have connection with my present journey, although the narrative may not possess much interest for uninterested strangers." We all placed ourselves in a listening attitude, and the old man began as follows: "I was born in the town of Littleton in this State, and when a boy, I had one school-mate, whom I could have loved no better had he been a brother. His name was Arthur Sinclair. And the affectionate intimacy which existed between us for many years is yet to me a green spot in the waste of memory. I was about twelve years of age when Arthur's parents came to reside in Littleton. That now large and thriving village then contained but a few houses, and when the Sinclairs became our neighbours, we soon formed a very pleasing acquaintance. I was an only child, and had never been much given to making companions of the neighbouring boys of my own age; but from the first I felt strongly attracted toward Arthur Sinclair. He was two years younger than myself. At the time when I first met him he was the most perfect specimen of childish beauty I ever saw, and added to this he possessed a most winning and affectionate disposition, and in a short time we became almost inseparable companions. My nature was distant and reserved, but if once I made a friend, my affection for him was deep and abiding. We occupied the same desk in the village school, and often conned our daily lessons from the same book, and out of school hours, shared the same sports; and I remember once hearing our teacher laughingly remark to my parents, that he believed, should he find it necessary to correct one of us, the other would beg to share the punishment. Notwithstanding the strong friendship between us, our dispositions were very unlike. From a child I was prone to fits of depression, while Arthur on the other hand possessed such a never-failing flow of animal spirits, as rendered him at all times a very agreeable companion; and it may be that the dissimilarity of our natures attracted us all the more strongly to each other; be that as it may the same close intimacy subsisted between us till we reached the years of early manhood. The only fault I could ever see in Arthur was that of being too easily persuaded by others, without pausing to think for himself; and being the elder of the two, and of a reflective cast of mind, as we grew up, I often had misgivings for him when he should go forth from his home, and mingle with the world at large. The intimacy between us allowed me to speak freely to him, and I often reminded him of the necessity of watchfulness and consideration, when he should go forth alone to make his way in a selfish and unfeeling world.

"He used to make light of what he termed my 'croaking' and say I need have no fears of him; and I believe he spoke from the sincerity of his good intentions; he thought all others as sincere and open-hearted as himself, and happy had it been for him if he had found them so. Arthur received a very good business education, and, when he reached the age of twenty-one, obtained the situation of book-keeper in an extensive mercantile house in the city of Boston. There was a young girl in our village to whom Arthur had been fondly attached since the days of his boyhood, and I need scarcely say the attachment was reciprocal, and that before he left home he placed the engagement ring on her finger, naming no very distant period when he hoped to replace it by the wedding ring. Belinda Merril was worthy in every way of his affection, and loved him with all the sincerity of a pure and guileless heart. I almost wonder that the shadows which were even then gathering in what to them had ever been a summer sky, did not cast a chill over her heart. In due time Arthur went to the city. I could not help my fears, lest his pleasing manners and love of company should attract to him those who would lead him into evil; but I strove to banish them, and hope for the best. Our pastor, an old man, who had known Arthur from his childhood, called upon him, previous to his departure from home, and, without wearying him with a long list of rules and regulations regarding his future conduct, spoke to him as friend speaks to friend, and in a judicious manner administered some very good advice to the youth who was almost as dear to him as his own son. The young man listened attentively to the words of his faithful friend and sincerely thanked him for the advice which he well knew was prompted by affection. During the first year of his residence in the city, we wrote very frequently to each other, and the tone of his letters indicated the same pure principles which had ever governed his actions. Time passed on, and by-and-bye, I could not fail to notice the change in the style of his letters. He spoke much of the many agreeable acquaintances he had formed, and of the amusements of the city, and was warm in his commendations of the Theatre. My heart often misgave me as I perused his letters, and I mentally wondered where all this was to end? After a two-years' absence, he returned to spend a few weeks at home in Littleton, but he seemed so unlike my former friend, that I could hardly feel at ease in his society. He never once alluded to any incidents of our school days, as he used formerly so frequently to do, and objects of former interest possessed none for him now. He called Littleton a "terribly stupid place," and seemed anxiously to look forward to his return to Boston. "Surely," said I to him one evening as we were engaged in conversation, "Littleton must still contain one attraction for you yet." He appeared not to comprehend my meaning, but I well knew his ignorance was only feigned. But when he saw that I was not to be put off in that way, he said with a tone of assumed indifference, "O! if it is Belinda Merril you are talking about, I have to say that she is no longer an object of interest to me." "Is it possible, Arthur," said I, "that you mean what you say; surely an absence of two years has not caused you to forget the love you have borne Miss Merril from childhood. I am very much surprised to hear you speak in this manner." A flush of anger, at my plain reply, rose to his cheek, and he answered in a tone of displeasure: "I may as well tell you first as last, my ideas have undergone a change. I did once think I loved Belinda Merril, but that was before I had seen the world, and now the idea to me is absurd of introducing this awkward country girl as my wife among my acquaintances in the city of Boston. I once had a sort of liking for the girl, but I care no longer for her, and the sooner I break with her the better, and I guess she won't break her heart about me." "I hope not indeed," I replied, "but I must be allowed to say that I consider your conduct unmanly and dishonourable, and I would advise you, before proceeding further, to pause and reflect whether it is really your heart which dictates your actions, or only a foolish fancy." Knowing how deeply Miss Merril was attached to Arthur, I hoped he would reconsider the matter, and I said as much to him; but all I could say was of no avail, and that very evening he called and, requesting an interview with his betrothed, informed her that, as his sentiments toward her had changed, he presumed she would be willing to release him from their former engagement. Instantly Miss Merril drew from her finger the ring he had placed there two years before, and said, as she placed it in his hand, "I have long been sensible of the change in your sentiments, and am truly glad that you have at last spoken plainly. From this hour you may consider yourself entirely free, and you have my best wishes for your future happiness and prosperity," and, bidding him a kind good-evening, the young lady left the apartment. Her spirit was deeply wounded, but she possessed too much good sense to be utterly cast down for the wrong-doing of another. Whatever were Arthur's feelings after he had taken this step, he spoke of them to no one. I never again mentioned the subject to him, but, knowing him as I did, I could see that he was far from being satisfied with his own conduct, and he departed for the city some weeks sooner than he had at first intended. Owing to the friendly feeling I had ever cherished for him, I could not help a feeling of anxiety after his departure, for I feared that all was not right with him. He did not entirely cease from writing to me; but his letters were not frequent, and they were very brief and formal — very unlike the former brotherly communications which used to pass between us. A year passed away. I obtained a situation nearly a hundred miles from home. I had heard nothing from Arthur for a long time, and, amid my own cares, he recurred to my mind with less frequency than formerly; yet often after the business of the day was over, and my mind was at leisure, memory would recall Arthur Sinclair to my mind with a pained sort of interest. About six months after I left home I was surprised by receiving from Mr. Sinclair a hastily written letter, requesting me, if possible, to lose no time in hastening to Littleton, stating also that he was obliged to take a journey to Boston on business which vitally concerned Arthur, and he wished me to accompany him. He closed by requesting me to mention the letter I had received from him to no one, saying that he knew me and my regard for Arthur sufficiently well to trust me in the matter. My fears were instantly alive for Arthur, and I feared that some misfortune to him was hidden behind this veil of secrecy: and I soon found that my fears were well founded. I set out at once for Littleton, and upon arriving there I proceeded directly to the residence of Mr. Sinclair. When he met me at the door I was struck by the change in his countenance; he appeared as if ten years had been added to his age since I last saw him, six months ago. He waited not for me to make any inquiries, but, motioning me into a private apartment, he closed the door, and seating himself by my side, said in a hoarse voice: "I may as well tell you the worst at once: my son, and also your once dear friend, Arthur, is a thief, and, but for the lenity and consideration of his employer, before this time would have been lodged within the walls of a prison." I made no reply, but gazed upon him in silent astonishment and horror. When he became more composed, he informed me that he had lately received a letter from Mr. Worthing (Arthur's employer) informing him that he had detected Arthur in the crime of stealing money from the safe, to quite a large amount. In giving the particulars of the unfortunate circumstance, he further stated, for some time past he had missed different sums of money, but was unable to attach suspicion to any one; "and, although," said he, "I have been for some time fearful that your son was associating with evil companions, I never once dreamed that he would be guilty of the crime of stealing, till I lately missed bank-notes from the safe, to quite a large amount, having upon them some peculiar marks which rendered them easy to be identified. For some time the disappearance of those notes was a mystery, and I was beginning to despair of detecting the guilty one, when I obtained proof positive that your unfortunate son parted with those identical notes in a noted gambling saloon in the city; and, as I have also learned that he has spent money freely of late, I have no longer any doubt that it is he who has stolen the other sums I have lost. Out of regard to you and your family I have kept the matter perfectly quiet; indeed, I never informed the parties who told me his losing the notes at the gaming-table that there was anything wrong about it. I have not mentioned the matter to your son, and shall not do so till I see or hear from you. I presume you will be willing to make good to me the money I have lost. Of course I cannot much longer retain your son in my employ, but he must not be utterly ruined by this affair being made public. I would advise you to come at once to Boston, and we will arrange matters in the best possible manner, and no one but ourselves need know anything of the sad affair; let him return with you for a time to his home, and I trust the lesson will not be lost upon him. When he first came to the city, I am positive that he was an honourable and pure-minded young man, but evil companions have led him astray, and we must try and save him from ruin."

I had never seen Mr. Worthing, but I at once felt much respect for him, for the lenity and discretion he had shown in the matter. To no one but his own family and myself did Mr. Sinclair reveal the contents of that letter; but the very evening after my arrival in Littleton we set out on our journey to Boston, and, upon arriving there, we proceeded at once to the residence of Mr. Worthing, where we learned all the particulars of Arthur's guilt. Mr. Worthing stated that he had ever entertained a very high opinion of Arthur, and, when he missed various sums of money in a most unaccountable manner, he never thought of fixing suspicion upon him, till circumstances came to his knowledge which left no room for doubt; but, owing to the high regard he entertained for his parents, with whom he had (years since) been intimately acquainted, he said nothing to the young man of the proofs of his dishonesty which had come to his knowledge, and still retained him in his employ till he could communicate with his father, that they together might devise some means of preventing the affair from becoming public. After Mr. Sinclair had listened to the plain statement of the affair by Mr. Worthing, he requested him as nearly as possible to give him an estimate of the amount of money he had lost. He did so, and Mr. Sinclair immediately placed an equivalent sum in his hands, saying: "I am glad to be able so far to undo the wrong of which my son has been guilty." All this time Arthur knew nothing of our arrival in the city; but when his father dispatched a message, requesting him to meet him at the house of his employer, he was very soon in our presence. I hope I may never again witness another meeting like that one, between the father and son. When charged with the crime, Arthur at first made a feeble attempt at denial, till finding the strong proofs against him, he owned all with shame and humiliation of countenance. The stern grief of Mr. Sinclair was something fearful to witness. "How could you" said he, addressing Arthur, "commit so base a deed? Tell me, my son, in what duty I have failed in your early training? I endeavored to instil into your mind principles of honor and integrity, and to enforce the same by setting before you a good example. If I have failed in any duty to you, it was through ignorance, and may God forgive me if I have been guilty of any neglect in your education."

Trembling with suppressed emotion Arthur replied: "You are blameless, my father; on me alone must rest my sin, for had I obeyed your kind counsels, and those of my dearest friend, (pointing to me) I should never have been the guilty wretch I am today." Turning to me, he said: "Many a time within the last few months have I called to mind the lightness with which I laughed away your fears for my safety, when I left home for the city. O! that I had listened to your friendly warning, and followed the path which you pointed out for me. When I first came to the great city, I was charmed with the novelty of its never-ceasing scenes of amusement and pleasure. I began by mingling with company, and participating in amusements, which, to say the least of them, were questionable; and I soon found my salary inadequate to meet my fast increasing wants for money; and, as many an unfortunate youth has done before, I began the vice of gambling with the hope of being one of the lucky ones. My tempters, no doubt, understood their business, and at first allowed me to win from them considerable sums of money; till, elated with my success, I began playing for higher stakes, and when I lost them, I grew desperate, and it was then that I began adding the sin of theft to the no less heinous one of gambling. But it is no use now to talk of the past; my character is blasted, and all I wish is to die and hide my guild in the grave, and yet I am ill-prepared to die." He became so much excited, that we endeavored to soothe him by kind and encouraging words. His father bade him amend his conduct for the future, and he would freely forgive and forget the past. In my piety for my early friend, I almost forgot the wrong he had done, and thought only of the loved companion of my boyhood and youth. I cannot describe my feelings, as I gazed upon the shame-stricken young man, whom I had so often caressed in the days of our boyish affection and confidence. Little did I then think I should ever behold him thus. The utmost secrecy was observed by all parties; and it was decided that we would remain for the night with Mr. Worthing, and, accompanied by Arthur, set out early the next morning on our homeward journey. But it was ordered otherwise. The next morning Arthur was raving in delirium of brain fever, brought, on doubtless, by the mental torture he had endured. Mr. Sinclair dispatched a message, informing his wife of Arthur's illness, and three days later she stood by the bed-side of her son. For several days the fever raged. We allowed no stranger to watch by him, for in his delirium his mind dwelt continually upon the past, and no one but ourselves must listen to his words. Mr. Worthing was very kind, and shared the care of the poor young man with his parents and myself. At length came the crisis of his disorder. "Now," said the physician, "for a few hours, his life will hang, as it were, upon a thread. If the powers of life of are not too far exhausted by the disease he may rally but I have many fears, for he is brought very low. All the encouragement I dare offer that is, while there is life there is hope."

He sunk into a deep slumber, and I took my place to watch by him during the night. Mr. Worthing persuaded his parents to seek a few hours rest, as they were worn out with fatigue and anxiety; and exacting from me a promise that I would summon them if the least change for the worse should take place, they retired, and I was left to watch alone by my friend. All I could do was to watch and wait, as the hours passed wearily on. A little before midnight the physician softly entered, and stood with me at his bed-side; soon after he languidly opened his eyes, and in a whisper he pronounced my name. As I leaned over him, and eagerly scanned his countenance, I perceived that the delirium of fever was gone. The physician, fearing the effect upon him of the least excitement, made a motion to me enjoining silence, and mixing a quieting cordial, held to his lips. He eagerly quaffed the cooling draught, and again fell into a quiet slumber. "Now," said the physician, "I have a faint hope that he may recover, but he is so weak that any excitement would prove fatal; all depends upon keeping him perfectly quiet for the next few hours." The doctor departed, and again I was left alone to watch over his slumber. Before morning, anxiety brought Mr. and Mrs. Sinclair to the room, to learn if there had been any change. In a whisper I informed them of the favorable symptoms he had evinced upon waking, and persuaded them to retire from the apartment. When Arthur again awoke, the favorable symptoms still continued, and the physician entertained strong hopes of his recovery. By degrees he was allowed to converse for a few moments at a time. It seemed to him, he said, as though he had awakened from a frightful dream; and he begged to know how long he had been ill, and what had happened during the time. We were all very cautious to say nothing to excite him; and by degrees as his mind grew stronger, everything came back clearly to his mind, his father's visit, and the circumstances which had brought him to the city. It is needless for me to dwell upon the long period, while he lay helpless as an infant, watched over by his fond mother, who felt that he had almost been given back from the dead. But he continued slowly to recover, and being unable to remain longer, I left his parents with him, and returned to my home in Littleton, and soon after went back to my employer. Mr. and Mrs. Sinclair remained with Arthur till he was able to bear the journey to Littleton, and it was to them a happy day, when they arrived safely at their home, accompanied by their son, who seemed to them almost as one restored from the dead. The unfortunate circumstances connected with Arthur's illness were a secret locked up in the bosoms of the few faithful friends to whom it was known. Arthur arose from that bed of sickness a changed man, and it was ever after to him a matter of wonder how he could have been so far led astray, and he felt the most unbounded gratitude to Mr. Worthing for the kindness and consideration he had shown him. His father did quite an extensive business as a merchant in Littleton, and as Arthur became stronger he assisted in the store; and after a time his father gave him a partnership in the business, which rendered his again leaving home unnecessary. A correspondence, varied occasionally by friendly visits, was kept up between the Sinclairs and the family of Mr. Worthing; for Arthur never could forget the debt of gratitude he owed his former employer. I have little more to tell, and I will bring my long and, I fear somewhat tedious, story to a close, by relating one more event in the life of my friend. I resided at a quite a long distance from Littleton, and some two years after Arthur's return home, I was surprised by receiving an invitation from him to act as groomsman at his wedding, and the bride was to be Miss Merrill. I know not exactly how the reconciliation took place. But I understood that Arthur first sought an interview with the young lady, and humbly acknowledged the wrong of which he had been guilty, saying, what was indeed true, that he had ever loved her, and he knew not what infatuation influenced him in his former conduct. Many censured Miss Merrill for her want of spirit, as they termed it, in again receiving his addresses, but I was too well pleased by his happy termination of the affair to censure any one connected with it. The wedding day was a happy one to those most deeply concerned, and such being the case, the opinion of others was of little consequence; and the clouds which had for a time darkened their sky, left no shadow upon the sunshine of their wedded life. Arthur and his father were prospered in their business, and for many years they all lived happily together. In process of time his parents died, and Arthur soon after sold out his share in the business to a younger brother, as he had received a tempting offer to remove to Boston, and enter into partnership with Mr. Worthing's son, as the old gentleman had some time before resigned any active share in the business. When Arthur learned their wishes he was very anxious to return to them; "For," said he, "it is to Mr. Worthing I owe my salvation from disgrace and ruin." For many years he has carried on a lucrative business with the son of his former employer and friend. An interesting family of sons and daughters have grown up around him, and I may with truth call them a happy family. Old Mr. Worthing has been for some years dead; and his earthly remains quietly repose amid the peaceful shades of Mount Auburn. My own life has been a busy one, and twenty years have passed away since I met with Arthur Sinclair; but the object of this journey is to visit my early friend, who, as well as myself, is now an old man." As the old gentleman finished the story, to which we had all listened with much interest, we arrived at our stopping place for the night, and, fatigued with the day's journey, we were soon conducted to our several apartments. The next morning we parted with the kind old man, as his onward route lay in another direction, but I could not help following him in thought, and picturing the joyous meeting between himself and his early friend, Arthur Sinclair.

THE SNOW STORM

The event I am about to relate happened many years ago, but I have often heard it mentioned by those to whom all the circumstances were well known; and, when listening to this story, I have often thought that there is enough of interest attached to many events which took place during the period of the early settlement of that portion of Eastern Canada which borders on the River St. Francis, to fill volumes, were they recorded.

The morning had been clear and pleasant, but early in the afternoon the sky became overcast with dark clouds, and for several hours the snow fell unceasingly, and now the darkness of night was added to the gloomy scene. As the night set in, the snow continued to fall in a thick shower, and a strong easterly wind arose, which filled the air with one blinding cloud of drifting snow; and the lights in the scattered habitations in the then primitive settlement of D. could scarcely be distinguished amid the thick darkness. It was a fearful night to be abroad upon that lonely and almost impassable road; and Mrs. W. fully realized the peril to which her husband was exposed on that inclement night. He had set out that morning, on foot, to visit a friend, who resided at a distance of several miles, intending to return to his home at an early hour in the evening. It was a lonely road over which he had to pass; the habitations were few and far between, and, as the storm increased with the approach of night, Mrs. W. strongly hoped that her husband had been persuaded to pass the night with his friend; for she feared that, had he been overtaken by the darkness of night, he would perish in the storm; and the poor woman was in a state of painful anxiety and suspense. The supper-table was spread, but Mrs. W. was unable to taste food; and, giving the children their suppers, she awaited with intense anxiety the return of her husband. The storm increased till it was evident that it was one of unusual severity, even for the rigorous climate of Canada, and, as the wind shook the windows of their dwelling, the children often exclaimed in tones of terror: "O! what will become of poor father if he is out in this storm." Bye-and-bye the tired children fell asleep, and Mrs. W. was left alone by her fireside. She endeavoured to quiet her fears by thinking him safe in the house of his friend, but she could not drive away the thought that he had set out upon his return home, and she feared, if such was the case, he had met his death in that pitiless storm. She was two miles from any neighbour, surrounded by her family of young children; so all she could do was to wait and watch as the hours wore on. Sleep was out of the question, and the dawn of day found her still keeping her lonely vigil. As the sun rose the wind calmed, but the thick drifts of snow rendered it impossible for her to leave the house, and she watched anxiously if any one might chance to pass, to whom she could apply for assistance in gaining tidings of her husband. Alas! her fears of the previous night were but too well founded. He had perished in the storm. His friend tried his utmost to persuade him to remain for the night when the storm began, but he was anxious to return to his home, fearing the anxiety of his family: and he left his friend's house about four o'clock in the afternoon. The weather was intensely cold, as well as stormy, and, owing to the depth of snow which had already fallen, he could make but slow progress, and, when overtaken by darkness and the increasing tempest, benumbed with cold, and blinded by the whirling drifts of snow, he sank down by the roadside to die, and the suspense of his wife was at length relieved by the painful certainty of his fate.

About noon on the day succeeding the storm, as Dr. S. was slowly urging his horse onward, in order to visit a patient who resided in the vicinity, he observed some object lying almost concealed in the snow. Stopping his horse, he left his sleigh to examine it, and was horror-struck to find it the body of a man. Thinking that, possibly, life was not extinct, he took the body into his sleigh and made all possible haste to the nearest dwelling, where every means was used for the recovery of Mr. W.; but all was of no avail, he was frozen to death. It was the kind physician himself who first bore the sad tidings to Mrs. W. When the lifeless body of the husband and father was borne to his own dwelling, I have heard the scene described by those who witnessed it, as most heart-rending. On the day of his burial the settlers in the vicinity came from a long distance to pay their last tribute of respect to one who had been much esteemed as a friend and neighbour. The widow of Mr. W. is still living, but she now is of a very advanced age. His children grew up and settled in various places, and the elder ones among them retained a distinct recollection of the sad death of their father.

THE NEW YEAR

Another year has just glided away, and it seems but as yesterday that we stood at its threshold, and looked forward over its then seemingly lengthened way, and fancy was busy with many plans and projects for future happiness and delight. We looked forward through the whole border of its months, weeks, days and hours, and life grew bright with pleased anticipations. The year has now passed away, and how few, very few, of all our bright hopes have been realized. With how many of us have unexpected and unwished for events taken the place of those to which we looked forward with so much delight.

As the hours and moments of the past year have slowly glided into the ocean of the past, they have borne with them the treasures of many a fond heart. The sun shines as brightly as ever, the moon and stars still look placidly down upon the sleeping earth, and life is the same as it has ever been; but for these their work is over, and they have done with time. As I sat watching the fast gathering shadows over the last night of the old year, I fell into a sort of waking dream, and I seemed to hear the slow measured tread of one wearily approaching. Turning my eyes in the direction of the approaching footsteps, I beheld the form of a very aged man; his countenance appeared somewhat familiar, yet it was furrowed by many wrinkles, and on his once high and beautiful forehead were the deep lines of corroding care and anxiety. His step was slow, and he leaned for support on his now well-nigh failing staff. He bore the marks of extreme feebleness, and gazed forward with a manner of timidity and uncertainty, and on his changeful countenance was expressed all the multitudinous emotions of the human breast. His garments had once been white and shining, but they were now stained and darkened by travel, and portions of them trailed in the dust. As he drew nigh I observed that he carried in his hand a closely written scroll, on which was recorded the events of the past year. As I gazed upon the record, I read of life begun, and of death in every circumstance and condition of mortal being, of happiness and misery, of love and hate, of good and evil, — all mingling their different results in that graphic record; and I trembled as my own name met my view, with the long list of opportunities for good unimproved, together with the many sins, both of omission and commission, of which I had been guilty during the past year; but there was nothing left out, — the events in the life of every individual member of the human family were there, all recorded in legible characters. As the midnight hour struck the aged man, who typified the old year, faded from my view, and, almost before I was aware of the change, youth and beauty stood smiling before me. The old year gone, the new year had begun. His robes were white and glistening, his voice was mirthful, and his step buoyant; health and vigor braced his limbs. He, too, bore in his hand a scroll, but white as the unsullied snow; not a line was yet traced upon its pure surface, except the title, Record of 1872. I gazed on its fresh and gladsome visage with mingled emotions of sorrow and joy, and I breathed my prayer for forgiveness, for the follies and sins of the departed year.

EARNEST HARWOOD; OR, ADOPTED SON.

CHAPTER I.

It was on a pleasant afternoon, in the month of June, some years ago, that a small funeral procession might have been seen slowly wending its way to the church-yard from the dwelling of Mr. Humphrey, in the village of Walden in one of the Eastern States. Although a deep seriousness pervaded the small company, and the manner of each was subdued, yet there were no visible tokens of that strong grief which overwhelms the soul when the ties of nature are rent asunder; for, with the exception of a little boy, apparently about five years of age, whom Mr. Humphrey kindly led by the hand, no one present bore any relationship to the deceased. As the procession approached the grave, and the coffin was lowered to its final resting-place, the little boy sobbed bitterly as he begged of Mr. Humphrey not to allow them to bury his mamma in the ground. Mr. Humphrey took the child in his arms, and endeavored to quiet him by many kind and soothing words, explaining to him, so far as the child was able to comprehend his meaning, that the soul of his mamma was now in Heaven, but that it was necessary that her dead body should be buried in the grave; and that although he would see her no more in this world he would, if he were a good boy, meet her one day in Heaven. The child still continued to weep, though less bitterly than before, — and when the grave had been filled up he quietly allowed Mr. Humphrey to lead him from the church-yard.

In order that the reader may understand the event above narrated, it is necessary that I should go back a little in my story.

A few weeks previous to the circumstance related at the opening of this chapter a pale weary-looking woman, leading by the hand a little boy, might have been seen walking one evening along the principal street of the small village of Walden. Although her dress was extremely plain, yet there was a certain air of refinement about her which informed the observer that she had once occupied a position very different from what was indicated by her present appearance. The little boy by her side was indeed a child of surpassing beauty. His complexion was clear and fair, and a profusion of dark brown hair clustered in thick curls around his full white brow. His childish features were lighted up by large and expressive eyes of a dark hazel color. He was a child which the most careless observer would hardly pass by without turning to gaze a second time upon his wondrous beauty.

I have been thus particular in describing the little boy as he is to be the principal actor in the simple scenes of my story.

As they walked slowly forward the woman addressed the child in a voice that was weak and tremulous from fatigue, saying, —

"We must call at some house and seek a shelter for the night, for indeed I am unable to walk further."

It required not this remark from her to satisfy the beholder of her inability to proceed, for extreme fatigue and exhaustion were visible in her every motion.

She approached the door of a handsome dwelling situated in the central portion of the village, and rang the bell. The door was opened by an elderly-looking man, who accosted her civilly and seemed waiting for her to make known her errand.

In a low and timid voice the woman asked him if he would allow herself and child to rest for the night beneath his roof?

He replied, in a voice that was decidedly gruff and crusty, —

"There are two hotels in the village; we keep no travellers here," and immediately closed the door in her face.

Could he have seen the forlorn expression that settled on her countenance when, on regaining the street, she took her little boy by the hand and again walked slowly onward — his heart must indeed have been hard if he had not repented of his unkindness.

After walking a short distance further, the woman paused before a house of much humbler appearance than the former one, and, encouraged by the motherly appearance of an elderly lady who sat knitting at her open door in the lingering twilight, she drew nigh to her, and asked if she would shelter herself and child for the night.

The old lady regarded her earnestly for a moment; she seemed, however, to be impressed favorably by her appearance, for her voice was very pleasant, as she replied to her request, —

"Certainly you can remain for the night, for I have never yet denied so small a favor (as a shelter for the night) to any one who sought it. Come in at once, and I will endeavor to make you and your little boy comfortable, for you look very much fatigued."

The woman gladly followed the kind old lady into the house, and seated herself in the comfortable rocking chair which she had kindly placed for her; she also placed a seat for the child, but he refused to leave his mother's side, and stood leaning upon the arm of her chair. The old lady soon after left the room saying, as she did so, that she would soon bring them some refreshment, of which they evidently stood much in need.

Mr. Humphrey, the husband of the old lady, soon came in,

and his wife said a few words to him in a low voice in the adjoining room; a kind expression was upon his countenance when he entered the room where were the strangers. He coaxed the little boy to come and sit upon his knee, by the offer of a large red-cheeked apple which he took from his pocket. He stroked his brown curls and asked him to tell him his name.

"Ernest Harwood," replied the boy.

Mr. Humphrey told him he thought it a very nice name, and also that he thought him a very fine little boy. The little fellow blushed, and hid his face at the praise thus bestowed upon him.

Mrs. Humphrey soon after re-entered the room, bringing a small tea-tray, on which was a cup of tea and some other suitable refreshment for the weary woman; she also brought a bowl of bread and milk for the child. The woman drank the tea eagerly, like one athirst, but partook sparingly of the more substantial refreshment which Mrs. Humphrey urged upon her; but the sight of the brim-full bowl of bread and milk caused the eyes of the little boy to glisten with pleasure, and he did ample justice to the hospitality of the benevolent old lady.

Mrs. Harwood wished to give Mrs. Humphrey some account of the circumstances which caused her to be travelling alone with her child, but the worthy and considerate lady would not allow her to further fatigue herself by talking that night, and insisted upon her retiring at once to rest.

"Tomorrow," said she, "I shall be happy to listen to any thing you may wish to communicate."

Mrs. Humphrey conducted the woman and her child up stairs to a neat bed-room where, after making every arrangement necessary to their comfort, she bade them a kind good night, and left them to enjoy the rest which they so much needed.

CHAPTER II.

When Mrs. Humphrey rejoined her husband in the sitting-room, their conversation very naturally turned to the stranger who was resting beneath their roof. They evidently felt deeply interested by her delicate and lady-like appearance.

"I am sure of one thing," said Mrs. Humphrey, "that this woman has seen better days, notwithstanding the poverty which her present appearance indicates."

"And I am convinced of another thing," replied Mr. Humphrey, "that no fault of her's has reduced her to her present circumstances, for her countenance shews her to be a worthy and true-souled woman; and she shall freely remain beneath my roof until it shall be her wish to leave it."

Little did Mr. Humphrey think, when he made this remark, how soon the poor woman would exchange the shelter of his roof for that of the grave.

Next morning on visiting the room of the stranger, Mrs. Humphrey found her too ill to rise from the bed. She complained of no pain, but seemed very weak and languid. Mrs. Humphrey did all that lay in her power for the comfort of the sick woman. Taking little Ernest down stairs she beguiled him with amusing stories, as she attended to her domestic duties, so that his mother might be left in quiet; and when the child grew weary of the confinement of the house Mr. Humphrey took him to walk with him while he attended to some business in the village. Before returning home Mr. Humphrey called upon Dr. Merton, with whom he was intimately acquainted, and spoke to him concerning the sick woman at his house. He requested the physician to call to see her in the course of the day, saying, that if the woman was not able to pay him he would himself see him paid for his services.

"It makes no difference," replied the humane physician, "whether she is rich or poor, if she requires the attention of a physician she must not be neglected; I will certainly call in the afternoon."

The physician accordingly called in the afternoon, and, after some conversation with Mrs. Harwood, prescribed for her some medicines, and left her, promising to call again in a short time. Before leaving the house, however, he informed Mrs. Humphrey that he thought the woman alarmingly ill. "As near," said he, "as I can judge from her appearance, I think that consumption has been for a long time preying upon her constitution, and overfatigue has thus suddenly prostrated her. The powers of life," continued Dr. Merton, "are fast failing, and in my opinion a few weeks will terminate her earthly existence. I have prescribed for her some simple medicines, but I fear her case is already beyond the aid of medicine. All we can do," said the physician in conclusion, "is to render her as comfortable as may be, for she will soon require nothing which this world affords."

The lonely situation of the stranger had deeply touched the kind heart of Dr. Merton.

As the Doctor had predicted, Mrs. Harwood failed rapidly. She suffered but little bodily pain, but her strength failed her daily, and it soon became evident to all who saw her, that the day of her death could not be far distant.

She gave to Mrs. Humphrey a brief sketch of her past life, which will be made the subject of another chapter.

Mr. and Mrs. Humphrey had reared a family of five children; three of them now slept in the village church-yard; the remaining two had married, and removed to a long distance from their paternal home, consequently the worthy couple had for some years dwelt alone in the home where once had echoed the glad voices of their children.

They soon decided that, should Mrs. Harwood not recover, they would gladly adopt her little boy as their own, if she felt willing to leave him to their care. So great was the anxiety of Mrs. Harwood regarding her child, that it was long ere she gave up hopes of recovery, but when she at length became aware that she must die, she at first found it very difficult to resign herself to the will of Heaven.

"Were it not for my child," she would often say, "the prospect of death would not be unpleasant to me, for I have a comforting hope of a life beyond the grave; but who will care for my orphan boy when I am no more? I must not distrust the goodness of the orphans' God."

Mr. Humphrey, in reply to these remarks one day, said to her —

"I hope you will make your mind perfectly easy in regard to your child; for, should it please God to remove you by death, I have already decided to adopt little Ernest as my own son, if you feel willing to consign him to my care; and you may rest assured that while my life is spared he shall be tenderly cared for, as though he were my own son."

"Now," replied Mrs. Harwood, "can I die willingly. Since my illness it has been my daily and nightly prayer, that should it be the will of Heaven that I should not recover, God would raise up friends to care for my orphan boy, and that prayer is now answered."

Just six weeks from the evening on which Mrs. Harwood entered the dwelling of Mr. Humphrey, her eyes were closed in death. The last day of her life was passed mostly in a kind of lethargy, from which it was almost impossible to arouse her. Toward evening she rallied, and her mind seemed clear and calm. She was aware that the hour of her death had arrived; but she felt no fears in the prospect of her approaching dissolution. She thanked Mr. and Mrs. Humphrey for their kindness to her, and again tenderly committed to their care her boy, who would soon become an orphan.

"I am powerless to reward you," said the dying woman, "but God will certainly reward you for your kindness to the widow and orphan."

She requested that her child might be brought and placed by her side. Placing her thin wasted hands upon his head she said, in a voice scarcely audible, —

"May the God who never forsakes the orphan preserve my precious boy amid the perils and dangers of the sinful world!"

She drew the face of the child close to her own, and imprinted a mother's last kiss upon his brow, and sank back exhausted upon her pillow. A few more fluttering quick drawn breaths and her spirit had winged its way from earth, and no one who witnessed her death felt a doubt that its flight was heavenward.

CHAPTER III.

The following brief account of the early life of Mrs. Harwood I give as nearly as possible in her own words: —

"My earliest recollection carries me back to a small village in Scotland, about one hundred miles distant from the city of Edinburgh, where I was born the daughter of a minister of the Church of Scotland. I was an only child. The salary which my father received was moderate, but was nevertheless sufficient to support us respectably. When I became of suitable age I was sent to school, and continued to pursue my studies until I arrived at the age of fourteen years. At that period I was deprived by death of a fond and indulgent father. Previous to the death of my father neither my mother nor myself had ever experienced an anxious thought as regarded the future. The salary my father received had enabled us to live in comfort and respectability; and we do not often anticipate the death of a strong and healthy man. He died very suddenly; and when my mother's grief at our sudden bereavement had so far subsided as to allow her taking some thought for the future, she found that although my father had died free from debt he had been unable to lay by anything for our future support. During my father's lifetime we had occupied the parsonage, rent free, as had been stipulated when my father became pastor of the church over which he presided till his death. Consequently we had no longer any rightful claim to the dwelling which had been our home for so many years. They kindly gave us permission however, to occupy the house for one year, but my mother liked not to continue to occupy a home which, in reality, was no longer ours. After some deliberation upon the subject, my mother decided upon teaching, as a means of support, as her own education had been sufficiently thorough to render her competent for the undertaking. But, as the village where we resided was small and already well supplied with schools, she wrote to an old friend of my father's, who resided in Edinburgh, as to what he thought of her removing to that city, for the purpose of opening a school. She received a very encouraging reply from the old gentleman, in which he promised to render her all the assistance in his power in the way of obtaining pupils, and as the gentleman was well known and much respected in the city, we found his assistance in this respect to be of much value. The task of breaking up our old home proved a very sad one both to my mother and myself. The furniture of the parsonage was our own. My father had left quite an extensive library, considering his limited means. With the exception of a few volumes which my mother reserved for ourselves, she disposed of the books among our acquaintances at a fair value, as each was anxious to obtain some relic of their beloved pastor. The kind people, among whom we had resided, expressed many kind wishes for our future welfare, when we left them to seek a home in the great city. The school which my mother opened upon our removal to the city proved very successful, and soon yielded us a comfortable support. I assisted my mother both in the duties of the school-room and also in our household work. We were prospered and lived contentedly in our new home. We missed, it is true, the familiar faces of our old friends, but we soon found friends in our new home; we were cheerful, and should have been happy but for the sad loss we had recently sustained. Four years thus glided by, during which time our school continued to afford us a comfortable support. About this time I became acquainted with Mr. Harwood, who had a short time before commenced the practice of law in the city of Edinburgh, and one year later I became his wife. His pecuniary circumstances were but moderate, as he had been only a short time engaged in the practice of his profession. We resided with my mother, as she could not bear the idea of being separated from me. I continued as usual to assist her in the duties of her school. We, in this way, lived happily, till the event of my mother's death, which took place two years after my marriage. She took a sudden cold, which settled upon her lungs, and terminated in a quick consumption, which, after a short period of suffering, closed her life. She died as she had lived, full of religious hope and trust. Of my own sorrow I will not now speak; the only thought which afforded me the least consolation was — that what was my loss, was her eternal gain. About a year after the death of my mother my husband formed the idea of going to America. He had little difficulty in gaining my consent to accompany him. Had my mother still lived the case would have been very different; as it was, I had no remaining tie to bind me to Scotland, and wherever he deemed it for the best to go, I felt willing to accompany him, for he was my all in the wide world. We left the British shores on the tenth of June, and after a prosperous voyage, we found ourselves safely landed in the city of Boston. We brought with us money sufficient to secure us from want for a time, and my husband soon began to acquire quite a lucrative practice in his profession, and our prospects for the future seemed bright. For a long time my spirits were weighed down by home-sickness. I felt an intense desire to return to the home we had left beyond the sea, but in time this feeling wore away, and I began to feel interested in our new home, which appeared likely to be a permanent one. When we had resided for a little more than a year in our adopted country, my little Ernest was born, and the lovely babe, with my additional cares, doubly reconciled me to my new home. When my little boy was about a year old I was attacked by a contagious fever, which at that time prevailed in the city. By this fever I was brought very near to death. I was delirious most of the time, and was thereby spared the sorrow of knowing that my child was consigned to the care of strangers. But the fever at length ran its course, and I began slowly to recover. But just when I was considered sufficiently strong to be again allowed the care of my child, my husband was prostrated by the same disease from which I had just recovered, and in ten days I was left a widow with my helpless child. I cannot even now dwell upon this season of sorrow. All my former trials appeared as nothing when compared with this. Had it not been for my boy I could almost have wished I had not been spared to see this hour, but I banished such thoughts as wrong and impious, and tried to look the dreary future calmly in the face. I soon found it necessary to devise some means of support for myself and child. I thought of many plans only to discard them as useless. I once thought of opening a school as my own mother had done, but the care of my child prevented me from supporting myself in this way; and I would not consign him to the care of strangers. I at length decided to seek to support myself by the use of the needle, and accordingly rented two rooms on a respectable street, and removed thither with my child, where, by the closest industry I succeeded in keeping above want for more than three years, when my health failed from too close application to my employment. My physician strongly advised me to leave the city, as he thought country air would have a beneficial effect upon my health. I followed his advice, and, with the small sum of money which I had been able to lay by, added to what I received from the sale of my few articles of household furniture, I left the city. When I left Boston I had no particular place in view as to where I might find a home. I had decided upon opening a school in some country village if I could meet with encouragement in the undertaking. About fifty miles distant from this city I was taken ill, and for several weeks was unable to proceed on my way. When I was sufficiently recovered to allow of my again travelling I found it to be imperatively necessary that I should seek some place where I could earn a support for myself and child, as the small sum of money with which I left Boston was now nearly gone. The kind gentleman, in whose house I remained during my illness, informed me that he was well acquainted in the village of Walden, and he thought it a place where I would be likely to succeed in establishing a select school for young children, as he informed me there were many wealthy people residing here, who would patronize a school of this kind. With this intention I came to this village, and when I purchased my ticket for Walden I had but one dollar remaining in my purse, which, with the clothing and other articles contained in my trunk is all I possess in the world. But this matters little to me now, for I feel that my days on earth are numbered. I am unable to reward you for your exceeding kindness to myself and child; but I pray Heaven to reward and bless you, both temporally and spiritually. It is hard for me to leave my dear child, but I now feel resigned to the will of Heaven, knowing that whatever He wills is for the best."

CHAPTER IV.

And so the little orphan boy found a home and friends to love and cherish him.

Mr. and Mrs. Humphrey felt a tender love for the lovely and engaging orphan. Mrs. Humphrey, in particular, seemed almost to idolize him.

She had many years before lost, by death, a little boy, when of about the same age which little Ernest was when thus strangely cast upon her bounty; and this circumstance may have attached her more strongly to the child.

Mr. Humphrey was equally fond of the boy, but his disposition was less demonstrative than was that of his wife he was, therefore not so much inclined to indulge, the child in a manner which would prove injurious to him as he grew older.

Although the child had a very affectionate disposition he yet possessed a will that liked not to yield to that of another. Young as the child was, his mother had discovered this trait in his character and had, previously to her death, spoken of the matter to Mrs. Humphrey, and besought her — as she valued her own happiness and that of the child — to exact strict obedience from him when he should be left solely to her care.

"Even," said she, "should it require severe measures to break that will, it must be done. Remember it is for the best good of the child."

Had Mrs. Humphrey strictly followed the counsels of the dying mother in the early training of her child it might have spared her much after-sorrow.

Mr. Humphrey treated the child very kindly, but made it a point that he should yield to him a ready obedience in all things. But the little fellow was quick to notice that when Mr. Humphrey was not present he could usually, either by dint of coaxing or noisy rebellion, carry his point with Mrs. Humphrey.

Her husband often remonstrated with her upon the course she was pursuing in the management of the child. She used often to say —

"I cannot find it in my heart to punish the poor child when I consider that he is both fatherless and motherless, and I trust he will outgrow these childish ways."

Poor Mrs. Humphrey! She is not the only one that has been cheated by this hope, and has thereby allowed their child to grow up with an obstinate will that has marred their happiness for life.

In after years Mrs. Humphrey many times recalled to mind a remark which a friend made to her one day in regard to little Ernest, then six years old. He came into the parlor where the two ladies were sitting, and taking from the centre table an elegantly bound book, began turning the leaves with fingers that were none of the cleanest. Mrs. Humphrey gently requested him to replace the book, which request she was obliged to repeat two or three times before he paid the slightest attention to it. And then it was only to say in a coaxing voice —

"Ernest wants this pretty book; do let me keep it."

Mrs. Humphrey replied that the book was not suitable for little boys, and again requested him to replace it on the table. When a few minutes had passed, and he still continued to turn the leaves of the book, Mrs. Humphrey again repeated her request in a decided manner, telling him to replace the book immediately, when his childish temper burst forth in a regular tempest. He tossed the book from his hand, and threw himself on the floor in a corner of the room, where he gave vent to his anger by a succession of screams, which were anything but melodious. But his desire to retain possession of the coveted book was yet strong, and when the ladies again became engaged in conversation he quietly approached the table and, hastily taking the book therefrom, left the room, and Mrs. Humphrey, to save further trouble, appeared not to notice the act. The lady, who was an intimate friend, asked

Mrs. Humphrey if she were not pursuing a wrong course in thus allowing the boy to do what she had once forbidden him?

"Oh," said Mrs. Humphrey, "he is but a child, and will become ashamed of such conduct as he grows older."

"I sincerely hope he may," replied the lady, "but I very much fear you will see a day when you will regret not having been more firm in your government of this child."

CHAPTER V.

Nine years have rolled by the with their various changes since we first introduced Earnest Harwood to the reader, a child of five years of age, weeping at the grave of his mother.

Let us again glance at him when he has nearly attained to the age of fourteen years. We find him grown a strong healthy youth, still retaining that wondrous beauty which had rendered him so remarkable in the days of his childhood.

The reader will doubtless be ready to enquire if his mind and character are equally lovely with his person. Would that it were in my power to give a favourable answer to the question. But the truth must be told, and, at the age of fourteen, Ernest Harwood was decidedly a bad boy. When of suitable age he had been put to school, and for a time made rapid progress in his studies. From the first he was rather averse to study, but as he learned readily and had a most retentive memory he managed to keep pace in his studies with most boys of his age.

Mr. and Mrs. Humphrey exercised much watchfulness in regard to his companions, as, when he began to mingle with other boys, they discovered that he seemed inclined to make companions of such boys as they could not conscientiously allow him to associate with. But, notwithstanding their vigilance, it was soon remarked that he was often seen in company with boys of very bad repute. He soon came to dislike school, and often absented himself from it for a very trivial excuse, and in many instances played truant, when Mr. Humphrey refused to listen to his excuses for being allowed to remain at home.

Mr. and Mrs. Humphrey endeavored to discharge their duty to the boy; and more than that, they loved him as their own child.

I cannot describe the sorrow they experienced on his account, when, as he grew older, he seemed more and more inclined to the company of vicious boys, and to follow their evil examples. Many of his misdoings never reached the ears of his foster parents, for they were very much respected by their neighbors, who disliked to acquaint them with what must give them pain. He soon became so bad that if a piece of mischief was perpetrated among the village boys, the neighbors used at once to say they felt sure that Earnest Harwood was at the bottom of it. Often when among his wicked companions, those lips that had been taught to lisp the nightly prayer at his mother's knee were stained with oaths and impure language.

Mr. Humphrey, one day, in passing along the street, chanced to find him in company with some of the worst boys in the village, smoking cigars at the street corner. He was hardly able to credit his own eyesight. He requested him to accompany him home at once. He at the first thought of administering punishment with the rod, but as he had done so in former instances of misconduct with apparently no effect but to make him more defiant and rebellious, he thought in this instance he would try the effect of mild persuasion.

"My dear boy you little know the pain you are inflicting upon your best friends by thus seeking the company of those wicked boys who will certainly lead you to ruin, if you allow yourself to follow their example."

He talked long to him of his deceased mother, telling him of her many earnest prayers for the future good of her child.

For some time the boy maintained a sulky, defiant manner, but his heart at length softened, and, covering his face with his hands, he wept aloud. He begged of Mr. Humphrey to forgive his past misconduct, and he certainly would try to reform in the future.

For a time there was a marked change for the better in the conduct of the boy, and his friends began to indulge the hope that the change would prove to be lasting. But his resolutions of amendment soon yielded to the influence of his evil companions, from whom he found it very difficult to keep aloof. He was of a rash, impulsive disposition, and he soon forgot his good resolves, and became even worse than before.

Mr. Humphrey still maintained sufficient control over him to oblige him to attend church regularly, in company with himself and wife, but often, when they supposed him to be attending the Sabbath-School, would he join some party of idle, strolling boys, and spend the day in a very sinful manner. The Superintendent of the school hearing of this, called and acquainted Mr. Humphrey of the matter.

"I am obliged to you for your kindness in calling upon me," said Mr. Humphrey, "although I fear I can do nothing that will have any good effect upon the boy. I have endeavoured to do my duty by the child, I know not wherein I have failed. I have counselled, persuaded, and even punished him, and you behold the result. I am at a loss what to do with him. I have brought up children of my own, who never caused me a real sorrow in their lives. Why is it, that this poor orphan seems so strongly resolved to follow only evil ways? Would that some one could advise me as to what my duty is, in regard to the boy, for, unless a change for the better soon takes place, he will be ruined for time and eternity."

Mr. Humphrey sighed deeply as he spoke, and seemed oppressed with sorrow. The gentleman with whom he was conversing, endeavoured, as well as he was able under the circumstances, to comfort him; telling him that they could only give him good counsel, and pray for him, and leave the result to an over-ruling Providence.

CHAPTER VI.

Previous to her death, the mother of Earnest had entrusted to the care of Mrs. Humphrey, a closely sealed package directed to Ernest in her own hand-writing. She had left the request that this package should not be given to him until he had reached the age of fourteen years. Many surmises were formed among the few who knew of this package, as to what it might contain. Some were of the opinion that it contained papers which might lead to the possession of wealth. But from what Mrs. Harwood had related to Mrs. Humphrey, concerning her early life, she thought this idea to be highly improbable.

However, she carefully laid by the package, and was very careful that it should sustain no injury. In the meantime, the boy had continued to go on from bad to worse, till he became known as the leader in every kind of mischief among the bad boys of the village. He now seldom spent an evening in his own home. In one or two instances he narrowly escaped being sent to jail. The respect entertained for his foster parents by the people of the village was all that caused them to show lenity to the erring boy. The conduct of Earnest had borne heavier upon them than their years; they had fondly loved the beautiful and friendless boy, and it almost broke their hearts to see him go thus astray. Many there were who advised them to cast him off, as he seemed given over to evil, and even treated them with unkindness and disrespect; but with all his faults, they still clung to him, hoping almost against hope that he would yet reform.

"I promised his mother," said Mr. Humphrey, "that I would care for her boy so long as I lived to do so, and that promise I intend to keep." "And," added Mrs. Humphrey, "as long as we possess a home, he shall not be homeless. For if we can do no more we can at least pray for him; and I have a hope that the prayers offered in faith will yet meet with an answer."

Time passed on, till the evening preceding the fourteenth birth-day of Ernest. Mr. Humphrey sat with his wife by their lonely fireside, Ernest had gone out directly after tea, and the hour was growing late. They were speaking of him, for they felt very sad.

"I often wonder," said Mr. Humphrey, addressing his wife, "in what duty I have failed to Ernest. I have endeavored to set before him a good example, and to do by him in all things as I would have done by my own son. I have prayed with and for him; and yet since quite a little child, he has been a source of grief and anxiety to us, by his evil conduct."

"I am conscious," replied Mrs. Humphrey, "that I have erred in his early training, by too often yielding to his childish will, rather than administer punishment to enforce obedience from him. I meant well, and if I have done him a wrong it is now too late to remedy it. I can only pray that he may yet forsake his evil ways. Tomorrow will be his birth-day, let us hope that the contents of the package which so many years ago, his poor mother entrusted to my care, may have some influence for good upon his future life."

While they were yet speaking a rap sounded at the door. Mr. Humphrey rose and opened it, but stood speechless, when he beheld Ernest supported by two or three of his companions. At the first he supposed him either hurt or seriously ill. But upon going near to him what was his amazement when he discovered that he was too much intoxicated to allow of his walking without assistance. This was something entirely unexpected. Some had hinted that, added to his other faults, he was acquiring a taste for strong drink, but those whispers never reached the ears of Mr. Humphrey or his wife. And when he was brought home in this state, they had no words adequate to describe their feelings.

Dismissing his companions they assisted him into the house, and to his room, Mrs. Humphrey only saying, "poor misguided boy, what will become of him?"

When they returned to the sitting room their minds were too much agitated to allow them to converse. After some time passed in silence, Mr. Humphrey said, "we will not attempt to talk of this new sorrow tonight, but we will pray for the poor boy as well as for ourselves, before we retire to rest."

Opening his Bible, Mr. Humphrey read the forty-sixth Psalm, then kneeling, he poured out his troubled soul in prayer. He prayed earnestly for the poor youth now lying in the heavy sleep produced by intoxication. He also prayed for forgiveness, if they erred in the management of the boy, and for future aid in the performance of their duty. Could the boy have heard the prayer which Mr. Humphrey sent up to heaven on his behalf, hard indeed must have been his heart, if he had not from that moment resolved to forsake his evil ways, and by his future good conduct endeavoured to atone for his past sins and follies.

CHAPTER VII.

When Earnest came down to breakfast the next morning, neither Mr. or Mrs. Humphrey made any allusion to the situation in which he had been brought home the previous evening. They treated him with their usual kindness, but it was evident, by his subdued manner and downcast countenance, that he felt sensible of his shame and degradation. They intended to talk with him of the matter, but deferred it for the present. Mr. Humphrey advised his wife to give him the package herself, as it was to her care it had been committed. Soon after breakfast was over, he went up to his room, whither Mrs. Humphrey soon repaired with the package in her hand. Earnest opened the door when she rapped for admission. He looked somewhat embarrassed, and seemed by his manner to expect she had visited his room for the purpose of talking to him of the event of the last evening. She made no mention of the circumstance, but seating herself by his side, addressed him, saying —

"My dear Earnest, you have often told me that you retain a distinct recollection of your mother. I have never before told you that, previous to her death, she consigned a sealed package to my care, directed to you with her own hand, with the request that I should give it to you on your fourteenth birthday. The time has now arrived, and by giving you this package I fulfil what was a dying request of your mother." As she concluded, she placed the package in his hand, and immediately left the room, thinking he would prefer being left alone to open the package.

When some time had passed, and Earnest did not come down, Mr. Humphrey went upstairs, and softly opened the door of his room. He found the boy with his face bowed upon his hands, weeping bitterly. He approached him, and gently placing his hand upon his shoulder, enquired the cause of his grief.

He replied, in a voice choked with sobs, —

"Oh! I have been so wicked — so — bad — I know not what will become of me. It is well that my mother did not live to see how widely I have strayed from the path in which it was her last hope and prayer that I should walk."

Mr. Humphrey endeavoured to comfort the poor boy, wisely thinking this to be no time to reproach him for past errors.

Mrs. Humphrey, thinking that something unusual must have taken place followed her husband to the room of Earnest.

By the tearful request of Earnest, she examined the package, which had for so long a time remained in her keeping. First there was a Bible and Hymn Book, the books were elegantly bound, and had silver clasps. Then there was an old-fashioned locket of gold, containing a picture of the father and mother of Ernest, which had been taken many years before. Between the leaves of the Bible was placed a letter addressed to Ernest, in the hand-writing of his mother. The letter had been written at different times as her strength permitted, during the last few days of her life. It read as follows: —

> "MY DEAR LITTLE EARNEST, — Long before your eyes will rest upon these lines, the hand that traces them will have mouldered into dust. The contents of this package with my prayerful blessing, is all I have to leave you. As I write these lines you are playing about my room a happy, innocent child. Would that my knowledge could extend into the future, that I might know what manner of youth you will be, when this letter is placed in your hands. But I fear that I am wrong in thus wishing to know the future which a kind Providence has mercifully hidden from us. It is my anxiety for you alone that prompts the desire. I leave a request that this letter be not placed in your hands till you shall have attained the age of fourteen years. For should your life be spared to that period, you will then be capable of reflection. It is my earnest prayer, that you should grow up a good and dutiful boy, and by so doing, reward Mr. and Mrs. Humphrey for the care and instruction, which, I feel confident they will bestow upon you. But, O! my son, should it be otherwise, and you have been led astray by evil companions, I beseech you, my child, to pause and think. Listen to the voice of your mother as if speaking to you, from her grave. *Again*, I say, 'pause and reflect.' If you have evil companions, forsake them at once, and forever. But I trust that these sad forebodings are needless, and that when you read these lines, you will be all that the fond heart of a mother could desire. The Bible and Hymn Book which I leave you belonged to my father, who was a minister of the Church of Scotland. Is it too much for me to hope that you will follow in the footsteps of your deceased grandparent, and use this Bible as he did in the pulpit, as a minister of the gospel? The locket contains the likeness of your father and myself, taken a short time after our marriage. I commit you with many prayers, to the care

of your Heavenly Father, for I feel that the hand of death is upon me, and that a few brief days will close my earthly existence. My last prayer will be that my boy may so live on earth, as to meet his mother in Heaven. My strength fails me. I can write no more.

"From your loving, but dying mother,

"Charlotte Harwood."

CHAPTER VIII.

The reader who has got thus far in the narrative of the early life of Earnest Harwood, will doubtless learn, with pleasure, that the letter written by his mother, proved, under the blessing of God, the means of his salvation. The earnest persuasion of that letter, induced him to form a firm resolve, that he *would* amend his conduct, and cease from his evil ways. He was, at the first, fearful that he had lost the love of his foster parents, by his ungrateful conduct. He one day expressed this fear to them, and together they assured him, that although he had certainly caused them much grief and anxiety, their love for him had remained unchanged. They took this opportunity, when his feelings were thus softened, to urge him to be firm in his resolution of amendment. They also, for the first time, spoke of the fearful sorrow he had caused them by being brought to his home in a state of intoxication; and besought him never again to allow himself to be persuaded to taste of the intoxicating cup. Mrs. Humphrey pressed a motherly kiss upon his fine brow, and said, —

"My dear boy I hope that you will not again disappoint our fond hopes, and that you will yet do credit to the fine abilities with which our Heavenly Father has so liberally endowed you."

From this time there was a marked and decided change in the character of Earnest. Many feared that the change would not be permanent, but Mrs. Humphrey was very hopeful.

"I feel an assurance," said she "that the many prayers which have been offered to heaven on his behalf, are about to be answered."

It was even so. And they who feared a relapse into his former evil ways were happily disappointed. He again punctually attended school, and applied himself diligently to his neglected studies; and his teachers were surprised, as well by the astonishing progress he made, as by his correct exemplary deportment. As may be readily supposed, he had much to contend with from the vicious boys who had been his former associates. He shunned their company as much as possible, but he could not avoid occasionally coming in contact with them, and I am happy to say, that they found him immovable in his resolutions for good. They tried every means again to entice him into evil ways, but without success. As a last resort, they tried the effect of ridicule, but they learned now, that he had allowed his better nature to assert its power, for he possessed a spirit far above the influence of ridicule; and when they found they could by no means induce him to mingle with them, they were forced to give him up, and allow him to go his way in peace. When Mr. and Mrs. Humphrey found that the change in Earnest was likely to prove a permanent one, their gratitude and joy was heartfelt and sincere.

Two years have now passed away, since the beginning of the happy change in the life of the orphan boy. We now find him a fine, tall youth of sixteen, as much respected as he had formerly been shunned and pitied. His personal appearance was still as attractive as in his childhood. He was called by many the finest looking youth in all the village of Walden. He had attended closely to his studies, and had obtained a good English education. During the mid-summer vacation Mr. Humphrey asked if he had turned his mind towards any particular calling in life which he wished to follow, —

"For," said he, "it is my intention to assist you in fitting yourself for any profession you may feel inclined to pursue."

Ernest blushed deeply as he replied, —

"You know, sir, the wish which my mother expressed in regard to my calling in life, and I feel a desire to fulfill her wish in the matter. I deeply feel my unworthiness for a calling so sacred, yet I hope my unworthy services may be accepted, should I be spared to enter upon the Ministry."

When Mr. Humphrey learned the wishes of Ernest he gladly defrayed his expenses while pursuing the studies necessary to fit him for the Ministry.

He passed through his college course with much credit to himself, and then devoted the necessary time to the study of divinity in the seminary.

CHAPTER IX.

In conclusion I would ask the reader to accompany me to what is now one of the oldest churches in the city of Boston.

It is a beautiful Sabbath morning in the balmy month of June.

Let us enter the church. Something of more than usual interest seems to pervade the large congregation there assembled. As we enter the church we observe in one of the front pews an aged couple, whom we at once recognize as Mr. and Mrs.

Humphrey. They are now quite aged and feeble, yet the countenance of each is cheerful and placid. Notwithstanding their age they have made the journey of two hundred miles to be present upon this occasion. For their beloved Earnest is this day to be set apart to the Work of the Holy Ministry by the solemn service of ordination.

When the services were closed, and Earnest came forward to accompany his aged foster parents from the church, they felt themselves more than rewarded for all the care they had bestowed upon the orphan boy; and they might have said, as did Simeon of old, —

"Lord, now lettest thou thy servants depart in peace according to thy word, for our eyes have seen thy salvation."

To the boys who may read this story I would say: As you value your own well-being in time and eternity, avoid evil companions — for these have worked the ruin of many a promising youth.

Should this little story be read by any who are mothers of families, it is my hope that it may afford them encouragement to persevere in their prayerful efforts, for the good of the immortal beings committed to their care. The letter penned by the feeble hand of his dying mother, under the divine blessing, saved Earnest Harwood from ruin. Let this circumstance encourage you, never to grow weary nor discouraged in your labours for the good of your children, and "ye shall in no wise lose your reward."

THE END

www.ingramcontent.com/pod-product-compliance
Lightning Source LLC
Chambersburg PA
CBHW030343310726
48979CB00001B/164

9781557429001